TALES OF PERSUASION

Philip Hensher

4th ESTATE • *London*

HarperCollins
PUBLISHERS

4th Estate
An imprint of HarperCollins*Publishers*
1 London Bridge Street
London SE1 9GF
www.4thEstate.co.uk

First published in Great Britain by 4th Estate in 2016
This 4th Estate paperback edition published in 2017

1 3 5 7 9 8 6 4 2

Copyright © Philip Hensher 2016

Philip Hensher asserts the right to be
identified as the author of this work.

A catalogue record for this book is
available from the British Library.

ISBN 978-0-00-745965-0

Printed and bound in Great Britain by
Clays Ltd, St Ives plc

MIX
Paper from
responsible sources
FSC C007454

FSC™ is a non-profit international organisation established to promote
the responsible management of the world's forests. Products carrying the
FSC label are independently certified to assure consumers that they come
from forests that are managed to meet the social, economic and
ecological needs of present and future generations,
and other controlled sources.

Find out more about HarperCollins and the environment at
www.harpercollins.co.uk/green

PHILIP HENSHER's novels include *The Mulberry Empire*, the Booker-shortlisted *The Northern Clemency*, *King of the Badgers*, *Scenes from Early Life* and *The Emperor Waltz*. He is Professor of Creative Writing at the University of Bath Spa and lives in south London and Geneva.

Praise for *Tales of Persuasion*:

'He is an expert writer, and an expert tone runs through this vigorous collection. Hensher observes all human life with the detachment of a scientist ... He nails lust, hypocrisy, regret and hopefulness with an exquisite eye for detail. Unromantic, and dark at times, this collection is always interesting'
Daily Mail

'Hensher is deft at locating the moment of crisis when a character experiences a change of heart or a nasty surprise, and life is exposed in all its drab wonder ... Entertainingly varied in tone and setting, the stories combine quaint physical observation with a caustic intelligence ... Among the collection's many delights are the walk-on characters ... Hensher has always been an acute observer of modern life ... the 11 stories have real edge and distinction'
Evening Standard

'A brilliantly astute book ... every narrative is unified by Hensher's incredible eye for detail and effortless talent for multi-layered storytelling'
Attitude

'Hensher's adaptability as a writer and love of form brings us clever, ravishing and moving storytelling'
Monocle

'Every page delivers something enjoyable and even eye-popping; a vibrant exchange, a spry description, a tickling bit of indirect speech'   *New Statesman*

'Entertainingly varied stories'   *Literary Review*

'Hensher's prose can be painterly'   *Financial Times*

'Hensher has a pitch-perfect way with language and invented detail'   *Sunday Times*

'A comedy of manners with an occasional dark side'
Daily Telegraph

ALSO BY PHILIP HENSHER

FICTION
Other Lulus
Kitchen Venom
Pleasured
The Bedroom of the Mister's Wife
The Mulberry Empire
The Fit
The Northern Clemency
King of the Badgers
Scenes from Early Life
The Emperor Waltz

NON-FICTION
The Missing Ink: The Lost Art of Handwriting

To Nicola Barr

Contents

Eduardo

(i.m. J.C.)

The trains were simmering under the glowing glass roof. In a moment, one midnight-blue train to the airport would leave, and another would arrive, disgorging and absorbing voyagers. The express to Penzance, beyond the shining metal barriers, began joltlessly to move away, and at the same moment, an express from, perhaps, Penzance drew up at the platform next to it. All this coming and going, as Fitzgerald thought of it. He never went anywhere. He did not even own a car, having no need for one in London. He stood at the bagel concession stand where he had agreed to meet Timothy Storey. Most people arranged to meet at the statue of a bear from a series of children's books. Fitzgerald had thought there was too much scope for confusion in explaining to a foreigner that they would meet at a bear called Paddington, at a station called Paddington. He had no idea whether the adventures of Paddington Bear would be familiar to someone who had spent all his life living in Kenya. His mind filled with the affecting image of a grass hut, a bowl of meal, a runner approaching across the veld with a single, cellophane-bound library book, *Paddington*

Returns, its boards warped and damp, gripped under his arm.

His name was called. 'I thought it was you,' Daniel Bradbury said. Fitzgerald went over to speak to him. Bradbury was a neighbour of his in Clapham; one on the other side of a social divide, since he lived in a new gated community. It was the result of the conversion of an old red-brick board school into loft apartments and even whole vertical houses. No keypad and gate guarded the access to Fitzgerald's maisonette, and the door was on the street. They were both from over the water; they had met by chance, passing the time of day when they found themselves in the same space, but they might have inhabited different cities. 'I had to come down to meet Eduardo,' Bradbury said, with a friendliness that took Fitzgerald by surprise. Bradbury was by no means open and chatty with his neighbour Fitzgerald as a rule. 'He wasn't sure about the Circle Line and the Northern Line. He wanted me to come to Heathrow, but I thought that was absurd. I said I would meet him at Paddington, it wasn't hard. Did I tell you about Eduardo? He was living here last year – I knew him, we met at a dinner party – and then he got deported back to Argentina, his visa ran out, but I've invited him back, he's moving in. It's all so much easier than it used to be, getting a visa for a partner.'

Fitzgerald agreed with whatever it was Bradbury was explaining. 'What are you here for?' Bradbury said. Fitzgerald explained that he was expecting a visitor. It was a young man from Kenya, a sort of *au pair* who would be living with Fitzgerald and undertaking light household duties in exchange for a low rent for the next three months.

'You haven't met Eduardo,' Bradbury said, turning to a man who had sat down on his suitcases. Fitzgerald had noticed him – of course he had noticed him – but it had not occurred to him that even Bradbury could be with such a man.

Bradbury had a record of seductions and triumphs beyond the imagination – no, beyond merely the ambition – of Fitzgerald. He always had some delicious man in tow, installed in what Bradbury imagined to be the lavish white spaces of the converted loft apartment. But looking at this man, with his simultaneous quality of darkness and glow, with his unaffected grace of leg and jawline, even sprawled over his luggage where he had thrown himself, even tired and unwashed after so long a flight, Fitzgerald wondered at the unfairness of it all. Bradbury was not so very young or good-looking or charming; he was only rather rich, and thin. A man like Eduardo should not be sitting, unremarked, in Paddington Station on a weekday morning. Everything about him and his sulky plump lips implied fame, the red carpet, the shining cliff of flashbulbs, the swimwear shoot with a budget of half a million.

Bradbury went on talking, evidently wanting to show off Eduardo, to talk about him; the days and weeks to come would bring better and more highly placed listeners to the subject, but Fitzgerald was by chance the first to lie in their way, so Bradbury talked. Eduardo made no sign that he understood what was being discussed. In a moment, Fitzgerald said to him, 'Have you only just arrived?'

'Only two hours ago,' Eduardo said, slowly, complainingly. His voice, in the middle register, was sleepy and resonant, with an odd and unspecific rasp to it, as if an ancestor had once smoked too many cigars of provincial

3

manufacture. 'So long to wait at the visa. We don't have that in Argentina. You only show your passport and they wave you through.'

'Well, they wave you through in Argentina if you've got an Argentinian passport,' Bradbury said, laughing a little.

'Yes, of course I've got an Argentinian passport,' Eduardo said. 'And I'm so hungry I could eat anything.'

'They never give you enough to eat on planes, do they?' Fitzgerald said.

'I don't eat on planes,' Eduardo said seriously. 'If you eat food in a plane, it swells up in your stomach, you get fat, your stomach it swells, even it can explode and kill you. Everyone knows that.'

'Someone's been having a joke with you,' Bradbury said. 'I don't think that's really true.'

'It's true. It was the steward in an airline, he told me that.'

For some moments, a fat white girl with a bright red face had been standing by them, trying to attract their attention. 'Excuse me,' she said. 'Are you Mr Edmund Fitzgerald?'

Fitzgerald looked at her, up and down, at the brownish stain running vertically down her side – rust? Ketchup? – from gypsyish blouse to dirndlish skirt, both unusually fashioned in some undefinable way. He looked at her woven plastic square holdall and plastic rucksack. Bradbury and Eduardo were turning away. 'Yes?' Fitzgerald said.

'Timothy Storey,' the girl said.

'Yes?' Fitzgerald said, bewildered.

'No,' the girl said. 'I'm Timothy Storey. Did you think I was a boy? People have thought that before. Because of my name. My parents called me Timothy after my little brother, he died when he was only three months old and my dad said he'd name the next one Timothy to keep his memory alive.'

'But—' Fitzgerald said.

'We'll be off,' Bradbury said, looking the girl up and down and perhaps comparing Fitzgerald's visitor with his. 'Nice to see you. We must have lunch some time.'

'Bye,' Eduardo said, and Fitzgerald observed that Bradbury, despite his commanding and top-person manner, picked up both Eduardo's bags and followed his beautiful stride.

'That's funny,' Timothy Storey said, as they went towards the Underground. (Fitzgerald was not a generous or lavish man; he had had only a half-formed plan to impress a phantom wide-eyed and black Timothy Storey with a journey home in a London taxi but, aghast, he dismissed that now as not worth the candle.) 'I thought I said I was a girl. I always try to remember to say that I'm a girl because otherwise it confuses people. But maybe I forgot when I was writing to you. It's easy for me to forget that not everyone knows, you know what I mean? My mum says, "Always say, Timothy, that you're a girl, because actually it's a boy's name." But not many people are called Timothy in Africa necessarily, so they aren't as surprised as I guess people are here. It's because of my brother that I'm called Timothy. Do we buy a ticket here? Golly, it's costly here, I couldn't believe it, what they asked for the train fare., it was nice of you to say that you'd pay for that so I wouldn't have to get here on the Underground. Were those friends of yours? He was a handsome fella, I'd say.'

* * *

5

Over the next few days, Fitzgerald tried to find out more about Eduardo – he laboured at bumping into him by the purest chance – but though Eduardo was living with Bradbury, only a hundred yards or so away, he seemed never to appear in any of the usual places. Fitzgerald went in a craze of expectation around Clapham; he sat in coffee shops, he walked round and round the Common – surely everyone the first time they came to Clapham took walks on the Common. But it was not Eduardo's first time in London; he had seen it all; and presumably he never went onto the Common. Fitzgerald threw caution to the wind and went up and down the bars of Soho, looking everywhere for Eduardo, in order to produce the casual 'Well, and how are you enjoying London, then?' That would lead to a daytime invitation, to drop round while Bradbury was at work at his advertising agency, or going round his buy-to-let property empire chastising tenants. At the end of the evening, he found he had gone into twenty-three bars, paying a five-pound entrance fee in twelve of them, drinking first small glasses of beer, then glasses of Coca-Cola, then fizzy water, then tap water, then nothing at all. It had cost him a hundred and seventeen pounds and he had not caught a glimpse of Eduardo. He knew Bradbury at all only by chance – once, during a tube strike, they had been hailing a cab within yards of each other on Upper Street in Islington, and had discovered they were both heading in the same direction, could share the cab; the heavy traffic had turned even the longish journey from Islington to Clapham into an epic, and they had discovered at the end of the forty-quid trip that they lived, strangely enough, within a hundred yards of each other. 'We must keep in touch,' Bradbury had said airily, and Fitzgerald had agreed.

Timothy Storey was showing no sign of starting her studies. She was hanging around the flat endlessly, eating whatever Fitzgerald placed in the fridge. How had such an awful blunder been made? Fitzgerald could have sworn that something in what she had written indicated that she was a boy, and black. He had never specified, himself. In the adverts that he placed online, offering a room to overseas students in exchange for some light household duties, he had always said very carefully that he was a single man. He had believed that would discourage girls from taking up the offer. At first he had thought of saying that he only wanted to let the room to young men, but that seemed a little too lecherously open, and Fitzgerald had an unspecific belief that such a stipulation might prove to be illegal. Up until now, the question had never arisen. He thought of telling Timothy Storey that a mistake had been made, that she ought to find somewhere else to live, but he had overheard her telling her parents over the Skype that it was ideal, that her landlord was a gay man so it was all perfectly safe. He resigned himself to having her around the flat for the next three months, filling up the bathroom with her unguents and peering over his shoulder whenever he started writing anything on the computer. 'Journalist, are you? That's nice. I'd love to be a journalist,' she would say, through a mouthful of Fitzgerald's hummus and Fitzgerald's bread. 'I've always wanted to write in a book.'

There was no telling when Timothy Storey might slide up behind him. To quell his disbelieving heart, he decided that he could only check the statements she had made by going up to the internet café on Clapham High Street. Fitzgerald envisaged, vaguely, some one-man kangaroo court in his sitting room, confronting her with her deceptions, pointing righteously at the front door at its conclusion.

'I live in the country here, on a game reserve,' he read, having called up Timothy Storey's old emails. 'My father works as the manager of the general stores. I used to want to work there too, to "follow in his footsteps", as they say, but now I hope I have larger ambitions! I have never been outside Kenya in my life, but I have an adventurous spirit and I am looking forward to seeing Europe with my own eyes. It can be quite conventional living here, with not very many people, and I do not think that I am really a conventional person, deep down inside my heart. Perhaps I should admit to you that, although I have not seen very much of the world and have not had many opportunities, I love fashion more than anything! I do not know from where that interest comes, and all my family, especially my four brothers, are forever teasing me for my enthusiasm for fashion. But that is by the by.'

Fitzgerald read all of Timothy Storey's emails, explaining all about her life – those details he had found so extraordinarily interesting and absorbing, so full of erotic promise. He found it hard to remember. There was absolutely nothing in these stilted statements that suggested she was anything but what she was; and Fitzgerald struggled to construct once more the image of the lonely, sensitive boy living in the middle of nowhere with four hearty hunting brothers; a boy with a dream of elegance, the interest in fashion a gift from the gods of Gay to the plains of Africa; a gift that would send him off to Europe in search of adventure and like-minded people. Fitzgerald had precisely envisaged a thin black boy, sitting up at nights, making ruffles. On the other hand, Timothy Storey had definitely never said, not in so many words, 'By the way, I am not a boy.'

Some presence interrupted his thoughts, and Fitzgerald looked up. Over the thin screen and the MDF partition, on the hired workspace backing onto this one, was the face he had been looking for: was Eduardo's.

'Hello,' Fitzgerald said, and the face looked blankly back at his, not sure that it had been spoken to. 'Hello,' Fitzgerald said again, less voicelessly. 'We met. At Paddington Station. I'm a friend of Daniel's.'

'Oh, yes,' Eduardo said. 'Were you with a girl? Your girlfriend?'

'No, not at all,' Fitzgerald said. 'It was a mistake, a big mistake. She's not my girlfriend or anything.'

'Yes, I remember now,' Eduardo said. 'Daniel told me you live near him, but he doesn't know you.'

'Well …' Fitzgerald said: he would not normally insist on his friendship with Bradbury, but it was his only connection with Eduardo.

'Listen,' Eduardo said. 'How do I make this thing work? It won't switch itself on. I tried, and asked them, and they told me to try again, and it still doesn't work. Can you show me?'

Fitzgerald was delighted. He moved smoothly round, pulling a chair up to sit close to Eduardo. He had a curious, marshy, wet-earth smell, like an animal, not at all unpleasant; where he sat he could feel the radiant, almost artificial warmth of Eduardo's body. He took the little ticket from Eduardo, and typed the code into the box – that had not occurred to Eduardo to be the thing to do. The machine started up.

'What do you do all day?' Fitzgerald said, to prolong the moment.

'Oh, I don't know,' Eduardo said. 'I sit, and I watch TV, and maybe I listen to music, or I go on Daniel's rowing machine, his running machine, I have a shower, and then it's time for Daniel to come home, I guess.'

'Do you ever go anywhere in London?' Fitzgerald said. 'If you're here, you should definitely go and see the city. Did you ever go to Richmond Park? It's beautiful – there are deer there, and the Isabella Plantation …' He trailed off, struck by the ineptness of the offer.

'No, I never go anywhere,' Eduardo said. 'I never heard of that park. Tomorrow, Daniel goes away to Paris with his job, for two nights, maybe, I don't know, maybe I go then. He said to me too, "Why don't you go to a museum, go to see some palace, fill your day?" but I don't know. I don't think I like to go to a museum, I never went to any museum in Argentina, except maybe at school.'

'No,' Fitzgerald said. 'I wouldn't recommend that to you, not if it's not the sort of thing you wouldn't take any enjoyment in.'

His sentences were growing inarticulate, struggling, vague, the utterances of a man who had learnt English as his third or fourth language, and had no rational sentiment to voice in that or any of the others.

The next day broke with sun through the thin curtains, and Fitzgerald was awake before seven; he had a sense of something to do, somewhere to go. He went through to his kitchen; from behind the door of the spare room, obscure rumbles and murmured syllables were emerging. Timothy Storey snored, and talked somewhat in her sleep, which extended until nine or later – he wondered what she had done on the veld, or whatever it was called in Kenya. He took a bath and dressed, and by eight was ensconced in a café at the corner of two main roads, sitting in a window, reading the newspaper. He believed that Daniel Bradbury usually left for work soon after dawn but perhaps, if he were going to Paris— Just then, in mid-speculation, he saw Bradbury's silver Saab at the lights heading away from his flat, with Bradbury at the wheel.

At half past nine, Fitzgerald went to the gate of Bradbury's converted school, and rang the bell of Bradbury's flat. The long silence made him fear that Eduardo had gone out, but eventually the sleepy voice came over the intercom. Fitzgerald said his name; there was another pause, and then the gate buzzed open. 'Oh, it's you,' Eduardo said, when Fitzgerald had gained access. He was standing on the landing, holding the door open with his bare foot; he was in a short silky dressing-gown going halfway down his brown thighs, hanging open to reveal a dark half-shaven chest. 'Daniel's gone, he's gone to Paris. Did you want him? He didn't say you were coming for anything. You woke me up.'

'No,' Fitzgerald said. 'You told me Daniel was going to Paris, yesterday. I thought you might be bored. I've come to take you to Richmond Park.'

Eduardo considered the invitation, rubbed his sleepy fists into his eyes, like a cat. He seemed unenthusiastic. 'The place with the deers,' he said. 'Oh, all right. Come back in half an hour.'

11

'I could come in and wait,' Fitzgerald said.

'I have to shower,' Eduardo said.

'I could wait somewhere else while you do that,' Fitzgerald said.

Eduardo considered this, then went back inside, leaving the door open. Fitzgerald took up this ambiguous invitation. The flat was what he had expected, the tall windows of the school, and the double-height ceiling, and it was entirely white. The sitting room was furnished with two identical giant black leather sofas, and on the main wall was an eight-foot-square painting-cum-screen-print of a flower some interior designer had concocted in the style of Andy Warhol. Fitzgerald walked about, examined all the photographs on the shelves. None, as far as he could see, included Eduardo just yet. He took a seat. In the recesses of a flat, a door clanged; the waters of a shower began to hiss.

When Eduardo presented himself, he was in holiday wear; a pair of white low-slung jeans, advertising the wares, and a sexily much-washed and faded black T-shirt. On his hairy, broad, flat feet, a pair of sandals identifying themselves as Versace. 'OK,' he said. 'Where do we go?'

In the taxi to Sloane Square and the tube to Richmond, Eduardo was evasive, short-sentenced, hardly observing Fitzgerald's company at all from behind his sunglasses. Fitzgerald made a couple of observations about passing objects, but then left it; some people, or so he believed, were not at their conversational best in the morning. At Earl's Court, an acquaintance of Fitzgerald's got on – one of his commissioning editors from way back, when Fitzgerald was still writing for gay magazines at a hundred pounds a pop. He stood in front of Fitzgerald, his eyes wandering constantly to Eduardo; the train was full, and it did not appear to occur to him that Fitzgerald could be accompanied by someone like Eduardo. When Eduardo said impatiently, 'How many more stops?' Fitzgerald introduced him; he noticed that Eduardo was just as brief with the editor, whose eyes were wandering back to Fitzgerald, perhaps considering whether he had missed something vital about Fitzgerald in the first place.

'This is nice,' Eduardo said, once in the park. 'I like to walk.' Over there was the white-icing façade of the royal lodge – or was it the ballet school – or White Lodge? Somewhere in the park was the Isabella Plantation. Fitzgerald remembered being taken to it, the dense displays of magnolia and rhododendron, whatever. He recalled walls of white and pink flowers; he did not think it was worth while dragging Eduardo about the place in search of somewhere so pensioner-friendly. Over there was a copse, heading the hill, and a single white cloud in the sky, quivering still on this warm morning. Eduardo flung himself down on the slope, made a single twisting gesture with his fists at either hipbone, and drew his T-shirt over his head. In the open air, there was the brief gust of that smell of Eduardo's: clean, but animal, and suggestive to Fitzgerald. Eduardo screwed his T-shirt up into a pillow, and placed it beneath his head. Lying back, his torso was articulated like architecture. The twin lines headed downwards into his low-slung trousers as if towards the point of a V; they bracketed about his solid abdominal muscles, like the lines of a pendentive on a dome, lightly furred. Fitzgerald sat down too, drawing his knees up and hugging them tight.

'Look,' he said, after a while, more for the pleasure of seeing the concertina-fold of Eduardo's stomach as he sat up than anything else. 'There are the deer.'

They had been there for a while, in fact. They were a herd of does and month-old fawns; a great buck or two could be seen, much further off. The mothers were performing a small ballet of rush and delay: of eating, of raising their heads, then making a short communal run before stopping again. The spontaneous and sudden movements separated by pauses of still and quiet had something moving about it to Fitzgerald. He wondered whether Stubbs had ever painted does with their fawns.

Eduardo propped himself up on his elbows, inspecting the herd. 'They are big animals,' he said. 'You don't know deer, they are such big animals. I thought they were the same size as, I don't know, as a goose, but they are big.'

'Yes, they are big,' Fitzgerald said. 'The males are bigger.'

Eduardo took this without comment. 'You know, it's strange that nobody ever eats deer,' he said. 'Every other animal, they eat them. Sheep, they eat them. Beef, they eat them. Pig, they eat them. Veal, they eat them. Fish, they eat them. I never heard of anybody eating deer.'

'People eat deer,' Fitzgerald said. 'It's called venison. It's good. I don't know whether people eat the deer in Richmond Park, though.'

'I never heard of that,' Eduardo said. 'I don't think that's right. I never heard of anyone eating deer, or what did you say?'

'Venison,' Fitzgerald said. Presently, Eduardo lowered himself back onto his pillow, and behind his mirrored Aviator sunglasses, his eyes closed; in a few moments, his hands folded on his chest, his slightly open mouth began to emit faint whiffles. And Fitzgerald admired the view.

Fitzgerald went round to Bradbury's flat the following day at ten thirty in the morning – he didn't want to make a habit of waking Eduardo up, if he was not a morning sort of person. He went to his usual café first, and picked up two croissants and two cups of some take-out coffee – a cappuccino with skimmed milk and without chocolate on top for him, a double espresso, which was what he believed South Americans drank for breakfast, for Eduardo. A different voice answered the intercom – not Eduardo's, but not Bradbury's either. A small Vietnamese woman opened the door to him, dressed in a plastic coverall. She explained that Mr Bradbury was not at home, and that his friend who was staying had gone out. She looked at Fitzgerald, wearing a pair of white jeans, sandals on his hairy white Irish feet and a washed-out black T-shirt, carrying two paper cups of coffee, one in each hand, and the neck of a paper bag awkwardly between the fourth and fifth fingers. 'If you like, you can give me his breakfast,' she said. 'I think he's Mr Bradbury's boyfriend, the one who stays here,' and she made a small, amused expression on her small, experienced face.

Timothy Storey was lying on the sofa when he returned, some time after eleven. 'Was it with that handsome fella you went to Richmond Park?' she asked.

'Eduardo, yes.'

'Is he a half-caste?' Timothy Storey said.

'No,' Fitzgerald said, with distaste. 'He's Argentinian.'

'You know how you tell a half-caste – because some of them, they look really as if they could be white? You take

15

a look at their gums, and they're sort of bluish. It's hard to describe, but they never lose that.'

'I see,' Fitzgerald said. 'I must keep it in mind.'

On the television, a boy like a rat was assuring a girl very much like Timothy Storey that he had not slept with her mother; the girl was assuring the boy in return that the baby she had just given birth to was his. 'Do you ever watch this?' Timothy Storey said. 'We don't have programmes like this in Africa. This is great.'

'Normally, I have too much work to do in the mornings to watch television,' Fitzgerald said. 'When does your course start, Timothy? Shouldn't you be in college or something?'

'They're going to make them take a lie-detector test,' Timothy Storey said. 'I love it when they do that.'

'Where is your college, anyway?'

'I think it's in Canning Town,' Timothy Storey said. 'Is that close to here?'

'Not very,' Fitzgerald said. 'You'll need to be out early in the morning to get to classes on time.'

'Oh, I don't think it's really that sort of college,' Timothy Storey said. 'You pay them a fee and they get you a student visa, but I don't think they expect to see you at classes or anything. It's just to get you into the country, and then you see how long you can stay before they catch up with you. The visa don't know your address, though. I would reckon I'm pretty safe for a few months holing up here. Is that a coffee going spare?'

Bradbury came back from Paris the next day, and though of course he worked during the day, there would be more of a sneaking-around aspect to calling on Eduardo. The

16

combination of Bradbury being away and Fitzgerald knowing that Bradbury was away would not necessarily coincide soon. But before Fitzgerald could wonder how he was going to see Eduardo again, Bradbury's Saab was drawing up by the bus-stop where Fitzgerald was waiting for a bus. Fitzgerald involuntarily looked beyond Bradbury, but the passenger seat was empty.

'I heard you kept poor old Eduardo entertained while I was away,' Bradbury said. 'Good for you.'

'Yes, we had a nice day out,' Fitzgerald said.

'He's not got a lot of get-up-and-go,' Bradbury said. 'I think he'd stay in the house all day if it were left up to him. Poor soul. Listen, we're having some people round for a drink on Saturday night – do drop in.'

There was something insulting about Bradbury's total lack of curiosity about the day in Richmond Park; it was evidently, from Eduardo's account, not something to awaken anything like jealousy. Fitzgerald wondered what he had said. But all the same, he said, 'I'd love to,' rather fervently, and Bradbury drove off, not offering Fitzgerald a lift, wherever he was going to.

'Come in! Come in!' Bradbury called wildly, from his door, to Fitzgerald at the bottom of the stairs. An old Perez Prado track was playing deafeningly from the flat; a fashionable choice that year, but a mistake, Fitzgerald believed, since once you had got past the *Dolce Vita* one, the Bob the Builder one and the one from the Guinness advert, they were difficult to tell apart. 'Come in!' Bradbury said excitedly. 'It's all good!' With an immediate glance, Fitzgerald saw the array of champagne bottles on the glass console table by a vase of white lilies, and bent to deposit his bottle of Jacob's Creek behind the door. He was an old hand at that sort of thing: if you handed your inferior bottle over to the host, it would disappear and you would get sneered at.

The party was in its early-full stage; a couple were attempting to dance and falling over cushions; the food on the table was untouched, but not yet covered with stubbed-out cigarettes. Bradbury introduced Fitzgerald to a man; a decent-looking but bewildered man called Stephen, in a white jacket, who turned out to be a friend of Bradbury's youth in Northern Ireland, in London for the first time, he said, in five years. No, he was staying in a bed-and-breakfast in Clapham Old Town; he'd found it on the internet. Wasn't the internet a marvellous thing, for finding hotels and that? Fitzgerald agreed. 'Do you think these lads here'd be up for a suck and a bunk-up later in the evening?' Stephen asked, indicating three bulky men in vests, romping on the carpet. 'I heard they had some of that cocaine with them, I'd like to have a go on that.'

Fitzgerald excused himself, and made his way over to Eduardo, who was sitting without drink or company in the far corner of one of Bradbury's enormous sofas. 'Oh, it's you,' Eduardo said. He was in a white shirt, unbuttoned to below his nipples, and quite an ordinary pair of jeans from which the labelled waistband of a pair of white pants emerged, whether by design or chance; he wore no shoes, and once more Fitzgerald allowed himself to be dazzled by the broad dark feet, the dazzling emergence of the dark

18

breast from the flutters of a new white shirt. It was too much.

'Is anyone getting you a drink?' Fitzgerald said.

'I'm fine, I don't want one,' Eduardo said. 'I don't know why Daniel's having this party. They all come and say hello, then they leave me, they go off into their bathroom and they have a line. I don't like to drink, I don't like to do line. It makes you fat.'

'Don't you like a party?'

'Oh, sure, but I like to dance, and no one's dancing here. That's not dancing,' indicating the wobbling pair, whose attempts to mambo to Perez Prado had turned into a more or less successful attempt to hold each other up. 'No one wants to dance, or talk, or anything but get drunk and high and then go to a club, maybe. And they all sleep with someone who isn't their boyfriend. I never do that. I think if a man's your boyfriend, you keep yourself for him and he keeps himself for you. That's what I think. Daniel thinks I'm crazy but I know he's happy I'm a good boy like that.'

'Well, Eduardo,' Fitzgerald said. He was so much more beautiful than anyone else there, so much more. 'One day soon I'll have a party for you, and people will dance and talk, and not sleep with anyone who isn't their boyfriend afterwards.'

'Thank you, you're sweet,' Eduardo rattled off, scowling at the room.

'I don't think anyone here understands you,' Fitzgerald said.

Eduardo seemed to ignore this, but something in his demeanour, like a dog pricking up its ears at the faint noise

19

or sniff of prey two hundred yards off, encouraged Fitzgerald.

'I don't think you show people what you're really like,' Fitzgerald said. 'I think I know what the real you is like.'

'I don't think you do,' Eduardo said. 'I don't think anyone does. Sometimes I don't think I do, even.'

'Well, I think I have some idea,' Fitzgerald said. 'You're really beautiful, do you know that?'

'Oh, everyone says that,' Eduardo said, the air of the attentive dog suddenly switching off. 'It's so boring, people saying that, it means nothing. I'm going to dance.'

'Let's dance,' Fitzgerald said desperately, and leant forward; he meant to take Eduardo's arm as a dancing partner might, but some movement of Eduardo's, some inability of Fitzgerald's to execute a suave gesture, meant that first his right hand, then the other, landed on Eduardo's upper thigh.

Eduardo pushed him off angrily. 'Leave me alone,' he said, getting up. 'Daniel was right about you. You're just the same as everyone else.'

'Yes, he does that to people,' Bradbury said to Fitzgerald, gliding past. Humiliatingly, the episode had amused the whole party, including even the terrible Irishman, who was tittering behind his hands. 'Don't worry, Graham. It's happened before and it'll happen again. I'm going to Munich for four days next week. Take him to the zoo this time. He'd like that, I expect.'

Fitzgerald punished himself; he only had himself to blame. A little more leisurely, a few more compliments about his beauty, and Eduardo would be eased into his bed. That was how it was done, wasn't it? Involuntarily, he thought about his greyish crumpled sheets, the pillows and the holed duvet scattered about his fetid retreat, and revised the picture: seducing Eduardo onto the no-doubt immaculate and crisp sheets of Bradbury's vast and snowy bed. All the next day, he lay on the sofa, groaning when he thought of what he had said and done, in front of an audience who despised him anyway. Timothy Storey was out for the day, God knew where; he settled into the depression in the sofa, the buffalo wallow she had made in the previous weeks of lying down. He did not have the excuse, for last night's behaviour, of drunkenness, either; he hoped Eduardo might assume, as they did, that Londoners were drunk most of the time.

Around three o'clock on Tuesday afternoon, the telephone rang, and he leapt for it. He was conscious that Bradbury's 'four days' meant that he might have gone on Monday, but had definitely gone on Tuesday. He set about immediately constructing a scene in which Eduardo was offering him the opportunity to apologize, in which Eduardo was apologizing, in which Eduardo had considered his offer and, now that Bradbury had gone to Munich and Eduardo was alone in the house—

It was a woman's voice. 'Is Timothy Storey there?'

'No,' Fitzgerald said. 'She's out.'

'Well, could you pass on a message? Tell her that Mrs Baxter from Ealing called, and she'd very much like to know where her aubergine bath sheet and matching hand towels are. It's not a joke. Those were expensive towels she's waltzed off with.'

Fitzgerald knew those purple towels: he kicked them out of his way on the bathroom floor most mornings, wondering who on earth bought purple towels. 'I'll tell her,' he said equably.

'It's really too bad,' Mrs Baxter said, relenting as she talked. 'Have you let her a room? I'd just like to give you some advice. Count your towels before she leaves.'

'I'm puzzled,' Fitzgerald said. 'This is Ealing in London you're calling from, right? When was she living with you?'

'Till two weeks ago,' Mrs Baxter said. 'It's taken me that long to get this number out of her people in Kenya. She was with me for six months. I had to pretend to her family that I'd bought her a gold necklace and I wanted it to be a surprise for her. Otherwise they wouldn't give me her new number – they're no fools. She told me she was going back to Africa, but of course I didn't believe that. She came to me from a friend of a friend in Acton, and I've just heard she had concerns about some missing knives. Sounds like she's preparing to furnish a flat. At our expense, if you don't mind me giving you some advice.'

'I'll let her know,' Fitzgerald said, and put the phone down. Rage filled his soul.

'I said that,' Timothy Storey said, when she returned and Fitzgerald asked her for some more details. 'I do come from Kenya. Mrs Baxter didn't tell you that I didn't come from Africa, did she?'

'But you asked me to meet you at Paddington,' Fitzgerald said. 'I thought you'd come from Kenya just that moment. I thought you were coming on the Heathrow Express.'

'Oh, no,' Timothy Storey said. 'I was coming from Southall on the train. It's only fourteen minutes, it's quite convenient. Mrs Baxter says she lives in Ealing, but it's really Southall, she thinks it sounds smarter. It was nice of you to meet me at Paddington. I could have made my own way here, but I thought it would be good if we met somewhere neutral before you took me home – you hear such awful stories. Mrs Baxter, she was a bitch from Hell, I'll tell you. She was always complaining about me watching TV when she wanted to watch something, and telling me I shouldn't be lying on the couch eating snacks, and there was something on the other side she wanted to watch, like she owned the TV or something.'

'But she did own the TV,' Fitzgerald said, almost incapable of speech. 'Didn't she?'

'No, I mean the TV channels, like she owned the TV channels. She always had her own thing she wanted to watch. She was a prize bitch. I'm glad to be out of there.'

'You know,' Fitzgerald said, 'I think I'm going to have to ask you to move out. I don't think you've been truthful with me at all.'

'Oh, I wouldn't do that,' Timothy Storey said. 'I like it here. It's been nice of you to let me have the room for nothing, but some people might wonder why a single man wanted to have a girl to stay in his house and gave her a room for nothing. It looks a little bit fishy, don't you think? I would only have to say to someone that you've been touching me—'

'I'm gay, you know. Everyone knows that.'

'Yes, indeed, what people in my country and some people in this one, too, like to call a sexual pervert. And then I might have to show them the hole that you drilled in the wall to watch me getting undressed at night. It's there, that hole.'

'There's no hole in the wall.'

'Take a look. I think you'll find there is.'

'You've drilled a fucking hole in the wall of my spare bedroom?' Fitzgerald said.

'Of course,' Timothy Storey said. 'I'm not going to tell anyone any of those awful things. I like it here, I really do. And another thing – those towels Mrs Baxter was telling you about, they're my towels. I bought those towels. I swear on my mother's life, I bought those towels.'

Satisfied that the conversation was over, Timothy Storey pushed off her shoes and lay back on the sofa. Fitzgerald went without speaking into the kitchen. A voice through a microphone in the other room began to announce the results of a phone-in vote, to wild applause, yellings of names and long, dramatic silences. The kitchen table was covered with the detritus of a quickly arranged snack; a tub of taramasalata lay open with the edge of a cream cracker broken off in it, like a tiny Excalibur. Fitzgerald pulled it out. Small fragments of cheese, of bread, lay scattered like bleak waste across the surface of the table; an open carton of orange juice had spilt onto the floor. The fridge door stood open, waiting for Timothy Storey to return to graze some more. Underneath the cork message board, Fitzgerald looked, and there was, indeed, a new hole, drilled in the wall, giving onto the spare bedroom. How had he failed to notice that? The situation bore down on him; where people like Bradbury had a handsome half-naked beast like Eduardo lolling around waiting for Bradbury's attentions, someone like Fitzgerald would only have a Timothy Storey, spilling biscuit crumbs down the sofa, thinking up blackmail attempts, destroying the masonry and eyeing up the bath towels.

'Can you give me a hand?' a voice called from the sitting room. 'This seems to be stuck.' Hopeless and speechless, Fitzgerald went into the room. Timothy Storey was kneeling before the DVD player, jabbing at buttons. 'I've tried this and I've tried that,' she was saying. 'But none of it does anything.' Fitzgerald contemplated, with hatred, her enormous, lying, blackmailing, cotton-straining, homophobic, racist, idle arse. Then a joyous possibility occurred to him. There was no reason not to do it. With three fast and accelerating steps, he was behind her, and he did it. He had never been good at school at football or rugby, but there, with a single, confident, long smooth swing, he gave Timothy Storey's arse the single kick of a lifetime.

He took a detour on his way to Eduardo's flat, going to the fancy confectioner's on Clapham High Street and buying an expensive box of chocolates – two pounds of pralines and fruit creams. Only when he reached Bradbury's road did he remember Eduardo's obsession with not eating or drinking anything that might make him fat. But it was too late; and, anyway, he realized he had bought the chocolates for himself, really.

'I want to say sorry, Eduardo,' he said, coming into the flat. The sun was streaming through the long windows, and lighting up half of Eduardo's face. 'And also goodbye, I suppose.'

'Goodbye?' Eduardo said. 'Are you going away?'

'No,' Fitzgerald said. The pathos of his farewell almost made him lapse into tears. 'No, I just think it's better that I don't see you again. It seems like a bad idea.'

'But where are you going?' Eduardo said.

He hadn't understood, and Fitzgerald said, 'I don't know yet. You might as well have these.'

He handed over the box of chocolates, and from the way Eduardo took the bag, eagerly, peering in at the confectioner-wrapped box of ribbons and bright paper, Fitzgerald saw that he was a man who liked to get presents, to get a present every day, no matter what it was. 'It's only chocolates,' he said. 'You don't have to eat them if you don't like them.'

'You can come in,' Eduardo said. 'I'm on my own. Daniel went to Monaco and he won't be back until Friday night. He went away this morning. It's so boring here.'

'I thought he went to Munich?'

'Yes, he did, he went to Monaco.'

'That's not the same place.'

'OK,' Eduardo said. 'I didn't know that. You want a coffee?'

'Only if you're making one. I'll stay and fend off your boredom, if you like.'

'Excuse me?'

Fitzgerald looked around. In this setting, this golden late afternoon, with the sun falling through the windows and the lilies from Saturday night's party now full-blown and on the edge of falling, Eduardo looked more dark, glowing and healthful than ever. He had not shaved today, and a dark shadow around the jaw gave him the air of a beautiful navvy. Fitzgerald drew in a great breath, savouring Eduardo's warm, animal, marshlike odour. 'Beautiful,' he said. 'I love the scent of lilies.'

'Lilies are so ugly,' Eduardo said. 'Everyone else thinks they're beautiful. For me, they're ugly, the way they fall, the yellow thing in the middle. I think they're ugly.'

'You have interesting opinions,' Fitzgerald said. 'I always thought you had a lot of interesting views about things.'

'Do you think so?' Eduardo said. 'I think I have interesting opinions. I think you're right. But Daniel always says, "Darling, just shut your mouth and look pretty. No one wants to know what you think." And one guy, one friend of his, asked me once if I knew how to tell the time, or maybe if I could tell my right foot from my left foot, some shit like that. His friends, they all think I'm just stupid, I know.'

Fitzgerald's attention was drawn to Eduardo's feet, his left foot, his right foot, perfect, dark, hairy and masculine. He would agree to be walked over, by such feet, he truly would. 'I don't think you're stupid,' he said. 'I always think you have the most original views about things. Not everyone would say that lilies were ugly, but they are kind of ugly, as flowers, you're right. I've often thought you had interesting opinions about all sorts of things.'

'That's funny,' Eduardo said. 'Because I do. I do have opinions about all sorts of things. For like, I think what we do in our lives, it comes back and has an effect on what happens to you. Like, if you are bad and mean to someone, then maybe later, someone else will be bad and mean to you. That's my opinion. I don't know how it works, but it does. And I think we're all connected somehow, like maybe if you are friends with someone, and they are friends with someone else, and that someone else is friends with someone else, then you are connected, you have a connection with that person, and in the end maybe you have a connection with all the world.'

'So because I know you, I have a connection with all sorts of South Americans I've never met,' Fitzgerald said. 'That's really an interesting idea. You're really an intelligent person, Eduardo.'

'And I think there is maybe enough money in the world for all the people, the rich people and the poor people,' Eduardo said. 'So there is no need for there to be poor people and rich people, the rich people, they don't need so much, so maybe the money can be shared about and the poor people get money from the rich people, and then everyone has enough and everyone is happy.'

'That's so true,' Fitzgerald said, in an ecstasy of happiness. 'That ought to happen. That definitely ought to happen.'

In the sunlit sitting room of a South London flat, the beautiful man sat, his hands clasped between his knees, his eyes widening, his pupils broad and dark and empty. He dipped now and then into the full box of chocolates, and his brilliant teeth shone from between his full lips as he went on talking, explaining, eating the pralines, emptying his poor unindulged mind before Fitzgerald. And Fitzgerald, understanding at last what it was that Eduardo wanted, and how, in the end, he saw himself, sat, barely interrupting, saying from time to time, 'That's so true,' and 'You surprise me. I didn't know you were as intelligent as that,' and 'You're an intelligent person, you really are,' murmuring and encouraging from time to time, as the light failed and the warm blue evening surrounded them.

It was as simple as that.

A Change in the Weather

(i.m. M.W.)

The air was plump, cold, full of anticipation. Something would fall from it. He was walking along the famous street with a briefcase that was not new; it was empty. To the left and to the right, ministries stood like serious cliffs. Whitehall. At this moment, the people he had worked with all summer and autumn and half the winter, they were sitting down in their office chairs and asking each other whether they wanted anything from downstairs. Their lives were going on, unambitiously, teaching English as a foreign language. Today was the day he started work in the public service, at the centre of the public service, in a building just off Whitehall.

George had a pass to the building – his building, he must start to think. It was in his pocket. He felt it now, as he walked. He knew exactly where he was to go, on this first morning. Mr Castry – Bill, he was supposed to call him – had taken him round and introduced him to people the Thursday before. He had not remembered very much, but Bill had made sure that he knew exactly where to go the following Wednesday. Everything else can come after that, he had said. George had got up at the weekend and walked all the way from the flat in Bloomsbury he was sharing with the Brazilian girl and the American girl. It was a rehearsal of his first day. The streets had been empty at half past eight on a Sunday morning, apart from some tourists and people who might have been hurrying to a Sunday service, here and there. George had walked down to Trafalgar Square, down Whitehall, to the outside of the building where he was going to work. He wanted to make sure that it was still there, where he remembered it was. Nobody was there to see him, and he had walked away quickly, not pausing, his trainers making no sound on the pavement. He might have been walking past purely by chance.

The office where he had worked for the last eight months was a cheerful and undemanding place. A temporary place. It accepted applications from overseas students to study the English language, and it assigned them to the appropriate class. Julie was in charge. She had been there for donkey's years, she said. Her husband was something in business. Something to do with bacon or coffee, but he was in the City; he never saw any bacon or coffee unless it was in the snackbar by the tube. For most of his day, bacon and coffee were just figures on a screen, Julie explained. Great mountains of notional bacon and coffee. She didn't know how he could stand it, all day long. There was a sense of fun in the office. They had opened the letters, had filled in the forms that were needed and, twice a week, had gone to the communal meeting room where the biggest empty table was, and arranged the applications from the past few days in order of classes. Probably Julie could have done this on her own, but she liked to get everyone involved. Sometimes a student came to demand his money back or to complain, because he had not succeeded in learning enough English. Those, too, were occasions of fun, once the complaining student had been refused and pacified and sent on his way. Julie had a way of rolling her eyes and holding her hands up to heaven that everyone copied. That office had been only until Christmas, and George had understood that from the start. The office he was going into would be for his entire life, from today onwards. He curbed his spirit of fun. The door to his building was open.

'Good morning,' he said to the man in uniform sitting behind the desk. A walk-in cupboard behind him was piled high with documents, tagged and ordered. George pulled out his plastic pass from his pocket and showed it carefully, the right side up so that the guard could inspect it.

The guard looked at it briefly, then at George, more curiously. 'Morning,' he said. Of course George should have been more casual about it. He felt like a criminal who, gaining access to a guarded building, had made himself stand out in some way. 'Starting to snow,' the guard said. His tone was not friendly, but it made George feel that he was accepted, grudgingly, within the building; it explained, too, something about the day that he had not understood. The metallic sensation of weight and chill obscurity in the air was not, as it had seemed, official London welcoming George to his new life. It was what had happened many times before without reference to the lives of any men or women: it was the sensation of snow about to happen. But George did not have to answer: a woman came out from the cupboard.

'Is it now,' she said, only glancing at George.

'It won't settle,' the guard said. George was pleased he had not misunderstood and tried to start a conversation. The office he was to work in was on the third floor. There was no need to ask anyone's advice about how to get there. One day, quite soon, he would know the names of both these people, and greet them with kindly deference.

He took the lift, and in a moment there he was in the corridor where the committee's offices were. There were four doors, and there were labels on three of them, giving people's names or their job titles. The fourth stood slightly open, a strip-light on. From inside he could hear a woman's voice, slightly muttering, and the sound of heavy documents being moved from one pile to another.

Before he could knock, the noise halted, and the door was opened wide. A woman with white hair in a bob, a sharp nose and bulbous eyes was there; she was wearing a coat and a scarf, and underneath a skirt in a large floral pattern, which seemed to be too long for her. 'Oh,' she said. 'Oh, I say.' Her voice was light and metallic, grating. She was assessing him, not in an unfriendly way but without a welcoming smile. 'I know who you are. You're our baby Clerk, aren't you? It's George, isn't it? I was saying to Pam, only this morning – trust the powers that be to send us a baby Clerk to nanny through, just when *all this* is kicking off. Patrick's not going to be one bit pleased. He'll be tearing his hair out.'

There was a sharp ring from inside the office. The woman turned and went inside, picking up the telephone. 'Energy Committee, Andrea speaking – oh, hello!' Her voice went from stern to girlish; she giggled. 'No, Patrick, don't you be – I'll tell you something, there's a lovely surprise for you when you get in, a lovely surprise waiting, your favourite thing … Oh. Who told you? … Well, no one tells me anything … Oh, about the usual, I would say. I expect you're phoning to say you're late in, as ever. Well, let me tell you …'

George walked away, feeling he should not listen to this flirtatious conversation. The walls were hung with mezzo-tints; eighteenth-century politicians and bishops on the shiny magnolia walls. Another door stood open to an empty office: its windows were hung with dirty grey net curtains, too long for the space and falling to a pile on the windowsill.

'That was Patrick,' the woman said, coming out of the office with a dark blue document clutched to her bosom. 'What are you doing down there? Come back and sit down with your aunty Andrea. She'll tell you what's what. You'll never guess. Patrick's calling from the phone box at the top of Whitehall. He says— Well, did you hear that bang?'

'No,' George said. 'What bang was that?'

'That bang!' Andrea said. 'Half an hour ago, that bang. I wondered what it was so I went down and asked the front desk, they didn't know any more than I did. What bang, he says. It made me jump, I can tell you.'

There was a pause. Andrea was inspecting him in close detail, standing with her legs apart.

'Well, we can't have you standing in the corridor all day,' she said. 'I expect I'd better show you where your office is, and you can make yourself at home. It'll be funny not having Mike in there. Ah, well.' She sighed theatrically. 'Now, these are my keys. I've got a set for everyone's office. Don't waste your time asking me if you can borrow them when you forget yours – ooh, Andrea, pretty please, it'll only be this once, I've never forgotten them before. I've got a good reply to that sort of thing. No. Way. Sunshine. Because there's no way I let them, my keys, I mean, out of my possession. So you've just got to hang on to yours. Welsh, are you?'

George's office was quite bare: there was a desk facing the door, an empty bookcase, and nothing more but a desk tidy, and a pair of plastic trays, one labelled IN and the other labelled OUT. There was a pile of papers in the in-tray. There was a large, grubby white telephone on the desk, and a spiral-bound notebook with a chewed biro alongside. Everything was generic, except one thing: a miniature object, a range of five furled flags the size of a stretched hand. There had been a previous inhabitant of this office, who now had moved out and left this. At some point George was going to meet that previous inhabitant; at some point he, too, was going to leave some individual sign of his life for a new boy, a new girl, to wonder about. In two years' time, perhaps.

Andrea had gone back to her office, closing the door, without waiting for a response to her question. A red light on the telephone showed that she had started a call. George hung his coat on the back of the door, and put his empty briefcase down by the side of the desk. His father's professional life must have started exactly like this, thirty-five years ago. He had arrived in the office where he would spend the rest of his working life, moving from job to job, but always remaining loyal to the organization. George's life had led up to this moment, and he would never be unemployed or unattached again. The years at university, trying to get an essay exactly right, trying to fish a piece of overlooked information from the seas of the Bodleian had led up to this moment, with an empty desk and a tray full of stern, detailed information.

He had taken two days off from the language school in October to undertake the application process. He had filled in forms, and drafted polite letters to imaginary supplicants who were attempting to defraud the public purse; he had entered into discussion with other applicants and with the examiners; and he had been interviewed. The rooms in which the process had taken place were bright-lit and yellowish. Each of them had windows, which, like this one, were veiled by net curtains too long for the space. A middle-aged woman with a mop of ginger hair and an amber brooch on a green sweater had introduced herself as the psychologist on the team. She had asked him penetrating and quite personal questions until one question – George could not recall what the question had been – had made him reply that he didn't believe the answer was any of her business. The interview had come to an end promptly after that. At the time, George had wondered whether he had scuppered his chances by being rude. Afterwards, when the offer of a job came, it seemed to him that he had been firm and impressive in drawing a line. So he was in his office, not yet with his name on the door, preparing to start work.

Elsewhere in the city, Londoners were setting to work, exchanging insults and flirtatious suggestions with their colleagues, having a cup of coffee, getting down to their most ordinary business. To kick your shoes off under your desk, to hang your jacket up and straighten the photograph of your family in front of you. They would be taking it all for granted. They did not know how magical it was to have a job; only George, on his first day, knew that. In a moment, it occurred to him that he was being paid for what he was doing, even now. The thought made him dizzy.

He had been in only two or three rooms in the public service, and before, he had thought that the net curtains hanging over the windows were a matter of personal idiosyncrasy by the inhabitants or users of the rooms. Now he understood that it must have been a decision made by some central authority. He got up and examined the net curtains. They did not hang loose, but fell to a gathering pile on the windowsill. The hems of the net curtains held small lead weights, to hold the curtain down in any breeze. He picked them up; felt them in his hand. The window did not have any kind of view. It gave onto a well between buildings, and faced a high wall with yellow and brown glazed brick, broken by a single brightly lit window. It appeared to be a window on a stair or a communal space. Snow was falling thickly through the artificial light.

'You'll be wanting to get on with that,' Andrea said, leaning against the doorpost. She held a blue printed report, the size of A4. 'The dreaded in-tray. There's always more to be getting on with. One word of warning – Patrick's quite nice but he's a devil for punctuality. He doesn't like it if there's something sitting in your in-tray that he's waiting for and he's still waiting for it tomorrow or, God forbid, the day after. Another word of warning – if Patrick starts gently suggesting that perhaps we could make a start on work before ten, start coming in by nine thirty or nine, just agree and come in at ten anyway. He's hopeless about all of that, coming in early – he's not another Chris Leonard, if you know who that was, which you don't, I don't suppose. Don't be taken in by that demeanour, he's very strict about most things. I had an aunt who was Welsh, not blood, of course, she was my uncle Edward's second wife. Ooh, she was a bully. She sent him out to fetch her little things, all her errands, in all weathers right to the end of his life and her twenty years younger than him. He was an old fool, we always used to say, my mum whose brother she was. I don't know why, but I've never managed to fancy the Welsh since then, all because of my uncle's second wife, Phyl. Strange, isn't it? And speak of the devil!'

In the corridor, behind Andrea, was a thin man with grey hair flopping over a drained white face, both middle-aged and boyish; he grinned forcefully, brushing the snow from his shoulders. 'What a day,' he said. 'What a day. So you must be George! Welcome, welcome, welcome. I should have been here to welcome you. But Andrea was here, I'm sure. How are you, my sweet?'

'Don't think you can get around me as easily as all that,' Andrea said.

'There's the most extraordinary thing,' Patrick said – he must be Patrick. 'Out there, the whole of Whitehall's been closed off. Did you see? There's been some kind of mortar attack on 10 Downing Street. I'm amazed you got through. A very, very good start, George! You succeeded in getting through the mass of police cordons and security walls. Most people would have given up and gone home and started work tomorrow. But not George! A big gold star on your first day, George. I really doubted I was going to make it. Did you not hear anything going off?'

'You see?' Andrea said. She tapped a red-painted finger-nail sharply on the back of the report she was clutching. 'I said there was a bomb going off, didn't I? Didn't you hear it? I'm the only one who heard anything, but, oh, no, Andrea, you must have been hearing things. But there you are.'

'I was at the far end of Whitehall,' Patrick said. 'And there was a police cordon going up, and I phoned you then from the phone box. Then I asked the policeman in charge what was happening. He wouldn't let me through at first. I knew he wouldn't. But then all of a sudden there was the Clerk of the House. I can't think what he was doing at the far end of Whitehall at a quarter to ten, but he just sort of glowered at them and told them who he was, and they let him through and me as well.'

'Well, there you are, then,' Andrea said. 'A mortar attack on 10 Downing Street. I do hope that nice Mr Major is quite all right.' She stood for a moment inspecting George, her mouth slightly open, an expression of amusement in her eyes. As if with a snap of command, she turned and left, shutting what must be the door of her office with a bright slam.

'She's a good soul,' Patrick said. He thrust an index finger in his ear and waggled it furiously, extracting it with a pop. 'You'll find that she has her own ways of dealing with things, and they all work out in the end. Just don't try to suggest any changes, and everything will be absolutely fine. Well. Welcome! I'm not at all sure what we should be doing today. I need to make two or three phone calls, and then we can sit down and talk and I can explain things, about where the committee has got to and what you ought to be doing and so on. I won't be too long. One thing …'

Patrick came into the office, and noiselessly pushed the door to. 'If I could recommend something – if I were you, I would always find that I had something important to do at the close of business on a Friday. Andrea's a very good soul, but it's as well not to be drawn into her Friday afternoons and evenings. Just a word to the wise.'

'What are you saying?' Andrea's voice shouted from her office.

'Nothing! Nothing at all, my sweet!' Patrick called. 'I was just welcoming George to the office. It occurs to me –' his voice dropped to normal volume '– that the one thing that is supposed to happen this morning is John Slaughter, the bod from UCL, he was supposed to come in and brief us. About wave energy. I don't know anything about wave energy and I don't suppose you do either. He was meant to come in at eleven thirty but I don't know if that's going to happen. If you wanted, you could try to find out whether they're letting anyone through. He hasn't phoned, as far as I know. Andrea,' he called again. 'Has John Slaughter called? Well, no, then.'

Patrick left. George knew that the time had come to demonstrate initiative and efficiency. He picked up the biro, and wrote 'John Slaughter?' in the spiral-bound note-book. He thought the best way to discover the state of affairs was to go downstairs and ask the security staff. He left the office, leaving the door open, and walked to the stairs. At the bottom, the woman security officer was at the desk on her own. He noticed she had a large hairy mole on her left cheek. He wondered if the time would come when he knew her name, and could recognize her. There was no need to ask her anything. Her voice called out behind him: 'There's been a mortar attack on 10 Downing Street. Everything's sealed off.' He nodded at her, and left the building, checking that he still had his pass in his pocket. The side-street outside was deserted; the snow was falling heavily, and had now settled. The junction with Whitehall was sealed off with police incident tape. George walked up to it. It must have been sealed off since Patrick had made it through. The whole of Whitehall, to left and right, was deserted behind incident tape. The snow fell on untouched ground, and was now a pristine three inches deep.

Once, George had been out in the country after a heavy snowfall, and had seen a woman playing a trick on her dog. A wound-up, bounding, overwhelmed dog, a Jack Russell. The woman bent down, and took a fistful of snow, rolling it into a snowball, and threw it. The dog hurtled forward to find the thrown thing to fetch, but where the snowball fell into the snow, there was only snow, and nothing to bring back. The dog ran around, astonished, baffled, and returned. The woman bent, rolled, threw again. The dog fell for it again. She had been doing it for some time. The field of snow contained something to fetch, and the dog had run into it, again and again. Now, beyond the Cenotaph, two policemen stood in their dark uniforms, like picturesque figures in a snow scene. There was no possibility that anyone would reach them until the road block was lifted. George stood there. The boulevard was transformed. Nobody else was there, looking at it. There was a perfume in the air that was the absence of perfume:

London stripped of its odours and made to smell of snow falling through oxygen. Nobody else would ever see the sight of Whitehall as blank and clean and silent as a remote moor in deep winter, unpressed by the tread of foot. The sight was as unique as his first day at the work he was going to make a success of.

He was able to tell Patrick that he thought there was no possibility of receiving any visitors until the cordon was lifted, and he did not know when that might be. Patrick cursed amiably, and went away, promising that he would sit down and explain everything about the committee and its work later that morning. George sat down and reached for his in-tray. He opened the first document. It was the annual report of an organization that seemed to be something to do with nuclear energy. George began to read it. He understood almost nothing of what he read, and soon a feeling of mild satisfaction came over him at the image of dedication he must be presenting, if anyone walked past his office and happened to glance in. In time, he shut the document and placed it in the out-tray. It occurred to him to make a note of what he had read, and he did so, in the spiral-bound notebook. He picked up the second document in the pile, and soon he looked like someone who was making efficient work out of his inconveniently interrupted day. He passed papers from one pile to another, with the appearance of someone who was working hard, and beginning a new life. Anyone could see he had the capacity to be useful, and the thought gave George, head down, something rather like joy.

My Dog Ian

'No, I don't speak the lingo at all,' she would say. 'Just bono giorno, honey, bono sera, that's all it takes. What's the point? They rob you anyway, rob you blind. Take Paolo ...'

Those Florentine afternoons. And afterwards I was always the same. Some people are always on stage. Most are destined always to be in the audience. Realizing it, you can never change the fact afterwards. After Florence, I would always be in row F of the stalls, hands clasped, looking up as the lights pointed in a different direction, allowing myself to be persuaded.

I went to Italy because of love – no, guilt. I was twenty-seven. I had been working 'in the arts' for five years. It was the sort of job that had sounded immensely desirable once. 'Arts administration,' I had confidently said to careers advisers, friends of my parents at drinks at Christmas. It had sounded good, labour rooted in passion and exchanged, at the end of the month, for money you couldn't be ashamed of earning. My contemporaries failed, and had to settle for jobs as solicitors. Five years later, they earned three times what I did and were beginning to drop me. They could not be blamed. 'Arts administration' meant a narrow office in a Victorian museum in the north, kept going with public money and the promise of lottery largesse. I found, after all, that you could be ashamed of the money at the end of the month. It was so little. My grey walls teetered with box files; outside, you walked between the museum's doubtful Raffaelino and the still more doubtful school parties. I grew to detest the single Matthew Smith, lurid as the municipal flowerbeds, to hate, too, the multiple aldermen in committees, drab and important in appearance as the museum's solitary Stanley Spencer. *Last Supper in Maidenhead*. You may know it from reproductions.

It was a city of three hundred thousand people but, still, it hardly seems surprising that I noticed Silvia. In that city, she was like a panther at a Tupperware party. The society was less extensive than you might imagine. A small Italian woman, with expensive accoutrements and an expensive, contemptuous way of standing with her hips jutting forward, made herself conspicuous. I had formed the habit of going to concerts in the university hall every other Friday. The tickets were cheap, and the platform just about big enough for an orchestra. The timpanist had to sit beneath the conductor's podium, however, and guess at the beat. More usually, as tonight, it was a string quartet. In the interval, the audience sat in their seats or clustered in the chilly atrium drinking coffee. It was not a well-dressed audience. You noticed Silvia.

'Have you seen,' my colleague Margaret said. 'A footballer's wife?'

(It was a recognized social category, in that impover-ished northern town with two famous football clubs. It was used for any woman under thirty with a tan and a handbag.)

'I hope she enjoyed the Webern,' Margaret said bitchily. I went to concerts with Margaret. It was no more than that.

'I hope so too,' I said.

After the interval, I took more notice of Silvia. She was sitting three or four rows in front of us, on the other side of the aisle. She listened intently to the first two move-ments of the next piece. Then, with a sigh, just as the string quartet was raising its bows, she got up and left, clacking down the central aisle. The string quartet lowered its bows, waited for her to leave. They began to play again.

'A bit much for the Footballer's Wife,' Margaret said archly, when it was all over. 'The bitonal passage can be a little demanding for many music lovers.' I wasn't sure, and not just because I didn't know what Margaret meant. To me those decisive stilettos clacking towards the exit looked much more like someone who only wanted to hear the scherzo of the Ravel string quartet; had come for that, had left when it was done.

In fact, Silvia seemed to attend the university concerts fairly regularly. I started to notice her now, and wondered why I hadn't noticed her before. She rarely stayed for a whole concert. She would turn up at the interval, leave after a particular piece, or even walk out, as with the Ravel, in the middle of one. It was terribly rude. It was the behav-iour of someone, I decided, who had come to like music through a collection of CDs. She had the habit of skipping about, selecting favourite movements, and rejecting music with all its tyranny and gleeful infliction of boredom in favour of 'highlights'. Margaret had a great deal to say on the subject. I weakly agreed, though tried not to refer to Silvia as 'the FW'. I did not agree with Margaret as often as she seemed to assume, and sometimes rebelliously thought, as I clapped exhaustedly at the end of some juvenile assault on a great masterpiece, that it might indeed be quite nice to press a fast-forward button as the Diabelli Variations grew a little too pleased with themselves. There was no such fast-forward button at the museum, either. It took up as much time as you were prepared to grant it.

'I've found out about the FW,' Margaret said one day, popping her head round the door of my office. 'She's not an FW, a footballer's wife, I mean. She's a *lettrice*.'

'A what?' I said.

'A *lettrice* in the Italian department of the university,' Margaret said immaculately. 'The equivalent of a *lectrice* in French, *Lektorin*, I believe, in German. She's come to teach them Italian.'

'It's not a big department,' I said. In the museum, we liked to think we had a relationship with the university that extended to sending Christmas cards to given departments, as long as no Bunsen burners were involved, at which point snobbery came into consideration. We did not know them, but we went to their concerts and we very well might have known them personally. Margaret, for instance, constantly referred to the professor of English literature, a man she had never spoken to and who was not called Percy as 'Percy'.

'No, it's not,' Margaret said. 'She's the first time they've been able to afford a *lettrice* – they're cock-a-hoop about it.'

'Where does the budget come from, though?' I said knowingly.

'They'll have got sponsorship from an Italian company,' Margaret said. 'Fiat, no, I tell a lie, it's Buitoni.'

'They make ravioli,' I said.

'They're sponsoring all sorts, these days,' Margaret said. 'The Hallé had a *bel canto* evening in Manchester and there was a reception at the town hall here after – the whole orchestra went. Oysters, I heard, the cor anglais player was laid prostrate for a week.'

'Only to be expected,' I said.

'But they've funded a *lettrice* for the Italian department here as well,' Margaret said. 'I found out she's called Silvia. Do you think they'd be interested in giving us money, Buitoni, I mean?'

'What for?'

'Oh, I don't know, that's your pigeon, isn't it? Something Italian. *Futurismo*. Let's have a meeting. She's living with the professor of theology. She comes from Cremona. Ah, *la bella Italia*,' she finished, clacking her hands in the shape of imaginary castanets, for some geographically inaccurate but festive reason.

'You've been busy,' I said, giggling.

'You know who I mean, the Australian professor of theology, not that there's more than one,' Margaret said. 'Renting a room off him. Must dash.'

She dashed.

As often happens in life, once you have acquired a certain body of information about a thing, a place, a person, it is impossible not to enter into a more active relationship with them. Once Margaret had told me all of this about

Silvia, it was inevitable that I would meet her very soon. It is something to do with the quality of the gaze. Once you know that a woman lives in the spare room of the Australian professor of theology, that she comes from Cremona, a town that, though famous for violin makers, only called up in my more slapdash mind the idea of a vast pudding, creamy and lemony at once, a city, more realistically, of pale yellow churches surrounded by a perfectly circular crimped wall, the warm colour of baked pastry … To be in possession of all this knowledge, both factual and fanciful, and yet to know that she knows nothing about you, not even your name, such a situation must engender a curious, knowing, unequal gaze.

I finally met her in the museum. Having seen her only at concerts, I stared somewhat, trying for a second to establish her context. She was looking with apparent enchantment at a glass case of ammonites. She felt my gaze; she looked up.

'Hello,' she said. 'You go to concerts, don't you? I recognize you.'

So we started to become friends. Three days later, we were sitting in the museum café.

'But you work here?' Silvia said. 'That's marvellous. I love this museum, so wonderful. In Italy we don't have these things, so beautiful, you know?'

A day or two later we were standing, as we had arranged, in front of a stuffed model of a sabre-toothed tiger. It had been patched together forty years ago out of old bits of dog and plaster fangs. Its skin was split and leaking kapok. Its fur was bald and patchy. Underneath, a handwritten notice in fading ink told us that possibly ten thousand years ago this animal had possibly roamed the countryside here-abouts, possibly.

'Look, a woolly mammoth,' Silvia said, moving on. 'Or the tooth thereof. You would not know that I was not English, yes?'

'Excellent,' I said. 'But you really like all this stuff?'

'Oh, yes, lovely,' Silvia said. 'Where do you live? You live alone?'

'Quite near here,' I said. I went on to tell her – there was not much to tell, but I told her about the rented flat at the top of a big Victorian house, converted for four single people by the Irish doctor who owned it; the dingy communal spaces, with the floral wallpaper no one had chosen, the half-dead spider plants, the solitary undusted china ornaments, Irish cast-offs, a chipped and smiling Edwardian lady in her china skirts at each turning of the stair, the mail for departed tenants piling up in the hall.

'Oh, that sounds nice,' Silvia said dismissively. She abruptly looked at her watch – 'Heavens,' she said. The watch was so tiny and so heavily jewelled you could not imagine using it to tell the time from, but Silvia said, 'I nearly forgot. I call my mother.'

'Not in the museum,' I said, gesturing at the woolly mammoth's tooth. But no one was around, and Silvia whipped her mobile phone out pooh-poohingly.

'*Mamma,*' she said. '*Come stai? … Bene, bene. Fa freddo – sta piovendo … Si, si, sempre. E Papa? … E Luca sta bene? … E Luigi? … E Roberto? … Mauro anche? … Massimo? … Va bene, va bene, ci parliamo domani, va bene? … Ciao ciao, Mamma.*'

She switched off. I later learnt that Silvia made this exact phone call, at exactly the same time, every single day of her life. She said that it was raining in England, she found out what the weather was like in Italy, and she asked after the health of her father and, in order, her five unstoppable brothers, Luca, Luigi, Roberto, Mauro and Massimo, twenty-two years old down to five, before promising to telephone at the same time the next day for the same purpose. It seemed strange to me, who in the English way called his mother once a fortnight or so. I rarely had much more to say than Silvia, but the embarrassment happened much less frequently. Silvia, I guessed at the time, might be homesick. That was not, however, the case.

And a week or so later, sitting in a pub in the early evening, she continued this conversation about her room and told me about the Australian professor of theology. For some reason, I had thought that he was a single man, but I learnt that he had a wife and three children, two sons and a daughter. By the end of that evening, Silvia had invited me to dinner, the day after next, at their house.

'I would say tomorrow night but, you know, it's not my house. I can't tell them until tomorrow morning, I need to give them a day or two, you understand? Listen, you like Italian food? I cook you an Italian dinner.'

All afternoon the next day I felt feverishly burgeoning, down in my windowless office at the museum. I felt like a nineteenth-century girl in a Swedish film, throwing off my corsets and discovering my sexuality.

'We missed you,' Margaret said, sidling through the door with a clipboard.

'Oh, Christ,' I said. 'It was the— Christ, what was it?'

'The education and outreach committee's budget meeting,' she said. 'It's been in all our diaries for weeks.'

'I knew there was something,' I said.

'There was indeed,' she said. 'There was something, you're right there.'

'That's a catastrophe,' I said. 'I don't know how I could have forgotten it.'

'You'll get the minutes,' she said. 'Don't be hard on yourself.'

Of course she was right: people missed meetings all the time. It wasn't that she was concerned about me. She could just tell that something new had come into my life; it would have taken a bright guess to alight upon Silvia, but Margaret, hovering in the door of my office, could tell it was something of that sort. She just wanted to know. I just wanted not to tell her.

The professor of theology was called Professor Quincy. He lived, I discovered, in an absurd villa in the opulent inner suburbs of the city. The street was lined with vast, ancient beeches, never intended by the Victorian planners to grow to such a size. Their foliage met and struggled overhead, and the pavement writhed and buckled over the roots like a late chapter of *Moby-Dick*. In other cities, to live in a Victorian house of this sort would require some wealth. These houses had been built for ruinous, grasping magnates, but a hundred years on, few people in the city had much money at all, and they were lived in by mere professors of theology. Quincy's house had crenellations, battlements in the local orange stone, stained glass in the oddest places. In the street, two small girls were playing an unnecessarily picturesque game of pat-a-cake, slapping each other's palms fiercely. As I passed them, they stopped and silently watched me. Silvia had given me the address, but had not offered to pick me up and take me there. I rang the doorbell, holding a box of chocolates and a bunch of carnations, which, I realized too late, were artificially dyed into lurid colours, the sort that would probably last in the recipient's second-worst vase for several weeks.

A dog hurled itself at the other side of the door, yelling furiously. I stepped back into the neglected border, tangling myself in some dead vines. As I was pulling my foot out, a shape appeared through the stained glass, a feminine shape, though too short and dumpy to be Silvia's. The girl – the Quincy daughter, it must be – rattled the door free from its chains. It swung open. I quailed back. The dog, still bellowing with rage, threw itself past me and ran directly to the front gate. It continued barking at the street, which was empty of anyone except the two small girls, who ignored it.

'He does that,' the girl said. 'He wants you to think he was barking at something behind you all the time. It's really that he doesn't want to offend you, but the temptation to bark, it's just too much for him. He's called Joseph. He's got very good manners, really. He'll come back when he thinks he's made his point.'

'Hello,' I said, going in. The hall of the house was red as raw liver, the heavy, elaborate wallpaper torn away into yellowing scars and hung randomly with pictures, knocked off the level by the passing human traffic: cheap old prints, a painting by a child, solidly framed, a watercolour of Derwentwater, a disconcerting and conical nude that might be of either sex – the acquisitions of rainy days, the findings in junk shops, the exhibitions of local painting groups, of arguments concluded with a dashing purchase. Something was clinging about my feet. I looked down. It was a man's walking sock. I kicked it off discreetly, trying to appear as if I were shaking myself from rain.

'Are you a friend of the Lettuce?' the girl said. 'Silvia, I mean. We call her the Lettuce because she's a *lettrice*, sorry, not very funny, I know. I'm Natasha.'

'I'm Mark,' a medium-sized boy said, hanging over the banister. 'Who's that?'

I introduced myself.

'Why have you got flowers? You've not come for dinner, have you? No one said anyone was coming for dinner.' The boy came downstairs, slouching from side to side.

'Yes, they did,' Natasha said. 'Silvia said, this morning.'

'Oh,' the boy said. He approached me, looked at me with amusement and, with a considered gesture, wiped his wet and dribbling nose noisily along the sleeve of his home-knitted red sweater. I looked at his clothes, and at Natasha's, with compassion. They were the clothes of the children of theology professors the whole world over. 'I'm precocious. Do you know what that means?'

'I would say that being able to describe yourself as precocious at your age is a fair definition of it.'

'No,' Mark said. 'That's not really correct. That would be an instance of precocity, and not a definition of it.'

I agreed.

'Come through,' a voice called. I followed the children into what proved to be the kitchen. I wondered whether I was expected. From the ceiling, what seemed to be a week's washing was hanging on a wooden frame, the frills and collapses of much-washed intimates like some natural phenomenon of drip and accretion. On the kitchen work-top, a pile of unsorted socks threatened to fall into a bowl of salad. The only orderly thing in the kitchen seemed to be five neatly labelled recycling boxes, and they were near overflowing.

'Hi,' I said. Silvia was at the stove. You noticed the things of the kitchen before the people in it.

'Oh, hello,' she said, half turning from the pot she was peering into. 'You found the house.'

'Yes,' I said. For some reason, I could not walk forward and offer her the awful flowers. With the terrible clarity of a crashing driver I envisaged the small but ugly scene as Silvia accepted the dyed carnations from my hand and I struggled to remember what on earth you say when hand-ing over such a thing, and I stood there mute. But then Natasha took it from my hand, gently but persuasively, and removed it, and I never saw it again.

In time other people came in, and sat at the table. 'This is my mother,' Natasha said; she seemed to have taken over the job of hostess. Conversation of a sort came and went. 'This is my father,' she said.

'We've never met,' I said firmly to the professor, bedrag-gled from some labour in the study, or so it seemed. 'But I know you by reputation.'

'Admired him from afar,' Mark said. 'Stalked him for months, drawn by an inexplicable fascination.'

'You can behave yourself,' the professor said. 'Company.'

'This,' the girl said, with pained distaste, 'is my brother Kevin.'

'I prefer to be called Benedict,' the boy said, coming in through the garden door. He was dressed unusually for a seventeen-year-old, in a striped boating jacket and a lop-sided bow tie. I wondered what school he went to, and whether he risked such an appearance in the playground. 'After the saint and founder of the well-known order.'

'Oh, God,' Mrs Quincy said.

'How long is this going to go on for?' Natasha said.

'The Church has endured solidly for two thousand years,' Kevin/Benedict said. 'I see no reason why the name Benedict should not endure one more human lifetime.'

'Yours, Mummy, he means,' Natasha said.

'Oh, God,' Mrs Quincy said.

'He got religion,' Natasha said. 'He went to the church down the road, the ordinary one, and got religion. He was always awful, you know. But then he decided that wasn't religion enough for him. So he went on to another church, which was more religion. And then he ended up on his knees dreaming of the day when he can suck the Pope off.'

'Natasha,' Professor Quincy said.

'Well,' Natasha said. 'And it was then that he got the voice to go with it.' It was true that Kevin/Benedict talked in a way unlike the two other children, who had a faint, attractive Australian hovering in their voice. Kevin/Benedict was conspicuously posh in his manner, sounding as if he were working up to announcing Saint-Saëns on Radio 3 in hushed tones. 'It won't last. He's signed all sorts of pledges, alcohol, smoking, chewing gum, but they won't last and then he'll not be religious any more. Temptation, you see.'

Kevin/Benedict lowered his head, faintly smiling, pustular. He looked like the Book of Job, and you could imagine him spottily going to and fro on the earth, walking up and down on it, forgiving everyone in a pimply manner.

'Would our guest like to say grace?' Kevin/Benedict said.

I looked at him with astonishment.

'Oh, God,' Mrs Quincy said. I agreed. I had never said grace in my life, and had probably heard it said no more than ten times. 'I couldn't,' I said. 'I wouldn't know what would be the appropriate thing.'

'Well, shall I?' Kevin/Benedict said.

'If you're quick about it,' Silvia said. 'My pasta doesn't wait for no one, not God, neither.'

'Oh, Lord,' Kevin/Benedict began. The rest of the family began eating, and, after a moment, so did I. 'Thank you for a delicious dinner, which we can eat, conscious of the fact that many in this world, many even in this city, not a mile from where we sit, have no ravioli to eat, nor *sugo all'amatriciana* –'

'Very good, Benedict,' Professor Quincy said, through a mouthful of dinner.

'– with which to adorn their ravioli, and so we give thanks that we are so fortunate as to enjoy the fruits of the pasta-maker and the mincing machine, free of worries, and taking pleasure in good company, and new friends around the family circle –'

'He means you,' Silvia said. 'No, don't use the bread, bread with pasta, that's terrible, terrible.'

'– and thinking all the time of how through the good things of the table our different lands and cultures are brought together in happiness and enjoyment in the unity of mankind and the love of God, amen.' He opened his eyes and raised his head, murderously. 'You've all finished.'

'Yes,' Mark said. 'I was hungry. I wasn't going to let it go cold.'

'I wonder where the practice of saying grace comes from,' I said conversationally. 'It must be of considerable antiquity.'

'Yup, must be,' Natasha said.

I was smiling and nodding like crazy at Professor Quincy. I had been aiming the observation at the professor of theology.

'Pa,' Mark said.

'Hmm?' Professor Quincy said. 'Oh – you said something. Sorry, you were saying?'

'I was saying, I wonder where the practice of saying grace comes from,' I said.

'Oh, right,' the professor said, swatting a fly circling his head. 'It was one of those English things where you're really asking some kind of question. I thought you were just talking.'

Silvia got up, collecting the plates, as if inadequately appreciated. I was rather hoping for some more pasta. It was jolly good. My thanks were effusive, and strange at this family kitchen table.

'Grace, Pa,' Mark said.

'Are we still talking about grace? To tell you the truth, I'm off work, chum,' the professor said. 'I like to stop the theologizing at six, if I can. Let a fellow eat his grub. I've met people like you before, think I like theology so much I want to talk about it all the time. What's this, Silvia?'

'Agnello,' Silvia said, bringing a vast and incinerated joint, perhaps a shoulder, to the table, half buried in carrots.

'Looks yummy,' he said. 'I'll tell you a secret. I don't like theology at all. You want to know how I got lured into it? I'll tell you.'

'Oh, God,' Mrs Quincy said, but rather with relish, and the children's eyes were shining. You could tell this was their favourite performance.

'Do tell,' I said.

'You start off in year nine at school,' Professor Quincy said. 'And they say to you, "All right, what do you want to do? Do you want to go on with history, or do you want to do Sanskrit – because the Sydney public schools, they offer that now, these days – or do you want to be doing biblical studies or RE, as they'd be calling it? Now I tell you, I grew up in Australia, you know. So history in Australia is not much to be writing home about. And my old mum – your granny in Sydney who killed the funnel-web with the ping-pong bat, kids, I'm talking about – she said, "Do what you're good at. A qualification's a qualification." So I do RE and I get the top marks in it because, to be frank with you, it's not all that difficult to do well in RE. Well, the school says to me, "Do what you're good at," so I carry on with the old RE, and before you know it, there I am at Sydney University, which is one of the most distinguished universities in the world, as I'm sure you know, because you don't strike me as one of those stupid snobs that England specializes in, and my degree, blow me down, it's RE still, only they don't call it that by now. It's called theology.

'Now my professor-lady at Sydney University, she takes me under her wing, because I'm a bright lad, and I pick up the old Hebrew for the Old Testament, and I pick up the old Greek for the New Testament, and she says to me, "What about taking it a bit further, because you know, my dear, it fits you for all sorts of things a degree in theology? And I say, "Like what?" And she says, "Well, you could become a priest," to which I say, "No, thanks, love." And I say, "Like what else?" And she says, "Hmm." And it turns out that the other thing it turns you out for, fits you for marvellously, it's doing more degrees in bloody theology. So then she says to me, "I've got an idea for something you can write about for your doctorate, son." So, being a bit wet behind the ears, I say, "What's that, then?" And she says, "Well, I reckon that there's this book in the Bible called the Book of Kings – I don't expect you to know of it, son – and I reckon, if you look at it, there's bits that's been written by one fellow and bits that's been written by another fellow. Well," she says, "I reckon that the bits that were written by the other fellow, it wouldn't surprise me if they were written by a woman and not a fellow at all."

'So I says, "Why do you think that, then?" And she says, "You go and write your thesis and tell me why. And I tell you what, call the first fellow P and the other fellow Q." So there it was, and here I am, and for thirty years, I've been writing about this nutty old girl called the Q narrator in the Book of Kings and no one else believes in her, and if she existed, I don't know why you'd think she was a woman, and if she was, I guess she was fairly typical of her time and place, which means that she struggled with a major facial hair problem and took a bath maybe once in her life, like by accident. And she seems a bit slow on the uptake, because I tell you, the bits she wrote, she's missed the point a bit, I reckon. And it's taken me thirty years to work out that I hate a prehistoric old girl called Q who never existed, and I hate the Book of Kings, and I hate theology and, son, I'm not that keen on God in the first place. You ever think, we all end up doing the one thing – the one thing, mind – guaranteed to make you want to puke every day of your life?'

'Yay,' Natasha said. 'Listen to your father, Kev. He knows about God.'

'But God knows more about him,' Kevin/Benedict said, placing his knife and fork fastidiously parallel.

Mrs Quincy put her knife and fork down too, in a furious clatter. 'If you don't stop it now, this second,' she said, with real venom, to her son, 'you can go and sit on the naughty step.'

Professor Quincy's story – obviously a much-repeated one – had cheered him up. It cheers most people up to tell the story of their life, particularly if you can reduce it to well-paid catastrophe. He set about his lamb, now rather cold-looking, with beard-smearing gusto.

'No no no no no no no no no,' Silvia said. 'You can't say everyone hates what they do. Look at him. He works in the museum, he loves it.'

'I don't love it exactly,' I said, unheard. 'My job. That was a lovely dinner.'

'The naughty step,' Natasha said, in stages. Her face was purple; she had been in choking hilarity for a minute and a half. 'The naughty step.'

'The naughty step,' Mark said, in solemn tones. 'Do you hear that? Kevin?'

'Benedict,' Kevin/Benedict said, all fight out of him.

The next morning I lay in bed, listening to the radio wind itself up into early fits of irritation and denunciation. The specific repetitions of government ministers wound in and out of my dreams as I dropped in and out of thin layers of sleep, and the faces of old friends looked into my eyes, telling me with concern about dangers to the environment. I thought about the night before. Silvia's vividness had been lost somewhere in that family, and her spotlit personality subsumed in the execution of her fine national dishes. Most of what I had said to her had been mere compliments on her cooking. I might as well have told her how well she managed to be an Italian woman. But perhaps that was right. I realized, after all, that I had no concept of Silvia apart from her nationality. She was just Italy in Yorkshire, an idea complete enough in itself that it sounded like the title of a symphonic poem by Delius. No nation is as interesting as a human being. So I was late in the museum, and Margaret, loitering round the eland in the foyer with a pen on a string round her neck, had a word for me. 'So we're friends with the professor of theology now,' she said. 'Eating dinner round there. You live dangerously, I must say.'

There was an unexpectedly hostile glitter in her eyes. She'd been preparing herself to coruscate lightly over the details of my expanding social life.

'Dangerously?' I said.

'I've heard they use the dog's basin as a pudding bowl,' Margaret said. 'If there's more than a given number of guests. It's said that many an unwelcome guest's found "Bonzo" written at the bottom of the cherry trifle when, naturally, it would be too late to do anything about it.'

Sherry trifle, I silently and irritably corrected. 'No, it was very nice. Silvia cooked. It was very good.'

Margaret, huffing off, was premature in her suggestion, but after that evening, I did rather take to the Quincys. Less predictably, they seemed rather to take to me. I did my grocery shopping in Sainsbury's, a branch I'd always thought far too big for my bedsit needs. Like a child, I went up and down every aisle, even the sock aisle, generally finding something necessary in each one, and a few days down the line generally throwing out a pile of decaying compost, the evidently perishable remains of my excessive shop.

Going round a supermarket, one too big for your needs, is like a sad evening in front of the television, hurtling through the channels and seeing the same faces recurring, harassed and increasingly familiar. The OAP you greet absently like an old friend by the time you reach the whisky was a new face as recently as the organic peas. A White Queen-like figure was floating in and out of my awareness at the far ends of aisles, only doubtfully recognizable. But I did know her: it was the professor's wife. She was only vague because she was out of her initial context. I was standing in front of the milk display when Mrs Quincy hailed me, coming alongside with a gigantic and nearly filled trolley, like a docking liner.

'You look lost and confused,' she said, hoisting four six-pint cartons of milk into her trolley, the shopping of a materfamilias with milk puddings to make.

'I was looking for milk,' I said.

'Well, you're in the right place,' Mrs Quincy said.

'No,' I said. I gestured feebly. 'I only want a pint of milk. Just for my cup of coffee in the mornings. They've only got enormous ones.'

She admitted this to be true. There were the gargantuan cartons suitable for her needs, but nothing smaller.

'Well, that's no good,' she said. She looked around for an assistant. 'Excuse me. Excuse me. Yes. I mean you. Yes. Hello. Thank you.'

The assistant who came over unwillingly was a tall youth. He might have been a sixth-former doing a holiday job.

'Do you really not have any milk,' Mrs Quincy said, 'in any size smaller than this? My friend here only wants to buy a single pint.'

'It's really not that important,' I said, Mrs Quincy contradicting me. 'I could buy a pint at the newsagent's round the corner.'

'At considerable inconvenience to yourself and some increased expense, I imagine,' Mrs Quincy said. 'Pay no attention. Now. Do you have one-pint sizes of – what, full-fat milk? You should drink semi-skinned. You get used to it in no time at all, three weeks, max.'

'I don't like it,' I said.

There was a pause before the boy realized we were waiting for his answer.

'We've run out,' he said. 'The delivery comes at three, I think.'

'Nonsense,' Mrs Quincy said. 'How can you have run out? I want to talk to the manager. Fetch me the manager immediately.'

The boy disappeared.

'The trouble with the English,' Mrs Quincy said very distinctly, attracting some attention from passing shoppers, 'is that they never complain. Or they never complain at the right time. They sit around whining endlessly when nothing can be done about a problem, and then when they're offered the chance, they sit quietly. I've often noticed it. If you don't say anything, you don't get anything.'

'How's the professor?' I said, in order not to respond. 'And the children? I so enjoyed dinner the other night.'

'Oh, God,' Mrs Quincy said cryptically. 'Here he comes.'

She meant the manager, not the professor. The manager looked, frankly, too grand to be troubled with these things. He was approaching in his suit and tie, the original boy tagging along behind, his face purply embarrassed. He had never had to ask the manager anything directly before, and was now wondering, I guessed, whether he should have done so. But Mrs Quincy had worked herself up into a lather over someone else's dairy purchases, and she was going to have her moment.

'I understand that there's a problem here,' the manager said.

'There is a problem,' Mrs Quincy said. 'Now, look at these shelves. You have six-pint containers of milk. You have four-pint containers of milk. And those are very well and good for someone such as I, with a family who drinks milk all day long. But look again and ask yourself whether you see single pints of milk. No. You do not. And for many people a single pint of milk is what they need. Now, this is my friend and he lives on his own. He lives in a bedsit. He

64

has few friends and he never cooks. He lives on takeaways and similarly unhealthy things. But he likes a cup of coffee in the morning or sometimes a cup of tea. And it takes him probably five days to finish even one pint of milk. What is he going to do with a gigantic carton like this? He would never finish it. He would find it turning to cheese before he was halfway through it. And he's paid four times as much as he wanted to for it, which, considering that he's living on a very restricted budget, is not a trivial matter. Listen to me. Where are the single pints of milk for the single lonely people in this town? Where are they?'

'We've got delivery problems,' the manager said, as I made faint noises of demurral and objection to this poignant but honestly insulting account of my life.

'What rubbish,' Mrs Quincy said. She was delighted. 'Now come along with me. Have you finished here? Will you ever. Do your shopping.' (Over the shoulder.) 'Here. Again?'

'Well,' I began, drawn along in Mrs Quincy's wake.

'The thing is,' Mrs Quincy said, once we were in her car – it seemed a done deal that I was being whisked off by her, though whether she was generously offering me a lift home or abducting me was unclear, 'Silvia's really a sort of family. Well, not family at all. But Richard, my husband, you know, she's the neighbour of a cousin of his in Florence.'

'In Florence?' I said. 'I thought she came from Cremona.'

'Comes from Cremona, ran away, very naughty, but it's all made up now, lives in Florence in a flat next to Aunty Paulina. I say aunty, but let me get this straight. Richard's sister's second husband, his stepmother, it was her niece. Half-niece, is there such a thing, because of course their

65

mother, who was married to the stepmother's brother and used to be a McIntyre, one of the Mount Isa McIntyres, if you can imagine such a thing, she met a Melbourne dentist and moved to Melbourne with relief and married him, and that was Paulina's father. Didn't work out but she stayed on in Melbourne, can't think why. This is all ancient history now, though. Paulina must be sixty if she's a day.'

'Look out,' I said, as Mrs Quincy jumped a red light.

'Oh, they get out of your way,' Mrs Quincy said, on this occasion correctly. 'Well, Paulina gets in touch out of the blue in July, which is very odd, because the only occasion we ever hear from her is Christmas, a card and a bottle of fruit in mustard-flavoured syrup, which no one will ever eat and you can't in all conscience give it to anyone else, they've been piling up in the larder for years. Not even to a jumble sale. I tried.'

'So you heard from Paulina,' I said, seeing that Mrs Quincy had lost her train.

'Oh, yes,' Mrs Quincy said. 'And she says her next-door neighbour, a nice girl, she's coming to England and not just England, to here, to be a lettuce in the university as the kids will insist on saying, not funny, and can we help her find somewhere to live? So Silvia comes and we let her have the top floor because, frankly, we just don't use it. I can't even remember the last time I went up there. The children tell me she's made it quite nice now. And, as you see, she's no trouble and she cooks up a storm, so she stayed. She was in *West Side Story*.'

'Silvia?' I said.

'No, Aunty Paulina,' Mrs Quincy said. Then – she must have told this before, and often been told in response that her listeners had been in *Oliver!*, back at school – she said, 'The real one, I mean. The famous movie. Here we are.'

We were at the Quincys' house. I went in, carrying half of Mrs Quincy's bags and my own one; she was talking all the way. And I stayed all afternoon.

Silvia's hours at the university were irregular, and when, over the next three months, I saw her or I did not see her, it was when I was at the Quincys' house. I learnt more about her from Mrs Quincy and from Natasha than I did from our occasional independent outings. I did not suggest going to a concert with her. I knew that Margaret could hardly cope with my defection from her side to Silvia's, and with Margaret I contrived different outings altogether. With her sensible shoes on, Margaret came with me on buses out to the national park and hiked in well-planned ways. We hiked not there and back, but in great twelve-mile circuits round entire dales, with a stop in a pub half-way round, greeting all other walkers on the way, if they seemed from their dress to be taking it as seriously as we were.

Silvia's clothes alone would have disbarred her from any such outing. Our dates tended to be cultural, short of Margaret's territory of the concert hall. The heavily subsidized theatre in the town was safe, a concrete bunker with an apron stage and, every so often, Sir Derek Jacobi. It changed its offering only every six weeks – a period that thoroughly exhausted the fascination the city might have cherished for Goethe's *Egmont*, say. There was a university theatre, taken up with student productions and local amateur dramatic societies. The cinema of the town fastidiously refused ever to screen anything that had cost its makers less than thirty million dollars. We managed, somehow, though we left a lot of offerings halfway through.

It was over dinner after one of these unsuccessful outings that Silvia made her point. The offering had been a number about people falling in love against the odds and having to run through cities before being reunited at the check-in desk. We had stayed to the uplifting end. Silvia was silent and scowling all the way to the restaurant.

'I'm going back to Florence the week after next,' she said, not quite looking at me.

'Not Cremona?' I said.

'No,' she said. 'My flat in Florence. It's empty over the summer. I'm going there.'

'Ah,' I said.

'You like Mrs Quincy, and you like Natasha, isn't it?' she said, quite emphatically.

The restaurant was Italian, after its own fashion. It was not my choice – I would have hesitated to suggest it to Silvia. Even more oddly, we had been there before, and she had spent the whole evening denouncing everything about it, from the waiter's pronunciation of *bruschetta* to his kindly suggestion of a cappuccino to finish with. 'They're catering for what people want,' I had mildly protested. 'There's no point in being Tuscan purists round here.' But it was a terrible restaurant; everything, to the outer limits of plausibility, had been improved with the addition of cream, and unfamiliar foodstuffs had crept into unlikely dishes. In all of this I had been instructed by Silvia – I mean, I wouldn't have known that rule about not having pineapple with pasta – but her mood of denunciation this evening was only encouraged by the restaurant. Its purpose was directed straight at me.

'No, not yet,' she said to the waitress, returning to her theme.

'No, we're not ready to order,' she said again, five minutes later. 'And the other thing ...'

'Listen, I will call you when we're ready,' she said, still later, as the waitress sauntered over.

'All the same to us, love,' the waitress said. 'We're not busy. I'm enjoying it, to tell you the truth.'

But all the same, when we were done, I had agreed to come with Silvia to Florence in two weeks' time. The denunciation, I had been expecting for some time – the slammed door of the Quincys' kitchen, the scowls and the increasingly rebarbative style of her outfits when we met. I hadn't been prepared for this outcome.

The promise was easily made but, after all, I had a job. Silvia, so emphatic about my job at first, seemed to be under the impression that, like the university's academic staff, I was going to take off for three months in the summer. The best I could manage was a fortnight, and that, I was given to understand, was quite a favour at such short notice. Margaret, when she heard of it from some other source, obstinately asked me, quite near the beginning of one of our hikes in the country, if I would like to go on holiday with her, if, of course, I hadn't made other plans for the summer with any other person. My explanation cast a pall over the day; something I think she might have foreseen. It was all so tiring.

Silvia's attic at the Quincys' was an island of lucid clarity in that stormy household: a neat bed, two handsome chairs, some pretty pictures against a colour she'd chosen herself, and a small bookcase carrying her fifty favourite books. So it was not a surprise to discover the airy, even elegant quality of her flat in Florence. It was at the top of a modern building, with terraces the size of half a tennis court, crowded with pelargoniums, bright as a seaside landlady's garden. Inside, in pockets of air-conditioned cool, austere long chairs of chrome and leather treacherously invited the act of reclining. It was on the outskirts of the city, at the foot of one of the hills that rise and surround it. The geography of Florence, as I soon discovered, kept the worst of its weather unchanging and building, stiflingly, from one week to the next all summer. There were other things about the flat to be discovered. The building was at the very end of a long-buried and nearly mythical river, the Affrica; and if there was no way of our detecting it, the river was clearly an object of fascination to millions of mosquitoes, which had an ancestral habit of following its course all the way from the Arno to Silvia's building, then staying exactly where they were for the whole summer. I became familiar with great generations of mosquitoes as the weeks passed, thwacking at my own head in the middle of the night, sometimes in Silvia's spare room, sometimes not.

'And of course there's Paulina next door,' Silvia said. 'But I expect you know everything about her.'

Quickly, we settled into a sulky routine. Silvia had, in the past, spent a good deal of time playing the guide, she said. (She meant: pushing visitors around Florence with an out-of-date guide book.) So the first day, she came out with me, showed me the crucial bus, and took me briskly to four asterisked treasures.

'Duomo,' she said.

'*David* of Michelangelo, great masterpiece of *Italian* art,' she said.

'Out here in the rain?' I said. 'When it rains?' (It was actually oppressively hot.)

'In Florence, it never rains,' she said. 'Look, beautiful sunshine. Englishman, wanting his rain. Where's your umbrella and your bowler hat, Englishman? No, it's not real, anyway. The real one it's inside Accademia, up that street. We don't have time.'

'Uffizi,' she said. 'Look at the queue!'

'And Ponte Vecchio,' she said, the unopened guide book firmly in her hand.

'I see,' I said. That evening, she phoned up all her Florentine friends at length, and complained with great gusto about me. She spoke in Italian; I understood quite well enough. After the first day, I left the flat in the morning and dutifully visited churches, palazzos, museums – more museums; I started with the postcard sights and steadily worked my way downwards. In time, I surprised the attendants of museums named after nineteenth-century Englishwomen, residents of Fiesole, with an unaccustomed ring on their doorbell. How Silvia passed her time, I don't quite know. I returned to the flat after an invariably unsuccessful sort of tourist lunch, often a sandwich at a bar by the bus station, a one-armed bandit's electric fanfares in my ear. The afternoons, she was incommunicado, and I read. We met at six each day.

'You know a funny thing,' she said, when we were settled in a bar the third night. 'I asked an English boy to stay here last year, and at the end I said to him, "What do you like most in Florence?" Because, of course, I think maybe he's going to the Duomo, the Uffizi, the Ponte Vecchio, maybe. But he says, "Most of all, I like the bars, where you go, you buy a drink, there's nice little bits of food there you can eat, it's all free." You English! Crazy for something free, always, always.'

I laughed politely, but I rather agreed with last summer's Englishman. The bar was laid out with such substantial nibbles, as Margaret would have called them, I was rather wondering in my impoverished way whether we could get away with not having dinner. Not the least of the issues that had arisen was that Silvia, considering the fact that I was saving on hotel bills, clearly thought that I ought to buy her dinner every night at a restaurant of her choice.

But that night I finally met Paulina. Silvia, I divined, had decided to keep her from me: enough of my friendship with the Quincys, or any potential one with their sister's second husband's stepmother's half-nieces. The door to the flat next door was open when we got home, though inside there were no lights. It was a stifling evening. A languid wail came out of the open door, followed by a middle-aged woman emerging from the darkness in aquamarine kaftan and turban.

'Oh, not again,' Silvia said.

'Oh, honey,' Paulina said. 'Be an angel. You know how hopeless I am. And I'd ask Paolo, honest to God, but—'

'It's not very difficult,' Silvia said.

'You say that, but— Well, hello there, I'm Paulina, how do you do – you remember, honey, the last time I somehow managed to put everybody's lights out, it was simply a disaster,' Paulina said. She had a curious voice, emphatic on each word, and with an accent not quite American, not obviously Australian. She could have been the product of a thorough elocutionist in any one of a dozen colonies. 'You see,' she explained confidentially, as if I were alone, 'the lights here, they sometimes go out for no reason at all, and I know there's something terribly simple you need to do in the basement …'

'There's just a switch, that's all, and you pull, no – what is it you do with switches? You turn, you flick – is that right? You flick it and then it's all OK, it's simple,' Silvia said, almost jumping up and down with rage.

'Thank you a cartload, honey,' Paulina said. 'I know you don't mind one bit when I need you to help me out.'

'You, come with me,' Silvia said. 'Then you know what you need to do in case it happens again.'

It was as simple as Silvia had said. Paulina must have been some kind of genius to make a mess of it.

'So that's Paulina,' I said, down in the basement.

'Yes,' Silvia said. She was decisive on the subject. And when we got back upstairs, Paulina's light was restored.

'I can't imagine what I'd do without you,' she said effusively, looking me up and down openly. 'Come in and have a drink. I've got …' her voice sank seductively '… I've got some Campari.'

'Perhaps some other night,' Silvia said.

It seemed to me, as the days went on, that the only understanding I had had of Silvia disappeared in her proper context. If in England she possessed a vivid and fascinating character, in Italy it was clear that I had not got much beyond discovering her to be Italian. In Italy, her reality dissolved, like a glass full of water in the ocean. I had no access to her real character, not having had the practice at reading it. It was partly my fault, for being satisfied with an exoticism that, after all, was banal even in Yorkshire. But partly, I think, it was hers, since in Yorkshire, in the Quincys' house above all, she defined herself so entirely by what she was not as to appear nothing but an embodied foreign culture. In Italy, having nothing much in her repertory to fall back on, she settled for being sulky. So it was, inevitably, that at a loose end in Florence, I found someone who was conspicuous in her culture, like a photographic negative of Silvia clacking noisily down the aisle of a concert hall in England.

The next morning, as I was leaving Silvia's flat, I saw that Paulina's door was open again. Round the door unfurled a long white arm, like the frond of a fern, followed by Paulina's head, the hair braided and twisted. Inside, the curtains were still drawn; she was in her peignoir.

'Honey,' she said huskily, her voice lowered for the sake – I guessed – of Silvia, 'you couldn't do me a favour, could you?'

'Of course,' I said.

'Thank you so much, darling,' she said. I noted the upgrade in the category, from *honey* to *darling*. 'I'm all out of bread and milk. You couldn't just pop down to Andrea's by the bus-stop and get me – I don't know – a loaf and some of that vile Italian milk? Otherwise I'll have to get dressed and I loathe getting dressed before breakfast, you know how it is. It wouldn't take you a moment, I swear.'

'No trouble,' I said, and did as she asked, coming back up the stairs rather than in the lift. The wheezy comings and goings of the lift echoed in Silvia's empty flat, generally awakening her curiosity.

'Thank you so much,' Paulina said. 'Now come inside while I find some money for you. How much was it?'

'Four euros,' I said, determined not to let it go. Paulina had drawn the curtains, and her flat was heavy with plush and stuffing, the marble floors covered with neatly tessellated red-and-purple rugs, the windows hung with yellow velvet curtains. On the available surfaces, dolls, stuffed animals, signed photographs in rococo silver from some previous age of splendour and café royalty. Paulina's face, when she turned to me, was broadly painted, an old wrinkled apple with brash blue eyeshadow, asymmetrical pools of rose-pink blusher, a tremblingly applied gash of bloody lipstick. She was agonizingly thin, a blotched skeleton splashed with Rimmel colour here and there.

'I can't seem to find it, not just at this exact moment,' she said. 'You're not in a great hurry, are you?'

'I've got a church to go and see,' I said. 'That's it.' Then it seemed rude not to tell a Florentine resident where you were going, and I added 'Santa Maria del ... del something. Anyway. Don't you have someone to do this stuff for you? Paolo, is it?'

'Paolo?' Paulina said. 'How d'you hear about Paolo?'

'I thought I heard you mention him last night,' I said. 'I thought he was your—'

'You thought he was my lover?' Paulina said, though I hadn't been about to say that. 'That is the world's biggest laugh. I'll tell you about Paolo, the rat fink. Well, when I moved here, I didn't know anything, not one thing. I didn't know how to get anything done. I had no idea – this was the first thing that started off the whole Paolo thing – I had no idea how to get one of those darling little brass plates engraved, you know, and put on your front door once you've moved in. Not a single solitary clue. Of course I could care less but the only thing I had succeeded in achieving, though Heaven knows how I did that, darling, was to find me an apartment to live in. Well, I can tell you, after a few days, I had gotten myself into a terrible state and a business over this silly little brass plate and so I went straight back to the realtor to throw myself on her mercy, try to found out how the hell these things are done.

'Well, the realtor, she turned out to have Paolo on her Rolodex, and she suggested that he was the world's most useful human being, and I should make a *loooooooooong* list of things in the apartment that needed his attention. Because there's always a million and one things when you first move into a place. No, honey, Paolo's certainly not my lover. He's my factotum, you might say, if we were in an eighteenth-century opera, which we aren't. He turned up the next day. He's a funny little man – you'd like him. He's like a jockey, five feet tall, with a big nose and knobby old arms. That's from all the cycling he does at weekends. It's just so bad for anyone of his age but I gave him the list and he did everything on it. He is a fink and a rat fink and a liar, but, honey, I give him this credit. When I gave him the list to do, he did that list.

'So, about a week later – I wish I knew where my purse was, do put the coffee on – I thought, That's a nice terrace out there, but it would be so much nicer with a few plants on it. But I have no idea whatsoever how on earth you would find someplace that sells plants, and how you would arrive there, and how you might transport all your plants from there, wherever there might be, to here. So again I telephone to Paolo, and he says, right away. Pistoia. And he took me to Pistoia where every plant under the sun grows, and we loaded up that funny little van with plants, with lemon trees and orange trees and lilies and *'erbs*, which he practically insisted I buy, and this *immensely* costly watering system, which didn't seem to do much good, because the only things that grow out there are olive trees and lavender, which is too depressing. Everything else died. Don't ask me why, darling.

'But at the time I was grateful,' she went on, following me into the kitchen like a lapdog, her pug in turn following her, 'even when he gave me an enormous bill, charging me by the hour, which, you know, hadn't been mentioned at all, and I was even grateful when, out of the blue, a lady turned up at my door with a bucket and a mop saying – I've got to tell you, Silvia had to come in and work out what the hell she was saying, because I was just reduced to smiling – that Paolo had arranged for me to have a cleaner because, you know, he'd worked out for himself that I'm really quite a slut and would need one. That was Nicoletta, who it turned out months later was Paolo's daughter and the most costly cleaner in the whole of Italy, I guess. Well, Paolo turned up the next weekend, and you know, that was kind of a surprise because I hadn't asked him to, and he looked at the plants on the terrace and, my God, he just yelled at me. I've never seen anything like it since I made my farewell to the stage—'

'You were on the stage?' I said, even though I knew this. I carried the coffee in from the kitchen.

'All in good time. Somehow, according to Paolo, I'd planted the plants all wrong – putting different plants in the same big pot so that they'd grow over each other. That's all wrong, according to Paolo. You should have one big pot here' – massive downwards gesture – 'and another one here' – second massive downwards gesture. 'And all my flowers were white or mauve, very tasteful, and naturally, Paolo just hates hates hates that. So, anyway, he set about all sorts of different household tasks. Another enormous sum of money! And later that morning, bing-bong, it's the door. And now it's Paolo's wife Luciana, and you know what, he knew she was coming, I didn't. I guess she was jealous or something like that – it's crazy, I know, Paolo spending all his time with this famous old foreign actress. She wanted to come over and see for herself there was nothing to be concerned about. Well, within the hour, that fink Luciana, she was sitting down and writing out in her own hand half a dozen recipes for me to make and promising that she was going to take me grocery shopping next week. I could see what it was. It had started with an apartment and no obligations anywhere. And three weeks later I was supporting Paolo and his entire fink-like family out of my tiny resources. I was having to dip into capital to keep going. Whatever they decide I need, I end up paying for. Look! You think I wanted to have my *salone* this shade of yellow? I can tell you, when I was growing up, I never thought I would end up – well, let me tell you about the goddamn place I grew up, and you'll understand …'

I stayed for three hours, entranced, and by the time I tiptoed out and down the stairs again, it was nearly lunchtime. I walked to the next bus-stop into town, in case Silvia should see me and wonder how I had spent the morning. My hands were buzzing after many cups of strong coffee. I had planned to visit two churches that morning, but there was time only for the first, the nearest. I had half an hour. It was some kind of monastery. There was nothing going on; they were all long transported, the monks. In the line of cells, a holy painting in each one, some pink and green and blessed, with girls standing weeping below the cross. But some were stranger: a floating eye and hand in a pale green fog, and what that meant I did not know. At the top of the stairs, a sign pointed to the cell of Savonarola. The name of Savonarola was somehow familiar to me, a name from history. I knew nothing whatever about it or him or her. I wished I did. But the monastery was closing.

I didn't have much to tell Silvia about my day, half a monastery and a terrible lunch off a *menu turistico*. She only half listened, though, and was nearly as vague about Savonarola, when appealed to, as I was.

'Beautiful, San Marco,' she said. I doubted she had ever been there, and felt as glossily invulnerable as an adulterer in possession of a good alibi. Our unspoken hostility to each other, without any kind of obvious cause, was making the evenings terribly long. Silvia had taken to improving them, for herself at least, by importing various monoglot Italian friends to entertain her and make me feel foolish. If there had been any obvious topic of disruption between us, we could have raised it; there seemed so little, however. Just the fact that I had mildly lost interest in Silvia. You could not blame her for being irritated at this. It was what anyone might be. It was no surprise to me at all when I found myself the next morning walking downstairs, as if to the bus but instead going into the dusty grocer's and buying bread again, and returning quietly to Paulina's as, indeed, she had asked me to the day before.

'I must give you the key to the mailbox,' she said vaguely, letting me in. 'And then I wouldn't have the awful bother of going down to pick up letters myself.'

After that, there was no more nonsense about churches and monasteries. In the evenings, I made up my expeditions from the pages of the guide book. Silvia seemed satisfied. Afterwards, when people said to me, 'Did you enjoy your time in Florence?' I would say, 'Oh, yes,' rather than 'Actually, I spent most of it in an old actress's flat, drinking cups of coffee.'

It didn't take long for Paulina to get onto the subject of *West Side Story*.

'Well, I was in New York City, and I was making my way as a dancer. You know, the old five six seven eight. I'd done ballet classes at home and some stage work as a cute kid before I'd run away and talked myself into the lead in an off-Broadway show where their standards weren't any too high. It's like being in the army – you learn the moves, and when the run finishes, you find yourself another job if you haven't dropped the baton. Well, I don't say it was because the producer, a weasel named Wollheim, didn't have an eye for my talents to the point where some of the other girls just hated the ground I five-six-seven-eighted on. I say some and there were only four of us girls so – imagine. But the next show I knew a little more what was expected of me and I'd dropped Wollheim and I guess I didn't drop the baton.

'At this time I was living in the Village with two boys from the chorus line. There had been three, but Preston had to leave in quite a hurry. You see, we had a party one night, and somebody dropped a gold and blue vase out the window to see the smash it would make on 12th Street, and everyone put the blame on Preston when it was some guy we'd never seen before and never saw again. And it turned out, it was the landlady's property and she said some kind of valuable heirloom. She was nuts. Well, one of the other boys, he had a friend who was fairly wealthy and backing a new show, and to make up for some disappointment over a watch that had gone missing in the company of a young man who was not all that he could have been, this wealthy friend fixed it up for Harry and I to try out for this beautiful new show. And that was *West Side Story*.'

'The movie?' I said.

'No, the stage show,' Paulina said. 'The movie comes later. You know, it's curious the thing that will stand out in your life, the one thing that defines you for ever. It's not teaching dance and movement in Buffalo to kids for thirty years, after all. Who knew? It was always going to be kind of a big deal, *West Side Story*, but so big a deal? Who knew? At first I was just a girl in the back line of the mambo, kick turn kick six seven eight, one of the Puerto Ricans with my hair dyed black and gravy browning on my face. But after it had become a big hit, and we settled down for a long run, I worked my way up. You know, it wasn't lavish like it is now to live in New York, but even so, you were glad when you got into a big musical, and you didn't walk away from it any too easily.

'So I worked my way up – I understudied Anita, imagine, and in a good long run like that, I had a few cracks at it. I may say, she took care never to fall ill on a Saturday night for a good long time. It was a couple of years before I had to admit all that skirt twirling and stomping and Latino stuff was getting on top of me, hell on the tendons, darling, and I persuaded Kit, the wealthy backer who knew my friend and me, to talk to the producer. And they moved me back to the Anglo side where I stayed, and when the movie came along, I got myself a speaking role all of my own.'

'Wow,' I said.

'You've seen the movie?' Paulina said. 'Well, you'll remember me. I'm the girlfriend. And I loved it. I was the girlfriend on the stage for a year, and when they cast the movie, they cast me in the part, which I had the honour to reprise on screen.'

Paulina's voice had been rising towards a pitch of excitement, but just then, she seemed to accept the great honour, and it dropped sombrely. Her gaze was somewhere else. The flat was silent and muffled. I almost jumped when a carriage clock chimed, began to ring twelve times. Simultaneously all the jets of the terrace's watering system came on with a cross pissing spurt. She looked over at me, a little confused. She had forgotten whom she was talking to.

'And as I say,' she said, as if cheerfully winding up, 'you never know what it'll be, the big fact of your life. Because if I thought anything about it, I thought that'd be the step to real fame and living lavish, to the mink coat and the fancy car, to people yelling my name outside premières, to the villa with the security guys outside, going from one triumph to another. I turned down a dozen proposals of marriage, some from some quite wealthy and charming guys. And then that was it. I don't know why. I tried out for one movie after another, and I was always the second choice. I went into another couple of shows on stage, then cut my losses and opened the dancing school, and that kept me going for years, until just now, I decided I wanted to come and live in Italy and I sold up. That was the only film I was ever in, the whole of my goddamn life. It paid for all this' – she gestured round at her one-bedroom flat, stiff with mementoes – 'and I have the fantastic memory of being a star in one of the greatest films ever made. How many people can say that, huh?'

'Do you keep in touch with them?' I said.

'Who?'

'The guys in the film,' I said. 'The others. That must be something you want to share?'

'You know what?' she said. 'I don't. You know why? They're all dead, mostly. Those chorus boys – they had kind of rackety lives. Picked up something nasty, murdered, fell sick, went missing. I met some amazing people – I met Mr Bernstein, and Mr Wise, and poor Miss Wood, she had a sad ending ...' She was falling quiet again, perhaps not remembering all their names. You could see that, for Paulina, nothing was so remarkable about her history as her finding herself living it. 'Well, let me tell you something about Mr Wise. When we were making a film together, the film of *West Side Story* ...'

There was a noise behind me, and I swung round. The door to the flat, I must have left it open. '... the film of *West Side Story*,' Paulina said again, with less conviction.

Silvia was standing there, with a look of mild disgust on her face. 'You silly old woman,' she said. 'You're doing it again.'

'Doing what again?' Paulina said.

'Telling them stories,' Silvia said. 'I've told you about this before. You have to forget about it. And don't you start telling all those stories to just anyone who happens to walk past your door.'

'Forget about what?' Paulina said, but she looked a little bit ashamed.

'About that kick turn kick six seven eight,' Silvia said. Her malice was exact, and her memory of a phrase. In a moment I realized that there was nothing special about me at all in Paulina's eyes. No wonder she had not troubled to ask me about the Quincys, about her distant relations, or anything at all about myself. I was just a one-man non-paying audience, middle of row F in the stalls when the theatres had emptied, the matinée audiences died, disappeared, turned into ghosts. She had told her story in exactly the same words, and many times. That was what she liked doing best, the performance that, after all, defined her life.

As it happened, my ruthless eviction coincided more or less with the end of the fortnight. I had a couple of extra days in an awful hotel before my return flight, and then I came home in time for the weekend. Of course I did not visit the Quincys. I spent the time washing the contents of my suitcase in time for Monday morning. And when I went into the museum, Margaret was waiting for me.

'You're not very brown, I must say,' she said happily. 'Have a nice time in Florence?'

'Lovely, thanks,' I said.

'Did you see Santa Rita delle Castagne?' she said, or possibly that, since I don't remember exactly what she had so exactly prepared.

'I think I can honestly say it was the highlight of my entire trip,' I said.

And the same day I went out after work and bought a DVD of *West Side Story*. Of course I had seen it before. I hadn't remembered 'the girlfriend', Paulina's speaking role. There was a good reason for that. It was really only a dancing role, and once I had eventually identified Paulina, I waited for her to say anything or do anything except posture behind the principals in a marvellous aquamarine frock. (She had evidently concluded that the colour suited her.) Finally, she did say something. It was her one line, it turned out. I thought she would say something else, but when the film reached the end, I concluded that I ought to understand what it was that she'd been saying. I rewound the film, and listened again, and finally it more or less coagulated into sense.

'Warts a Bee Goy Dear,' she said, but it's no good. The alphabet won't stretch to what she did with her mouth. You want phonetic symbols, groaning with colons in odd places, upside-down letters, inexplicable markings, and then, with practice, you might capture what she did to her one line. It was amazing, Paulina asking what the big idea was, a noise from a dialect never spoken by man, woman or child. You could see, as she sashayed through the crowd and brought out, projected the line, like her one big chance, the thirty or so takes that had preceded this one. You could read the impatience in the shoulders of the dancers behind her, and even in the faces of the bigger stars. They ought to have been more professional. Yes, this was the thirtieth take, and the end of a long afternoon under lights, a long time ago.

That was a peculiar time. I feel very much settled now. I was being led from one woman to another, and every one so resentful of her successor, and all the time the one at the end was going to be the one who was there, unrecognized, all along. I never thought my life was going to be so much like a terrible Oriental fable about Happiness being at Home. Most of those women, though not all, I slept with, and most of them I left in something like tears or rage. I think of them from time to time, though I don't keep in touch. I google them sometimes.

But now Margaret and I live in another northern town, not so different from that one, and we have a dog. A King Charles Spaniel, overbred and rather delicate in health, and expensive, I may say, at the vet. But Margaret always wanted one, and she always wanted a dog called Ian. 'Hilarious,' she says. 'A dog called Ian.' And this morning I was taking him for his morning walk – it was raining, but it was my turn, not Margaret's – when he stopped dead on the pavement. I looked away tactfully, feeling in my pocket for one of the lemon-scented bags you pick up poo with. But he was making an awful noise, like a rusty engine going unwillingly into reverse. Not again, I thought, but Ian was coughing and choking, and then, in a single moment, he vomited hugely. A huge lake of green dog-sick. God knows what he'd been illicitly devouring. 'Christ, Ian,' I said, to explain to any passer-by my anti-social behaviour in leaving it there. I didn't expect a response. 'How do you expect me to deal with that?' And then I decided to go home, to shut myself away with some quite private task, and not to come out again for quite a while.

The Midsummer Snowball

The school had been opened only two years before, in 1975. It was a low, long, complex structure of smoked glass, yellow brick and bright green and red pipes. Built at the corner of two main roads, it was conspicuous and striking, even to those driving past who had no children at the school. It had been entered for awards for both architecture and educational practice; the architects had consulted widely, and had built an exterior with elements of both nursery and factory. The interior was hardly divided up at all: classrooms opened up into each other around a central area, devoted to craft work. The offices of the headmaster and the administrative staff were up a short flight of stairs, but without divisions from each other or the teaching areas, and in practice without any privacy. The noise was terrific, the heating costs *colossal*, and professionals had been coming to look at it more or less ceaselessly, one party every ten days on average, for the last two years.

For the children of the affluent western suburbs of the industrial Yorkshire town, the school was not anything so very remarkable. Most of them lived near each other, in the detached houses of the 1920s suburb of Satterthwaite, and the large executive development on the town's outskirts, Moor Hills. Their houses were a little older than they were; the *school*, they knew, was younger. They could remember it going up from when they were little, months of bare mud and a huge square hole in the ground, and then, quite suddenly, the yellow walls *had* gone shooting up and you could see the building it would be within a couple of weeks.

They had forgotten the old school almost as soon as they had moved in; now, what they were proudest of in their new school were the social innovations. Children in the last year could volunteer to be the social patrons of new first-years, supervising their play and listening to their miniature troubles – 'Like a big brother or sister would,' the headmaster said. His fresh face, spiked hair and usual bright-coloured jumper made him seem like a big brother himself. Each class elected one member to serve on the school council, with teachers and governors, though the adults held meetings without the pupils, too. Worry boxes, in which any pupil could place a written comment, complaint or confession of misery, were placed at regular intervals throughout the school. But there were not many unhappy pupils at Fisher Fields Middle, or so the head-master said to his frequent official visitors and inquisitors. The visitors sometimes thought, but did not say, that it would be an odd child who would both admit and exacerbate his social failures by being seen to post a letter in a box like that.

The children mixed well, even – the headmaster said – the twenty or so children bussed in from the old Powell's

Bottom flats, in the interest of social inclusion and spread. ('Social inclusion and spread?' his visitors wrote in their notebooks, balancing them awkwardly against their wrists.) Apart from the Powell's Bottom children, the majority of the pupils caught the same number 51 bus home, up the hill to their 1920s brick crescents, executive avenues with their still spindly trees or, sometimes, a Victorian cottage marooned amid more recent development. The parents were doctors, university teachers, librarians, bank managers, accountants or, at the very least, shopkeepers. Their children played together in the undeveloped woodlands around their houses, exploring the moorlands that ran up to the edge of the city. They knew each other, and mixed in their avenues, closes and crescents without much reference to their own age or year. In these circumstances, crazes and fashions spread quickly: a solitary inherited pogo stick might sound out like a woodpecker from the bottom of Sandygate Avenue one Saturday afternoon. It would quickly attract a curious crowd, and by the end of the week, thanks to birthday money, advances on birthday money, sums cadged off grandmothers or, rarely, saved-up pocket money, the whole estate would echo and rebound to the pick-ah-puck-ah of a dozen pneumatic ride-ons.

It was a Thursday morning, and geography, the last before lunch. The class had taken over the crafts area to work on a contour map of a glacial valley, one per table. 'I don't care,' a child was saying, over and over. 'I just don't care, not a bit.' 'Now, Two C,' Miss Clarke called. 'Now – attention, please – please, attention – stop chattering and listen – now – I said …'

Teresa was sharing a table with the twins, Cathy and Sam; at the next table were the boys they usually sat with at break and lunchtime, Joshua, Michael Brown and Santosh. There was also James Collins, who had been put on their table by Miss Clarke. He was the only boy in the room at a girls' table. He came from Powell's Bottom, the only one in their class; if he got put on your table, he would sit back cautiously, as if he were in church. His face was white and thin, mean-looking, his eyes large and watchful in the bony face. His hair was utterly black, and hardly ever properly brushed at the back. It stuck out horizontally behind him, like a dirty black jet trail. Always, when he was at your table, after a while, slowly, slowly, his thin white fingers, his thin white arm with the blue pullover rolled up to the elbow, always the same blue pullover, those horrible fingers would reach out waveringly, like some blind underwater tentacled thing, and start to move the Plasticine about for some reason of their own. Once his fingers started at their work of destruction, they would continue, mesmerized, systematic, until he was told to stop. He shouldn't have been in their class: he should have been in Remedial. Joshua said he had heard a teacher say so once. They had all heard a teacher say, 'James Collins!' or overheard one saying, expressively, 'That James Collins ...' He would never go on a table on his own: was always having to be put on one, unwillingly.

'What are you doing, James Collins?' Cathy said. 'Stop that. That's my glacial ridge. I'd got it just how I wanted it.'

'I'm starving,' Teresa said. James Collins withdrew his hands, let them sit on the table, the splatter of Plasticine on them like wounds on small animals. 'It's an age since breakfast. I'm starving. I hope it's cottage pie. I love cottage pie. I could eat it for every meal.'

'Could you eat it for breakfast?'

'Cold from the night before?'

'With cold peas and cold ketchup!'

'Could you eat it for your birthday treat?'

'Could you eat it for Christmas dinner?'

'Because—'

'Because—'

'It's *always* cold, ketchup is!'

The twins burst out laughing, abandoning their inquisition.

'I could,' Teresa said. 'I don't like turkey at all. I could eat it for Christmas dinner, easily.'

'School cottage pie,' Sam said, in mock awe. 'For Christmas dinner.'

'No, we don't know what's for dinner,' Cathy said. 'We're not eating school dinners any more. We talked about it, and we decided that we wanted to bring packed lunches from now on.'

'"A hot, heavy lunch at midday isn't at all necessary,"' Sam said, quoting someone.

'Where do you keep your lunches till you eat them?' Teresa said, and from their bags, first Sam, then Cathy brought out a plastic box, one blue, one green. Initials S and C were carefully painted on the top with correcting fluid.

'We know which is ours,' Sam said – she wanted to be a boy.

'But Mummy gets it wrong, she's always going to get it the wrong way round, she said,' Cathy said, who wanted to work in a garden centre, when she grew up.

Miss Clarke was at the other side of the classroom, and over the noise you could hear her voice crying, 'I just don't understand why you would ...' Her hair was flying, her fat face and arms in her short-sleeved floral dress were red and scrubbed-looking.

First Sam, then Cathy, opened their packed lunches; on top, there was a banana for Cathy, an apple for Sam, who said bananas furred her teeth up and made her want to be sick; two sandwiches with tuna and cucumber, and two with ham, cheese and pickle, only without the pickle for Cathy; there were two bags of crisps to share, and a boiled egg with a little twist of salt in foil, and, wrapped up in clingfilm, a handful of dried fruit, a lobe of dried mango, a dark confusion of raisins, some dull-gold coins of dried banana. 'Mummy said when it's cold, she'll make soup and put it in our Thermos flasks,' Cathy said, perhaps unnecessarily. 'Or we could go back to having school dinners.'

The opening of the lunch boxes had drawn the boys from the next table, who were craning to see this elegant independence, this choice to picnic like shaded gentry, rather than gorge at a long bench at hot communal messes, indoors.

'You've got salt and vinegar crisps,' Santosh said.

Then there was Miranda, who could never bear for there to be anything exciting going on that she hadn't started, who had come halfway across the classroom. She stood and sucked her hair, a long blonde wet strand, nodding and looking. 'I might do that one day,' she said eventually. 'I thought of doing it last week, but I decided not to in the end.'

The two lunch boxes sat on the table amid the half-built wreckage of a Plasticine geography. In a moment a pale finger started to creep towards them; a thin arm followed. Cathy snapped the box shut, and hugged it to her bosom.

'Don't think you can steal my packed lunch, James Collins,' she said.

Sam snatched hers, too, the apple falling out and rolling across the table landscape. 'I know you'd like to,' she said.

James Collins looked down; his fingers busied themselves with pills of Plasticine, rolling thin sausages of green and blue and brown clay. 'You can get salt and vinegar from the school shop,' he could be heard to say, which was stupid: those wouldn't be crisps you'd brought from home in a box with your initial on it. And then they closed their boxes, not to reopen them until dinner time.

Even Miranda felt a little shamefaced today at going in to eat a hot dinner, served by dinner ladies, where you couldn't choose what you wanted and didn't like what they gave you. It was lamb stew and dumplings, which no one liked. There were always fatty bits floating around. And out there in the sunshine, sitting on the steps as if it was a real picnic, there were Sam and Cathy, resting their elbows on their knees, Sam putting her sandwich down in her own box with her own initial on it, showing Cathy a new move she'd worked out for the hand-jive to do in class when the teacher was facing the blackboard. You could see it. They were all too old for games and chasing: they'd done all that, oh, years ago, played everything. And Sam and Cathy had moved on to packed lunches and their own choice.

If they made an impression at lunchtime, it was still more impressive at the middle of the afternoon when, at break time, the twins opened their boxes and compared their teatime treat, a chocolate bar each; they found they had different ones, but snapped them in half, compared again, and swapped. By Friday of the same week, everyone – Santosh, Michael Brown, Teresa, the twins and Joshua – had all started bringing packed lunches. Miranda had a bigger box than anyone else, with her full name, not just her initial, painted on it very neatly, in curly copper-plate writing, though she didn't have any brothers or sisters and her mother wouldn't confuse her lunch with anyone else's. They sat on the steps outside the dining space; they once went on sitting in their form area, perching on tables. They tried some of the odd fried confections and cold rice dishes Santosh's mother sent him to school with. They swapped sandwiches – turkey and cheese for Philadelphia and grapes, tinned salmon and mayonnaise for beef and tomato. As the week went on, a certain jostling competitiveness entered into the contents of the sandwiches. Miranda – it would be Miranda – opened her box nonchalantly, looked and said, 'Oh, it's Coronation Chicken.' One day when Michael Brown forgot his bag and his packed lunch with it, they all chipped in, donating a sandwich each, and he had a bigger and more interesting lunch than anyone else. Sometimes their lunches went on all lunch break, leaving no time for anything else; they sat on the steps and were conscious of being, in the eyes of the school running about the playground, an elite.

* * *

Teresa Fynes, her brother William and her parents lived in a tall witchy house with gables, triangulated windows and even a turret; it was just at the border where the dentists' art deco of Satterthwaite gave way to the young executives' brick and glass modernism of Moor Hill. It, and half a dozen other Victorian houses, had been surrounded by later buildings, the gardens growing smaller and smaller with time; previous owners had sliced off areas of an ample lawn for building on, and now the garden of the Fyneses' old house was exactly the same size as the gardens of the houses that surrounded it. People driving past the house often wondered about the turret, and envisaged a child, sitting with a book in a curved window seat. In fact, though the Fyneses had bought the house four years ago largely because of the turret's romantic appeal, they hadn't yet found a use for it, and it was full, still, of packed boxes from poor Granny Pineapple's house.

There was a room that had always been called, by them, the dining room, just as there was a room on the second floor, beyond the three bedrooms and the spare bedroom, that they had called the library, at first ironically and then just neutrally, because it had all the books in it. They hadn't eaten in the dining room, however, until poor Granny Pineapple had died and left them her dining table. The old one had been cast onto the street for the bin men to take away –Teresa would never forget the glum appearance of the square old table on the street, like a cow in a field in the rain. And then they had taken to eating their meals in the dining room, Teresa's mother at the head and her father at the foot, Teresa and William facing each other. Even breakfast.

'So what have you got planned for today?' her mother said.

'I haven't got anything planned,' her father said.

'There's a surprise.'

'Just pass the sodding butter.'

Teresa and William began to giggle. 'If I pass you the sodding butter,' William said, 'can I have the bleeding jam back?'

'Charming,' their mother said. 'I can't think where they get it from.'

'No, nor can I,' their father said. 'Actually, I did have something I wanted to do. I was going to pop down to the builders' yard.'

'Oh, the builders' yard. What a lovely idea.'

'Yes, I thought so. And then I thought about popping in to see that exhibition of Burne-Jones and having lunch in the pub.'

'If I were these two,' their mother said, 'I can't think of a single thing I'd rather do than go to the builders' yard, followed by some old paintings, followed by lunch in the pub. You really know how to keep children entertained, Derek.'

'Oh, they're coming with me, are they?'

'You bet they are. You really know how to give your children a morning out to remember, don't you?'

Teresa and William sat, absorbed in this, their eyes going from one end of the table to the other, dragged between mother and father, like the spectators at a tennis match. Teresa was always impressed by her parents' ability to have an argument without actually disagreeing at any point with each other. As for herself and William, she realized that neither of them could do any wrong, not really, because whatever one parent said about what they had done, the other could be guaranteed to say the exact opposite.

'Can I go and work in my flower patch after breakfast?' she said. 'William can do the weeding.'

'Don't you want to come out with me?' her father said.

'Yes, to a builders' yard, then to some old art gallery, then—'

'Thanks, Chrissie,' her father said. 'It might be fun.'

'Don't you listen to your father,' her mother said. 'You go and work in your flower patch. Do some weeding. In the rain. That's a very good idea. That sounds like more fun than your dad's day out. You too, William. Pull out some weeds. See you at lunchtime.'

'Christ, are there any weeds left in that flower patch?' her father said. 'They were at it all last Sunday. You'll be pulling out the flower shoots if you do much more weeding.'

'I'm sure they're very good at telling the difference,' her mother said. 'And they could always start on the rest of the place if they run out of little weeds to deal with.'

'The rest of the garden.'

'The rest of the garden.'

Later that morning, Miranda phoned and invited Teresa round to what she called a 'gathering'. 'We've got boys coming round,' she drawled. 'I invited Joshua, and Santosh Chatterjee. I wouldn't ask some of the other boys. They're so immature. But Joshua and Santosh I think are all right. I thought I just would, just on the spur of the moment. Have some people round for a gathering.'

It was not like Miranda to start inviting people only an hour or two before she wanted to see them arrive. A Saturday-morning invitation for a Saturday-afternoon gathering at her pink-and-white house, the glass surfaces gleaming, her awed parents withdrawing from the sitting room, once they had arranged the mounded-up trays of refreshments about the place for their prodigious daughter: that was unheard of. The smallest of Miranda's gatherings usually meant a week of giving and taking away invitations, as she played current favourites off against each other, holding out the possibility of an invitation, threatening another with exclusion. The pleasure of the party, for Miranda, was obviously in the anticipation. Once the guests had arrived, Miranda had no more power over them; they could only either leave or stay; and her parties, even her smallest gatherings, had a dissatisfied aspect that radiated from Miranda herself.

The big blue car of Santosh's parents overtook Teresa as she was walking up the hill; it slowed and stopped, waiting for her to catch up. Mrs Chatterjee asked if she wanted a lift, but Teresa said she would rather walk, and the car drove slowly by her side up the hill, Mrs Chatterjee talking all the while. At the window of the house, Miranda stood, her arms folded angrily. She didn't like people to talk to each other independently when she wasn't there to supervise.

But while white, nervous, bald Mr Cole was welcoming them in, ushering them into the sitting room and asking them what they fancied, what he could get them, Miranda's mother must have been having a firm word with her. Because in a moment the Miranda who was presented to them was gracious and smiling, her plump outer appearance sparkling with green eyeshadow, blusher and pink lipstick – her own, not borrowed from her mother. Every detail of Miranda's Saturday appearance had been forbidden specifically for wear at school, so she wore it. It was early in the gathering for her to be told to stop showing off, or so Teresa considered. But the word had worked, and Miranda for the moment was plump, smiling, adorned and generous with bright green facepaint.

'You're on time,' Miranda said. 'But Joshua's not here yet.'

'Perhaps he's fashionably late,' her mother, a fat woman in a strappy summer dress, said, raising her plump hands to her cheeks in amusement; both nails and dress were a brilliant, pillar-box red.

'I don't think so,' Miranda said. 'I think he's forgotten I invited him.'

'How can he have forgotten if you only thought of having people round this morning?' Teresa said, and then, halfway through her question, she understood a hundred signs. Santosh wriggling in his seat, Miranda blushing, the oval dishes of heart-shaped and diamond-shaped sandwiches and other delicacies, the tidied and cleared sitting room, the china-lady ornaments on the top shelves of the bookcase. She saw what had really happened: that Miranda had asked Santosh and Joshua round for a mature and perhaps even a naughty afternoon; that something had happened to disclose the guests to Miranda's parents, and her mother had insisted, that morning, that Miranda phone Teresa and include her, too.

To confirm this, Mrs Cole now said, 'It's so nice to see you, Teresa,' and, putting her dish down, gave her a special but rather undecided one-sided embrace, somewhere between a tousle and a full hug. Mrs Chatterjee was all shine and surface, Teresa's mother untidy, impractical, skinny in jeans, but Miranda's mother, a warm and toasty bundle of flesh, curls, powdered skin and a warm patchouli-ish, Christmas-spice smell, was the most obviously mother-like of any of them.

'Have you seen my new trolls?' Miranda said, when her mother had retreated. They went upstairs to see the three new trolls that Miranda had bought that morning, plastic squashed dolls with hair like a cypress on fire. The door-bell went; it was Joshua, and she dashed down and brought him straight up. Without breaking her stride, she showed them a new pair of shoes she'd bought the week before, white slingbacks from Chelsea Girl. 'I'm not wearing them for school,' she said. 'They're too good for that. I'm wait-ing until the weather improves, and I'll wear them out some evening, for a special occasion, or possibly at a week-end gathering in the garden, if my parents decide to hold one.'

'Can we see your dad's rubber johnnies again?' Santosh said, because once before, when Mr and Mrs Cole were out, they had gone into their room and found a pack with 'Durex' on it; they had passed it from hand to hand, marvelling that something so known to them through playground jokes should have a more than mythical existence.

'No, of course not,' Miranda said. 'I don't know what you're talking about.'

Then she played them a new record, by Elkie Brooks, that she'd got in town last week, and showed them her collection of postcards, and her holiday photographs from the South of France from the summer before. 'That one didn't come out so well,' she said, of one in which an explosion seemed to be overwhelming a table in a café. They had seen all of these before, but Miranda was always a bit like that; in a while, once everything had been shown, she would calm down and they would start to be normal together.

'Gosh, it was hot,' Miranda said. 'In the South of France.' Then a thought came to her: 'If only it would hurry up and turn into summer, we could get the snowballs out and have our snowball fight at last.'

'What?' Santosh said. 'What snowballs? How can you have a snowball fight whenever you feel like it?'

The other three looked at him, but of course he was only recently their friend, and he didn't know about the snow and the snowballs, preserved for the July snowball fight.

'What happened,' Teresa explained, 'you know last year, there was that really big snow, where it came up to your knees and we didn't have to go to school even. We went up to the top of the road, William and me, in our wellingtons, and we thought that the main road would be clear even if our road wasn't, but the main road was really blocked too, so we just went home, and when we got home Mummy said the school had phoned to say that there wouldn't be any school that day. So we all stayed in and went down to the lower crags and sledged, and everything.'

'And I said,' Miranda butted in, almost shouting, 'because it was my idea really, I said, "Wouldn't it be great if we didn't have to wait for it to snow for us to have a snowball fight, if we could just have a snowball fight whenever we wanted, whatever the weather was like?" And then I thought, it was my idea, that we could make a lot of snowballs, and bring them back here, and put them in the chest freezer, and keep them cold until it was July, even, and then one day we'd take them out and we'd have a snowball fight, in the middle of summer.'

'But why?' Santosh said. 'Why do you want to have a snowball fight in the middle of summer?'

The two girls looked at each other, and Miranda made her eyes go wide, and her shoulders rose in a huge shrug. Why would they? 'Heaven alone knows,' Miranda said. 'Maybe I'm just completely insane, that's probably it. Loopy, round the twist, fit for Middlewood Hospital. *I* don't know why.'

'Where are they?' Santosh said.

'In the chest freezer, in the utility room,' Miranda said, delighted to have something else to show her guests. They trooped downstairs together – Miranda's parents were sitting cautiously in the kitchen, out of the way, like servants waiting for the bell to be rung by their mistress. 'We're just going to have a look at the snowballs,' Miranda told them.

'They're still there, I know,' her mother said. 'I haven't touched them.'

'I wouldn't dare,' her father said.

And there they were, in a Ziploc bag, to the side of the family's immense entombed holdings of ice-stiff food; an organic, fungi-like form. Here, surrounded by the white blossoms of ice creeping up the silvery wall, the snowballs seemed less impressive than in their description. But they were definitely snowballs. Miranda unclipped the bag, and let them look inside, and there, you could see the hand's mouldings that had shaped them, the fingers' marks, the detritus of black and green fibres all over their surface from Miranda's winter mittens, or – was it? – William's gloves: he had been with them that day, trailing along.

They all looked at them, one after the other, and it seemed to Teresa that a breath of winter rose from the bag's secrets. She could not imagine what it might be like to toss one of the snowballs on a hot summer day.

'Listen,' Miranda said. 'I found something out. You know that James Collins, that awful James Collins? He doesn't live in a house. I found out. He lives with his mum, just the two of them, and they live in a maisonette.'

On Monday, Miranda had plenty to say about her successful Saturday-afternoon gathering. The weather was better, and they were sitting on the steps to the hall, comparing their packed lunches: samosas and a little box of rice salad, another with some chopped pineapple, another with hunks of beef from, the twins said, their Sunday roast, Sam's with piccalilli, Cathy's with mayonnaise, because she liked that with almost everything. Teresa turned – she didn't know what had taken her attention – and there was James Collins. He, too, was holding a plastic box; not a Tupperware picnic box, but a plastic box made originally to hold ice-cream, and still with some rags and tatters of its original label. He held it to his chest and his musty blue pullover, bloomed over and faded with something like mould. The others turned round too, and saw him, nervous, unspeaking, not knowing what he should say. Embarrassment and pity claimed Teresa for their own.

'Do you want to sit with us?' she said. 'You can eat your packed lunch with us, if you want.'

They divided in the middle, making a space for James Collins, and he sat down, squatting awkwardly without saying anything. He opened his box with a sudden, unformed, almost angry gesture.

'But you've got …' Miranda said, glancing into it.

In James Collins's box there was not the variety, the abundance, the evidence of care that the others had found in their boxes, all last week. In it there were only six sandwiches, squashed and malformed as if sat upon, all out of damp, cheap white bread. The filling was seeping through, like blood through a shirt, and smeared all about the inside of the box. It was red jam that James Collins had filled his sandwiches with, and nothing else.

'Haven't you got anything else?' Joshua said, tactless and incredulous. 'Have you only brought jam sandwiches for your lunch?'

'James Collins brought nothing but jam sandwiches for his lunch?' Miranda said.

'Shut up, Joshua,' Teresa said. 'James Collins likes jam sandwiches. He can have jam sandwiches for his lunch if that's what he wants.'

She thought that was helpful and kindly, but James Collins shot her a look of pure hostility. He had made them himself – that was obvious: no mother's hand had been responsible for those sad torn objects – and perhaps had not been able to take more than the end of the loaf and a few knifeloads of jam, what he might be expected to eat anyway when he got home from school.

'I've got tuna,' Michael Brown announced. 'I don't like it that much. Do you want one of mine? Do you like tuna?'

'I've never had it,' James Collins said. His voice was harsh and mechanical, grinding out the words one by one; he spoke like a poor reader, making sense of the page before him as best he could.

'You've never eaten tuna?' Miranda said. 'Tinned tuna, Michael means, not fresh tuna. I've only had fresh tuna once, on holiday in Italy. It was gorgeous. He doesn't mean he's got tuna sandwiches from fresh tuna. That would be really stupid.'

'I've definitely had it,' James Collins said. 'It was a long time ago, though. I can't remember exactly. What is it? Is it fish?'

'It's not really fish,' Michael said. 'I don't know what it is. It's not like the fish you get in fish-and-chip shops, but I think it might be a fish originally.'

'I've had tuna loads of times, hundreds of times, but I don't know that I like fish,' James Collins said, his tone not changing at all with the change of his statement, but in a moment he reached out his hand, his thin fingers trembling, rippling towards the out-held sandwich, its gestures all tentative and deniable, as if prepared to snatch itself back if the offer turned out to be a humiliating joke. But it was not, and he took it. Michael released the sandwich gently. They all watched as James Collins brought it to his mouth, sniffing discreetly. Then he put it into his mouth and they all started to talk at once.

Somebody must have spoken to Miranda during the afternoon. The class was supposed to be doing a poll on how much TV they were allowed to watch during the week, so everyone was milling round the teaching area. Miss Clarke was sitting at the front of the class – there was no front and no back, that was the idea, but there were still parts where the teachers stood or sat, and parts where the naughty boys clustered to be out from under her eye. Miranda, going round with her notebook, approached James Collins first, talking to him quite earnestly, then the others. 'We're going to have the snowball fight tonight, I've decided,' she said, sitting down with a great tired adult flump at Teresa's table. 'And I've asked James Collins to come, too.'

'You hate James Collins.'

'No, I don't. I don't hate anyone. Don't be so immature.'

'You said he's poor and he lives in a maisonette, and today you laughed at him for bringing jam sandwiches for his lunch.'

Miranda gave rather an affected sigh. 'I would never say anything so immature. Whoever said that, I'm going to ask James Collins to forgive them.'

'Do you think he cares what you say about him, anyway?' Teresa said.

Miranda stared. 'Of course he cares. He wants to be our friend. Why do you think he brought his raspberry jam sandwiches, anyway? He wants to sit with us, and I for one …'

Teresa left it: when Miranda said, 'I for one,' there was no further argument to be had.

So they found themselves, three hours later, in Miranda's garden. It was shaded by two large trees, a holly tree and an elm, both much older than the house or the estate, one to the left, the other to the right. A bench circled the trunk of the elm, and a filigree green-painted cast-iron table stood by the side, loaded with two jugs of squash, some crisps and – Mrs Cole had almost gone too far with her spontaneous and party-like offerings – a plate of cold chipolatas. In the middle of the lawn, in a perfectly circular island of gravel chippings, a cherry tree, the fruit, like bright vermilion marbles, scattered among the foliage.

'Where are the snowballs?' James Collins said. He seemed determined not to look around him at the smooth garden, the eight-windowed back of the house under the Tudor roof, the shining expensive carp pond or the Japanese bridge over the rockery.

Teresa decided to put him at his ease. 'Miranda will get them,' she said. 'Let's get into teams for the fight first.'

'It doesn't work like that,' Miranda said. 'A midsummer snowball fight doesn't work like that. Don't you know anything?'

She did not wait for an answer, but went into the house, trotting on the white slingbacks she had changed into. 'How does it work?' Teresa said.

'Miranda says it's different,' Sam said. 'She's going to tell us how.'

She was coming back with a large plastic picnic hamper, made to preserve frozen goods, and a length of twine on top of it. 'It's quite easy,' she said. 'This is the way a midsummer snowball fight goes. There's one person who agrees to stand up against a wall, or a tree, or something

109

like that. And the others agree that they'll throw snowballs at him. It's easy, really.'

'Who's going to be the one person?' Santosh said, but he was looking already at James Collins, and Teresa found that she, too, was looking at James Collins. Over the surface of his face was running the memories of humiliation: of the jam sandwiches of that day, all that could be contrived to get him into their company; of lawns and Japanese bridges and a maisonette in Powell's Bottom; and of what must be endured. Perhaps all of that, and the knowledge that on the other side of some humiliation might lie acceptance. Or perhaps none of that at all was on his face: only fear.

'Now,' Miranda said, 'James, you stand here against the tree, and we'll fasten you to it. Like that. Yes: just stand still.' There was a croak of excitement in her voice. 'Hold the end of the string, and Joshua, you run round till he's tied fast.'

In five minutes the thing was done; James Collins stood wrapped fast against the tree, his head and shoulders left free, his arms tied against his sides. They had done it silently, and with none of the Red Indian yelps that might have come in different circumstances. Miranda opened the box, and inside were the preserved snowballs. Teresa took one; it did not feel like a winter snowball, but hard, frozen, stone-like. On its surface were the marks of some other hand, she did not know whose. It was already beginning to slick and to melt, the ice of its casing liquid under her warm palm, in that warm afternoon.

'Santosh, you throw first,' Miranda said, and Santosh threw underarm, from five yards distance; it hit James

110

Collins's side and bounced off without breaking or disintegrating, as snowballs do in winter when thrown in fun. 'That was pathetic,' Miranda said, and Cathy threw hers harder, just missing his head, landing on the lawn beyond intact. Sam and Joshua were next, Joshua scoring a direct hit on James Collins's head. Then Teresa, then Miranda, who threw hers harder than any of them, running up almost to James Collins, and throwing it directly in his face. He gave a little grunt, but no more noise of pain; he seemed determined to get to the end of this without showing weakness. Only Miranda's snowball had broken on impact, and it was soon discovered that these midsummer snowballs, preserved in the chest freezer for the moment of their liberation, could be thrown more than once, could be picked up and chucked again, and again, until the midsummer sun melted them. There were more snowballs in the picnic box, and soon they were picking them up, dirty, tainted with handprints and the fibres of mittens, and throwing them without much sense of order, one after the other in James Collins's face.

'Look,' Miranda shouted with joy. 'He's *crying*.' And he was, but not only that: about his mouth, blood was running from where a lump of hard ice had hit him in the eye, or the nose. 'I know where you live,' Miranda was calling in a fit of savage joy. 'I know you only live in a maisonette, James Collins.'

'He's hurt, stop it,' Teresa cried; her missile had dropped to the ground, half melted. But Miranda paused, took stock of James Collins's mask of tears and blood, raised her last snowball, ran up to him, and almost smacked him in the mouth with a mess of fist and ice and blood. Santosh was already behind James Collins, untying him.

And then, all at once, James Collins was gone, pushing his way past Mrs Cole, at the garden gate with some more crisps in a bowl. 'Let me call your mother,' she was saying. 'I'm not happy about letting you make your own way home. I'm sure your mother would be happy to come and pick you up …

'Oh dear,' she said. 'I hope he hasn't got far to go.'

'He lives in Powell's Bottom,' Sam said.

'Powell's Bottom? Does he really? That's near Tattercliffe, isn't it? I don't really know. Oh dear. I haven't seen him before – whose friend was he?'

'We don't really know him,' Miranda said, flushed and breathless. 'I don't know why he came.'

'Well, it's a shame things had to end like that,' Mrs Cole said. 'I expect he'll be all right in five minutes, no harm done. Who's for some more nibbles?'

Many years later, Teresa – nowadays Tess – was at a dinner dance in the city. Her marriage hadn't worked out: she had been persuaded there by a colleague. 'Get a babysitter, leave the kids,' the colleague had said. 'How are you ever going to meet another man, staying at home?'

In the hotel ballroom, she went from group to group. She saw herself, a small, nervous woman with a practical haircut, wearing the same posh frock that she had worn last year and the year before, always on the edge of a group, always late for the joke. After half an hour, she was standing between much taller men in a circle, when one of the group said, 'James Collins.' The name was familiar, she could not say why.

'I used to know someone called James Collins,' she said, when the conversation seemed to have run its course for the moment and her associations had pinned the reason down.

'I hope it's not the same one,' the man who had spoken said, a sweaty-faced accountant type with a white carnation in his dinner jacket. 'This one ran off with half my clients and then came back for my wife.'

'Let's be fair,' a woman with a hard face and a geometric bob said. 'Your wife ran after him. He didn't have to do much running in that direction.'

'That's as may be,' the fat man said. 'But he's got a nerve, showing his face here tonight.'

The group turned, and their collective subdued attention focused on a man alone at a table, tapping impatiently on the white cloth. 'Bit of a smoothie,' someone murmured. Tess had no memory of James Collins's appearance, of the one she had known and seen pelted with the midsummer snowballs in Miranda Cole's garden. She had only a collection of verbal attributes, and this one – neat-faced, bold-eyed, his smooth grey head the possible consequence of pitch-black hair – did not contradict those descriptors, that was all. She had no idea. What struck her was that the boy's flight, whatever had happened to him, had left such a trough of guilt and repentance in her mind. The guilt grew as she acknowledged that the boy James Collins could have died at some intervening moment, that his life could have disappeared into the mass of humanity, or it could have led him to a table in the same northern town, tapping his fingers on the tablecloth, and not caring whether he was observed or not. Yes: it could be him. But it was a common name – she had seen it on other occasions and in other contexts, and in a moment the man stood up and walked in another direction.

In Time of War

The Germans had stayed only one night. Fred was glad of it. They had arrived in a mood of resentful ruddiness, and had kept it up until their departure the next morning. Here, at the southern end of India, they had been discordant and unwelcome. Fred's eye had grown used to a different human scale, to seven-stone Dravidians in crowds, and even his morning reflection in the wardrobe mirror had started to strike him as indecent. The manager of the lake-side hotel, tapping away in his office trying to get onto the internet, had taken the same view. Far from being pleased at this addition, he had looked the two Germans up and down and done his best to get rid of them immediately. He refused to give them any discount, although he had only one other guest. He gave way grudgingly – there were no other hotels for miles – and showed them to the worst room. Fred had glimpsed it when the door had been left open earlier that day, and knew it was horrid, dark and dirty, with a view over the kitchen dustbins. It was quite unlike his top-floor room, empty and luminous with a balcony giving over the lake. Perhaps it was kept for such a purpose as this, and a colony of cockroaches tenderly nurtured.

The war, a few hundred miles north, had emptied the hotels of India. All that long hot night Fred sat by the side of the lake, thinking nothing very much, enjoying each new eruption of complaint from the Germans. The food, the towels, the bed, the light-switches, the nation. It was as interesting as the battles of small-scale wildlife. They ignored him. There was the noise, calm as milk, of the lake lapping at the shore beyond the villa's veranda, and then absolute starry blackness. Moonless unfeeling felt. In the morning, the Germans paid their bill with noisy outrage and departed in a taxi, a white Ambassador, which, with its squashed front and its engine complaint, reminded him of an old boxer trundling into a boastful retirement. Fred and the manager watched them go, and enjoyed a moment of sly, unspoken satisfaction. The manager sat on one of the benches, and raised a smiling eyebrow at his only guest. They sat listening to the car groan up the track and away. There were the ghosts of two quite different smiles on each face. When the car's noise had quite faded away, the manager turned to the lake and gave himself up to the luxuriant, old-fashioned poetry of the day. It was as if the two of them were quite alone. Fred found that flattering. He would stay a while longer here.

When people told Fred he was a dizzy tart, he could not plausibly deny it. But if they referred to his 'gang', his 'crowd', his 'cronies', he would counter the distaste with a short smile and by saying, 'It's more of a posse, really.' He was always pleased to know that the arrival or assembly of the posse in one of their five regular London bars attracted not just attention but often alarm. They had gravitated towards Fred, one by one, until he was at the centre of a little court; noisy, handsome and scathing, they were the object of envy of strangers who, finding them impermeable by duller or plainer applicants, often described them as a clique. Fred was rather thrilled by that, and even egged acquaintances on when they voiced their resentment. He had always preferred the company of foreigners to that of his own nationality, and the posse, made up as it was of half a dozen nationalities, might have been assembled for the purpose of making him shine in public. His most cherished evenings were those that began at eight in a Soho bar, and ended twelve hours later, as the posse lay about on the sofas of some bewildered boy they had somehow acquired on their yellow-brick route, and shouted, indefatigably, with laughter.

As the years went by, however, the posse had begun to shrink as, one after the other, the foreigners took a graceful bow, and returned to their birthplaces, summoned by promotion, love or duty. Christian, who for years had been intermittently pursuing some tiny academic point in the British Library, finally exhausted the munificence of the German government and had to take a job as an administrator in the Pinakothek at Dresden. Max went to Chicago for three months to take the lead in a new play, was discovered and never came back. Each departure was marked by a Soho bender in the grand style, and from time to time a new member of the posse was acknowledged, in order to fill a gap. Still, Fred's posse was not what it had been, and

117

sometimes, at thirty-five, he was uncomfortably aware that those who had remained were the least adventurous and dashing of the original group. From always being the one who would pursue the evening to its last moment, Fred became the one who, quite often, would go home before closing time, on the tube. When two of the staunchest members of the posse fell in love with each other and started living a life of quiet domesticity, Fred said to himself that enough was enough. He decided to take radical action before he found that his life had diminished to a quiet pint up the road on his own in a cardigan, farty old Alsatian at his feet.

Fred had always longed to have a career of a random and unlikely nature, the despair of his parents, but in the event had worked steadily for the same clothing chain for fifteen years. He had slowly risen to a position of responsibility, managing all the chain's London shops. Just as he had decided that the state of his social life justified some radical alteration, an event took place that would make this possible. The firm he worked for had, for many years, existed almost outside fashion, the dowdy butt of urban jokes and the safe choice of country matrons. It was acquired by a conglomerate. The conglomerate was newly under the control of a viciously successful young American designer. Fred knew what that meant.

It would not be true to say that Fred, in those fifteen years, had not changed. In some respects, he had altered a great deal. His name, which at school had been something borrowed from a great-uncle, changed its nature in the early eighties. As Freddie, Fred rode the snobbish aspirations of the time. It was now perfectly incredible to him that he had once gone to nightclubs with a cricket sweater draped round his neck. Later, he reverted to Fred. In the interim that had become a name of fascinating urban style. With his name, he scrupulously altered his dress, his behaviour, even his accent.

Two months after the takeover, he was summoned by the new director of the subsidiary – a mild, nervous man, whose milky blue eyes, disconcertingly suggesting, of all things, grief, would not connect with Fred's. Fred learnt, after hearing a great deal about the future of the company, that he was being sacked. The future of the company now did not interest him: he wondered why the man had told him all about it.

He was not surprised. He was one of the last of the long-serving staff of the company to be dismissed in this way. Nor did it worry or frighten him. He saw in this sacking an opportunity to carry out the change in his life he had come to see as necessary. The settlement was generous, amounting to fifteen months' pay; the new owners were impatient to begin work, and had little stomach for legal disputes.

With this neat exchange of years for months, and months for money, Fred saw a way to do something he had always wanted to do. He prepared for departure. He let his flat, bought a plane ticket, packed his bags. He had it in mind, for the first time in his life, to take a holiday for some other purpose than getting a suntan.

'It was either that or Morocco,' he said to the posse. 'There was just this great deal going on with business class to India at the moment.'

'That'll be because they're in the middle of a war,' someone said. 'You dizzy tart. At least you've got the combats.'

'Of course,' he said. 'I'm not about to discover myself, or anything.'

They grinned at the idea that there was anything much of Fred to be discovered. Like the globe, by the beginning of the twenty-first century that terrain had been thoroughly gone over by all sorts of amateur explorers.

Fred had arrived at the hotel in the dark. In England, the idea had been to have a butch, unplanned sort of holiday, rather than one with coaches and an itinerary. His vague general idea of working around the coast of the southern half of India had deposited him at Kollam towards the end of the afternoon. He didn't quite know why he'd left the train here. Every time he heard someone mention the town, they gave it a different pronunciation. Quilon, Kwee Lung, Co-Lamb, Column. The ragged guide book had not been enthusiastic, saying only that it was a convenient point from which to explore the surrounding countryside. In fact it was a dirty, squat, scrubby little town, like any other. He hailed an auto-rickshaw, and told the driver to take him to a good hotel. Tomorrow he would set off for somewhere better. 'Where are you coming from?' the driver asked, after a mile or so.

'Trichy,' Fred said absently. The driver fell into a puzzled silence, but it was five minutes before Fred saw his mistake and said, 'I mean, I come from England.' The driver left the answer where it lay, wary of a man who was unsure of his origins. They drove on in silence.

There were no hotels of any sort here, and they were soon in dark, wooded country. The driver appeared confident, and Fred did not query their direction. 'Not very Thomas Cook,' he said to himself, but it was hard to be camp and ironic on your own. After half an hour, they turned off the main road onto a rough track. By now it was dark, and the only light came from a few bungalows set back from the road. The few people they passed peered curiously into the rickshaw. A European now, in this time of war, counted as an event for them. Drowsily, Fred entertained the possibility that there was no hotel here, that he was about to be robbed and murdered.

But the rickshaw climbed the slope, whinnied at the crest of the hill and, taking a steep descent into near darkness, came all at once upon the villa. They stopped, and the driver unloaded the bags. Fred offered him a hundred rupees, which he took without comment, driving off. The manager came out. Previous hotels had treated Fred like royalty instantly on his arrival; trains of anxious-eyed bearers had greeted him with ornamental drinks and floral tributes, promises of reduced rates and volumes of hand-written commendations. This man was indifferent. He did not even call Fred 'my friend'. No one offered to carry Fred's bag for him; no one emerged as they went into the hotel. It proved cheap, and the top-floor room plainly furnished and clean. The silence all around was absolute. For one night it would do. He went early to bed, sleeping without dreaming until eight in the morning.

Fred made his way downstairs to breakfast. He wandered about the ground floor of the hotel before noticing that a single table had been laid on the lawn; clean and much-darned linen, and plastic-handled cutlery. He sat down in solitude, looking at the lake, the low sun, the forested hill at the far shore. Someone appeared. It was not the man from the night before, but someone younger. His hair was slicked down, and he was wearing a green velvet suit with a purple cravat. He was carrying a pot of coffee and a jug of milk, which he set down in front of Fred. Without saying anything, he went back into the hotel, and in stages brought out a breakfast: a plate of that pink-orange Indian fruit with its cotton texture and faint feety smell of Parmesan, a salty glass of brine-coloured lime juice, and a hot dish, a soft pancake filled with a sort of potato curry. Fred ate it all steadily, like a patient, his eyes on the eventless lake. No request had been made of him, no decision required. A boat drifted into view, a small canoe with two fishermen in it. They raised their hands, and Fred waved back. There was nothing to do, and nothing to think. When he had finished, and the dishes had been cleared away by the velvet dandy, he lit a cigarette peacefully.

The day passed without narration or commentary, and for most of it, Fred sat by the lake, watching the sun move through the sky. He fetched his book, but after a few minutes, his attention lapsed; there was nothing in the landscape to watch, but all the same he watched it. Some time after ten, he remembered his camera, and got that from the room. Over the next hour, he took fifteen or so photographs, hardly moving from his chair. It was just when the view struck him as suddenly beautiful that he raised the camera. Sometimes he was photographing something new, a cormorant landing on a floating branch, a fishing boat. But mostly he was photographing the same thing, the lake. He could see how corny the photographs were going to look. It was more like a tribute to beauty than a record of it.

Lunch came in the same way breakfast had, without consultation, and it was all delicious. Afterwards he fell asleep for a time in the sun. He considered going for a walk, and actually got up and strolled round the grounds; but then decided that it was too near sunset, and sat down to read a page or two more. The sunset held his attention, like pornography. It was odd to see a whole day like this, and when it was over, he gave a sigh and went inside to shower and rest before dinner. He had more or less forgotten that he was supposed to go on today, to the next place. Beyond the lake – beyond the hill – out there, the world was burning, the earth was beginning to roar. For the first time in his life, Fred felt something of all that, out there.

The next day the Germans came, and quickly went. It was only on the fourth or perhaps fifth day that he came down in the evening and there were two tables set for dinner. Fred felt a tang of surprise and disappointment. Five minutes later, a girl emerged. She was white, deeply tanned, and tiny in her backpackers' vest and khaki cargo pants. She looked at him, her nose wrinkling, and grinned. He started mildly – he supposed he must have been staring – as if some unobserved animal had slinked itself about his calves.

'You had a quiet afternoon,' she said. 'Snoring, you were, when I got here. I thought, There's a man without a care in the world.'

'You should have woken me up,' Fred said, but that was absurd.

The girl raised an eyebrow. 'I don't suppose you've ever met anyone who the first thing they said it was about your snoring.'

'No,' Fred said, reflecting that this was not so; that quite often the first proper conversation he'd had with someone had begun with a breakfast complaint about his snoring, after the brisk Soho pickup, the taxi snog, the efficient one-off shag. No, it was quite often the first thing someone said to him. 'Second impressions are best. Shall I sit here?'

'Don't mind,' she said. Fred picked up his knives and forks, and transferred them to her table. The girl snorted with laughter – he couldn't think why. 'Where have you come from?'

'England,' he said.

'Just now, I meant,' she said.

'Oh, right,' he said. Where have you come from, he thought. Where are you coming from; where do you come from. Odd that. A silence fell. He noticed after a time that it was his silence.

'Sorry,' she said. 'Boring question, I know. People always say that when they meet you here, where have you come from, where are you going. Sorry.'

'That's OK,' Fred said. 'Madurai, it was. No, Trichy.'

She made a gesture with her hand, as if winding up an invisible crank, encouraging him to go on. 'It was nice,' Fred said helplessly, and smiled, shrugging.

'How long's it been?' the girl said.

'Long?' Fred said.

'You're funny,' the girl said. 'Don't look so scared. I'm not going to eat you. I mean since you've been in India, since you've opened your mouth and had a conversation,

124

you know, with words. Me, it's just a couple of weeks. I'm still normal, I can still talk, you know, but I've seen it before. After a bit, you get so you can't talk or you can't stop talking, one or the other. I've seen it before, don't worry, I don't mind. Oh, boy, that man – where was it? Madras – I just said hello and it was like you'd pulled a plug out, he couldn't shut up, and then half an hour later he was following me down the road. Couldn't shut up. You're the other way, I can tell. Hello!' she said quite abruptly, in a Minnie Mouse voice, grinning and waving with both hands from three feet away. 'My name's Carrie, what's yours?'

'Fred,' Fred said. He was appalled.

'Oooh,' the girl said. 'Here comes dinner.' But then the waiter, who had been coming out of the villa with a tray of food, appeared to think twice. He turned back. 'Ah, well,' she said. 'Why don't you say something?'

'You know,' Fred said, 'people are always saying to me, why don't you say something. Well, not always, but I can remember a few times when someone's said it to me and I couldn't think of anything to say back. I did German in school, years ago now, and I don't know why – well, yes, I do, it was that or geography or technical drawing and I thought, You never know when you'll need a bit of a foreign language, do you? Four years I did it, but the only thing I can remember is the one afternoon Mrs Thornton said, "And what goes in the gap in this sentence, Frederick?" and I just sat there and then she said, "Why don't you say something?" and I said, "What would you like me to say?"

Funny, really, because there have been quite a lot of occasions in my life when someone has said to me, "Why don't you say something?" and I always say back, "What would you like me to say?" And you know what? They never tell you. There was once a boy, and I'd been seeing him for a while, a year or two even, suddenly said to me that he'd met someone else, and then we had the why-don't-you and the what-would-you-like conversation, Richard his name was. But what would you say? Good luck, I hate you, oh, fancy that? And then a month or two back, when I got the sack, I knew it was coming, I did, so I didn't have anything much to say, and my boss said it. "Why don't you say something?" Funny, really. It doesn't really matter who it is but they tell you something. You know it's coming whatever it is, or you don't know it's coming but there's nothing to say. And they want you to say something. They always do. And you don't know what to say and they don't know what to say but still they say it. Why don't you say something? Why don't you say something? And sometimes you want to shut your eyes and close your mouth and say nothing because there's nothing to say. Nothing.'

Fred stopped talking for a moment. He was out of breath. It was eight in the morning, the next day. He was alone in his room before breakfast. A sound had attracted his attention outside. He cocked his head; he lowered the fist he had been making to the empty room. The bed was rumpled with his sleep, the blue canvas bedspread tossed to the floor. On the bedside table was a green plastic flask of boiled water, his watch and his untouched book. The noise came again, a call. He didn't know how loud he had been. There was no telephone in the room to blame his talking on. Stealthily, like someone stalking a cockroach in the dark, he went step by step through the balcony doors into the day. Down there was the girl from last night, her face upturned like a flower, her hands behind her back. He waved uncertainly down at her.

'Hello, Mr Fred,' she called up. 'Look!' She spun round and pointed, there, there, there, lake, trees, villa, before turning back to him with a great smile. The morning woke again for him with the clean magic it had displayed on his first morning, and she had woken it for him with a sorceress pointing. 'Look!'

'I know,' Fred said, smiling despite himself. 'Yes, I know.'

'Oh, you're dressed,' Carrie said. 'Come down. I was just thinking—'

'Hang on,' Fred said. It was true, it was beautiful; the long lax passage of days had veiled the lake's beauty without him noticing, and the girl had shown it to him again. He hurried, gratefully. She was already talking when he came out onto the lawn.

'... wouldn't be a bore, I mean, I was going to head off today, but I might as well stay, and I've got no plans otherwise. You're not going on today, are you? You didn't say. I mean why not? It could be fun, the guide says it's fun.'

'I'd love to,' Fred said, divining that at some point she had suggested something. 'But I wasn't listening.'

'You're funny,' Carrie said. 'You're not going on anywhere today, that's all I was saying.'

'No,' Fred said. He didn't know how long she had been standing there, but now that there were two of them, the waiter came out to lay the first stages of their breakfast.

'So I was wondering,' Carrie said, 'if you'd like to go somewhere today with me. It could be fun. Did you get a newspaper today? I didn't get one.'

'No,' Fred said. 'I don't think they give you one here.' He stopped talking and just looked. 'It's lovely here.'

'Laavly,' Carrie said, making a joke of it.

After breakfast, they had agreed to drive to Kollam together. Fred didn't mind the idea now. He had never been a solitary person, and already his lone travelling started to strike him as an uncharacteristic interlude, an attempt to be a person he could never be, like – what it was – a holiday from the self. He waited on the steps of the villa. Carrie might prove the beginning of some new posse, as if in a week or two he and she and five others, friends yet to be made, would be hilariously trolling the bars of some south Indian city.

It was true, what she said, that this hotel did not supply you with a morning newspaper. Every hotel he had stayed in until now had done so; the luxurious mock-Mughal palace in Madras, the overstaffed and dusty towers in Trichy, Madurai, Tanjore. They had been local papers, but still they were the same stories, the same slow terror that was on the front pages of every newspaper in the world in these black months. He had never been a habitual reader of newspapers; he preferred the sort of magazines that depicted the lives and taste and marriages of rich people. Even *Hello!*, however, seemed to find itself discussing threats and violence and bloodshed among distant people; even breakfast television's chipper sequence of innuendo and natter was intruded into, once an hour, by a minute or two of sinister declarations, of brisk body-counts. It could not be avoided, the outside world, and Fred had not missed the free newspaper.

But all the same there was a presence in his mind that had not been there before, an expanse stretching behind the immediate and particular events of his life, and this journey. It was like the lake, behind everything, like an atmospheric backcloth. Sometimes, in the last few days, he had found himself envisaging the crump and soar of munitions flying over borders only a few hundred miles to the north of the quiet Keralan lake. At first the images of war were as clean and swift as Hollywood fireworks, but he could not prevent the camera in his mind zooming in; the imagined ka-pow of the rockets always seguing into the noises people made. The thoughts ran their course, and perhaps for the first time in his life Fred found the vivid imagery giving way to intense fruitless speculation about wrongs and global grievances. He had not been paying attention, and could not answer his own questions, never having thought that they might one day become urgent to him. The questions would not go away. It surprised him; he surprised himself.

He waited for Carrie outside the empty hotel. The train of thought ran its course, but then it was exactly the unenvisaged emptiness of India that encouraged such speculations. Involuntary and inept, they were provoked by the painful absence of European tourists. The floral tributes were disconcerting enough, but it was a single recurrent gesture that most unnerved Fred. He would walk down a road in a temple town, and a row of faces would turn slowly and watch his progress. On his return, the faces would monitor that progress, too. It happened again and again. It was like a slow-motion film of the crowd at Wimbledon, swivelling their necks. The acclamations and curiosity his presence inspired puzzled him at first – it was more of a burden than a pleasure, this sudden celebrity. But there were no other Europeans around, or very few. It was then that he started to think about the war.

Fred was not a stupid man, but the furniture of his mind was randomly and unhelpfully arranged, as if supplied by others; a flat-pack of parts without the necessary tools, and instructions in Japanese. The sense that the mental furniture had been supplied by others was not so false. What he knew had been donated by the posse and people like them, and he had acquired little by his own efforts, but by listening to informed members of the posse going on about Tiepolo, or whoever. None of it had arrived by the more conventional routes of reading a book or a newspaper. Fred wondered how he had ever come to know the name of the prime minister without, as far as he remembered, anyone ever mentioning it over a vodka and Red Bull in a gay bar.

Most painfully, he realized that he knew nothing about politics and nothing about this war. It now seemed urgent to him. The posse, in general, tended to regard the subject as evidence of being, as they said, a bit *sad*. The long years of neglect had not struck Fred until he had found himself alone in India, without even the doubtful aid of the posse to keep him up to date with information about the state of the world. In the first stages of his holiday, he had taken to reading the newspapers left outside his door in previous hotels. He made an effort, but it was too late. The stories, with their long and lordly allusions to the BJP and the STU and the FRD (Fred! he thought, like the dizzy tart he was),

were opaque and, over a series of brow-wrinkling break-
fasts, did not become less so. It was like listening to an
inconsiderately detailed conversation between friends
about people you didn't know and would never meet. On
the third such attempt, Fred's attention had wandered
towards an impenetrable but well-drawn cartoon of two
politicians grappling with an octopus – he didn't have a
clue who the politicians were, but he could recognize an
octopus when he saw one. A waiter and an underling were
hovering by him.

'Komflix?' the waiter said.

'Yes,' Fred said faintly. 'Yes, lots of conflicts in the
newspaper.'

'Komflix,' the waiter said more decisively, and went
away. Five minutes later, he returned with a bowl of some
yellow mush. Fred accepted it; gave it a poke; tasted the
sugary mess. Cornflakes. Bugger.

The driver came at ten, and the driver's enquiries began
while Fred and Carrie were still settling themselves.

'You have left your children behind, sir, madam?' the
driver said.

'No, no children,' Fred said.

'Honeymoon?' the driver said.

'No,' Carrie said. 'No, we're not married to each other.
We're just friends. We just met.'

The driver digested this. 'You are married, sir?'

'I was married,' Fred said. 'My wife died, though, five
years ago. She was killed in a car crash.'

A reflective silence came upon the car. Poor Fred! Poor
wife of Fred! And then Carrie, all at once, without any
encouragement, told Fred the story of her life.

Fred had only taken this journey once, in the opposite direction. Although he remembered it being a long trip, it seemed longer today. Twice, he interrupted Carrie's story to lean forward and make sure that the driver really was taking them to Kollam. Perhaps there were, after all, no variations in pronunciation; perhaps Kollam and Quilon were really different towns. But the driver twice gave that side-to-side wobble of the head – not yes, not no, probably no more than 'I am going to rook you of an embarrassingly small sum of money.'

It was so strange, time: it passed more slowly when everything was interesting, and when everything was boring. Outside the car, everything he saw was interesting – cripples, crops, temples, crowds. Inside the car, Carrie was talking about a boy who loved her more than she loved him, which was sad when you came to think about it.

'And that's how I got here,' Carrie said eventually. Fred looked up. They had come to a halt. She smiled a brave, practised smile.

'I wait here for you,' the driver said.

'No,' Fred said. 'We don't know how long we'll be.'

'Best to wait,' the driver said. 'No problem.'

'It's best if we pay now,' Fred said.

'Pay later,' the driver said. 'I can wait, no problem, one hour, two hours, three hours, I wait.'

Later, Carrie said, 'That's so sad.' Fred was watching a bullock in the middle of the road, the devout, graceful choreography of orange rickshaws around it.

'What, the driver having to wait?'

'No,' Carrie said. 'I didn't know about your wife. You don't have to talk about it if you don't want to.'

'My wife?' Fred said. 'Oh, my wife, the car crash. No, I always say that. I should have warned you. It's not true. I just say that.'

'It's not true?'

'It shuts them up. They always ask if you're married, and then keep asking and asking, but if you tell them your wife's dead, they stop out of respect.'

Carrie just turned and gaped. 'It's not true?'

'Afraid not.'

All at once, Carrie began laughing. Around her, Indians stared at the laughing woman.

'We seem complicated to them,' Fred said. 'A boy said that to me, a few days ago, in Madurai. "Complicated," he said. I didn't know what he meant. "Wife, girlfriend, boyfriend, divorced …" You can see what he meant. They get married and then they have children and that's it. We have all these complicated arrangements. They understand a dead wife, though.' The boy in Madurai had not, in fact, said 'boyfriend'.

'That's terrible,' Carrie said. 'You're terrible, Mr Fred. You really are. What's your dead wife's name?'

'Fifi,' Fred said. 'They don't often go so far as to ask that, though. It really does shut them up.'

'Fifi, Christ,' Carrie said. 'And no wife? None at all?'

'No, none,' Fred said. 'I should have warned you. They always ask. You should try it. It really works.'

'We can't both say it,' Carrie said. 'It would look like the widows' outing. And they wouldn't believe me. I just don't look the type. I don't look like I've known pain and suffering.'

'Do I?'

Carrie turned and looked him up and down, as if he were a horse she were going to buy. 'Oh, I would say so,' she said. 'Deep pools of suffering, lots of silent pain in your soul, yes, I would definitely say so. You're deep, Mr Fred, deep and secret and sorrowful. No one ever told you you're a man of mystery?'

'You see that clock?' Fred said, overpoweringly embarrassed. 'It says here it was put up in 1911 when George the Fifth visited.'

'Swot.'

Deep pools of suffering and silent pain in the soul, and the clock, a fifteen-foot replica of Big Ben, reminded you that some things were only good when they were very big. Dicks, for instance, he attempted – but, no, you couldn't be smutty all on your own, either. Fred turned his attention to a roadside fruit stall. It was a sad little stall with only three sorts of fruit on it, each arranged in a series of neat pyramids on sheets of newspaper. By the stall, a boy squatted. All around the town, the forest grew, thick with fruit. The oranges and durian and mangoes glowed in the dark of the forests. But on the streets of India, there was only warty, dried, shrunken fruit to be had, piled up in hopeful pyramids. He supposed the best went straight to Sainsbury's, and the children of India reached five foot two and stopped growing.

He was about to suggest buying some oranges to Carrie, but she had been taken by something else. On the other side of the road, two figures were making their way through the crowd. Europeans, a boy and a girl like them, but weighed down with rucksacks – the girl, who led the way, was actually carrying two, the second over her front.

The boy was wearing the thin Indian skirt, the *lungi*, and both had beaded and braided hair. Under their loads, they were bent down towards the earth, and did not see Fred or Carrie or anyone else looking at them. Carrie, her mouth open, watched them go in the direction of the train station.

'Someone you met?' Fred said, when they had gone.

'Oh, no,' Carrie said. 'I was just looking. They wouldn't want to speak to us, anyway. I know the type. You know, they've come to see the real India, they're not going to speak to someone just because they've got the same white face. And they're not tourists, they're travellers.'

'I'm a tourist,' Fred said. Nothing Indian interested Carrie; only him and other tourists. 'I go to beauty spots and send postcards home and I buy souvenirs. I'm too old to be a traveller. I thought you were a traveller, though.'

'Oh, no,' Carrie said. 'You'd know I was a tourist if you'd seen my luggage.'

'I was asleep when you got there. Do you like India?'

'Ooh, yes,' Carrie said. 'I can't believe how cheap it is.'

Fred agreed, although whenever India had started to mean something to him, it was the glimpse of a monkey cavorting through a wild orchard of roadside pepper trees, not cheap but unbuyable, free. They walked in a slow way without map or plan. Their guide books were unhelpful, saying only that Kollam was a useful place from which to depart to explore Kerala's network of canals. Before long, they found themselves in a street full of ironmongers.

'I started this game,' Carrie said, as Fred was examining a tiffin-pail with a degree of scrupulous curiosity he had never, quite, been able to summon in the face of even the lewdest temple statuary. 'It was in Madras. Every day, I'd sit and watch the backpackers go up and down, and after a while, I started a competition, you know, for backpacker of the day. I gave them points and the one who came out on top won the competition for the day.'

'What do you think that's for?' Fred asked.

'I don't know,' Carrie said. It was a round tin box. 'You could keep things in it. You're not listening.'

'I'm listening,' Fred said. 'What did you give them points for?'

'Oh, if they were carrying a copy of *Lonely* fucking *Planet*, or for stupid hair, or for wearing Indian clothes and looking stupid in them, and for the size of their rucksacks. There was one boy who had a rucksack that was so big he couldn't get through the door of the backpacker café in Chennai. And for having a conversation about where they'd just come from and where they were going, and telling you where you should go to and where you should have come from, that was another point.'

'You're a very unusual person,' Fred said.

'How unusual? I'm not unusual,' Carrie said.

'Well, I've never met anyone like you before,' Fred said. It was not quite true; it would have been more true about almost any other person in this town. But he had not met those other people.

Carrie stopped. It was just another ironmonger's, and what she picked up was just another tiffin-pail. The shopkeeper, at the back of the dingy little space, wearily raised himself from his accounts book to deal with them. She set it down and turned to Fred. Did she have the beginnings of tears in her eyes? 'Don't say that, Mr Fred,' she said. 'I'm not going to fall in love with you. I always know – I always know whether I'm going to or not, straight after I first meet someone.'

'I didn't mean that,' Fred said. He was astonished. Perhaps he had been right; he had never met anyone like this before. He was glad of it.

'You don't know what you meant,' Carrie said. Anyone else might have sounded angry. 'Let's talk about something else.'

'How many points would you give those backpackers there – those ones?'

'Oh, we've done that,' Carrie said. 'Well, all right, four. Maybe five if they were Swedish. I know. Do you know what language they speak here?'

Fred attracted the attention of the shopkeeper. 'Malayalam, apparently.'

'Ma-lay-a-lam,' Carrie said. 'Hello! How do you say hello in Malayalam?'

The shopkeeper told them; they repeated.

'And goodbye? And thank you? And how do you ask how much something is, in a shop?'

The shopkeeper produced a bubbling stream of syllables. He gazed at them with a schoolmaster strictness, waiting for their repetition.

'All right,' Carrie said. They left the shop. 'We were only asking. Hey, Mr Fred. Will you buy me some oranges?'

'They're not that nice. I bought some a few days ago, but they were old and dry and full of pips. You don't want them, really. I only bought them because of how they'd set them out. But they weren't very nice. This was in Tanjore, though.'

'I'm trying to guess what you do for a living,' Carrie said.

'I'd tell you if you asked,' Fred said, reflecting that she hadn't asked.

'Whatever it is, it's something where you get to say, I liked how they'd set them out, all day long.'

'That could be anything, though,' he said.

'No, not anything,' Carrie said. 'For instance ...' she thought '... I don't think vets get to say it.'

'I like how you've set them out,' Fred said. 'Animal medicines. Or a line of anaesthetized hamsters.'

That was the way the afternoon passed. They looked at everything, and it all looked back at them. They had a glass each of iodine-flavoured Limca in the empty dining room of a blowsy hotel with posters of Switzerland on the walls. Carrie said the smell of the drink reminded her of swimming lessons at school. She had not had it before, and couldn't promise that she'd have it again. 'It's nice, India,' she said disconsolately. 'It's not as nice as Australia. It's nicer than China, though.'

'Have you been? Fred said, glimpsing the United Nations or something, arranged in order of niceness.

'China smells,' Carrie said.

On the way back to the waiting car, she started a game, of sorts.

'Would you rather be blind or deaf?'

'I've played this one before. Blind. People are sorry for you. They get annoyed with deaf people.'

'Would you rather be a hammer or a nail?'

'A hammer.'

'That's horrible.'

'But only because I'm really a nail.'

'That's okay, then. Would you rather be rich or famous?'

'Rich.'

'You're horrible. Would you rather have a cat or a dog? Wait, have you got either?'

'No, nothing. I'd rather have a cat if I had to. You don't have to bother so much about them.'

'A cat,' she said, and from the way she'd just repeated what he'd said, he could see that she was taking in the possibility that horrible was what he might actually be. A cat, because you don't have to make an effort for it. It was true and horrible.

'Is that it?' Fred said.

'Would you rather be gay or black?' Carrie said.

'Gay or black?'

'Okay, would you rather have a dead wife called Fifi or know that you were never going to have any kind of wife at all?'

'The question doesn't arise,' Fred said, his heart hardening. In any case, there was the driver waiting for them, squatting with a cheroot on the bonnet of the white Ambassador. How nice was India, or Fred, or Carrie? Nicer than China?

'You're not going to have to choose between being a hammer and a nail either,' Carrie said. 'The question never arises. That's not the point. Why doesn't it arise?'

'Well, I am homosexual,' Fred said, sidling into the car as their driver held the door open. Carrie was about to get in through the same door; he started to shift along to make room. It was strange to get into a taxi with no shopping. But then she walked around with regal, ballerina-like steps.

The driver, caught by surprise, ran around to open the other door. There was nothing wrong with saying that you were homosexual, but he could only have said it to Carrie when his heart was hard and cold towards her. It made no sense. He knew of no kindness or care in himself that would have stopped him saying it. She should have said something encouraging and sympathetic as she got into the car. But she said only, 'It wasn't really worth it, that town, was it?' It was in quite a different voice, perhaps her mother's decisive voice, wherever or whoever her mother might be. He hadn't heard it before.

All the way back, she carried on playing the game, but with a party brightness in her tone that kept him at a distance. He obediently chose at her whim. It was only when she had been reduced to making him decide between being an orchid or a lawn (lawn, naturally) that she finally said he might have mentioned it earlier. There was nothing accusing about the way she said it; she only shrank back a little from her social manner as if deflating. It was an absurd complaint. The fact was banal and conspicuous. But her comment made him see that, in her life, his existence would count as in itself interesting, pitiable, specialized in its appeal. In London, among the shrinking posse, the fact had been ordinary, and in India the least exotic of his qualities had been his habitual practice of sodomy, as some people might put it. It had been years since he had had a conversation like this one. She was doing her best.

'Have you got a boyfriend?' she said. The car turned off the main road, onto the dirt track that led to the hotel.

'No,' Fred said brutally. 'Not my sort of thing, darling.'

'I've got a boyfriend,' Carrie said accusingly.

'Great,' Fred said.

Then silence fell, and afterwards Fred could never understand how that was. It was as if he had had a clear idea of someone, a different Fred, who could change the subject and, at this pitch of hostility, would ask Carrie if (say) she'd seen a newspaper recently. He imagined himself, suddenly well informed, explaining the international situation to her. There was a Fred in his mind, in the silent car, who could talk about the violence and destruction to the north. If everything, every other thing, in his life had been different, he could have smoothed things over by exposition, setting out the wrongs on each side, lighting up a history of grievance by talking. This was a girl who knew nothing. That other Fred could have enlarged her life by showing her what she had never listened to: the reason the world was as it was. He had never talked in such a way. Much as he wanted to, he could not start now. They travelled in silence, since once her games had come to an end, neither could supply anything in their place. All at once they were together in front of the hotel.

'I'd never have thought ...' she said. 'I mean,' she said admonishingly, '*Valentine's Day.*' She stepped out and was away into the hotel.

To be alone was astonishing. She had been presenting him with choices all the way back, but the choice she hadn't offered him was the important one. Would he prefer to be the person who loves? Or the person who gets to endure being loved? Would you rather be a talker, or a listener? He asked himself the questions. He didn't know the answers.

He was far from home, but he had no idea how far. The only unit of measurement he had was the memory of one of the posse – Christian, was it? – moaning that with the prospect of a shag he'd gone all the way to Brighton, a good hundred kilometres. It had been a funny story. Fred heard Christian's voice, saying 'a good hundred kilometres'. He tried to see London and Brighton on a map, tried to multiply that hundred kilometres over an imagined globe to see how far India was from London. He couldn't do it. A hell of a distance, though, to travel in order to discover that he was bored with the lulling womanly topic of love, whether one person loved a second more than the second loved the first. Though he had devoted hours of his conversation to the subject, he now felt unutterably bored with its future applications, and felt in any case that nothing much in his life had prepared him to discuss love with authority. Deprived of that, he had nothing else to resort to. He could hear the vague, rumbling music of inquisitive and knowledgeable speech, but a man who, like him, could not turn those swells and crescendos into words, into an explanation of war and politics and the world, would always be vulnerable to an easy exchange. One says, 'Do you love me?' and the other replies, 'No,' before silence and incapacity swallow everything. Millions of books and films, billions of individual dreams had found love and nothing else interesting enough and, until now, the prospect of it and its attendant physical acts had been enough to keep him talking, all his life. Carrie entered the hotel, leaving him to pay the driver, and he saw the terrible poverty of the situation. Their lives: there was nothing in it but a CV, and a lot of going on about love.

She wasn't at dinner. He didn't blame her. It didn't seem important; after all, the next day he would see her. The night had descended, and the lake, which had so delighted him, had been put away for him to play with tomorrow. The dinner, too, which he ate self-consciously and with embarrassed attentiveness, turned out to be exactly the same sequence of dishes as the night before and the night before that. It hadn't disappointed him until now, this unambitious regularity. Carrie had just fallen asleep, he assured himself. But when he came down the next morning, she had gone, and he was, again, the only guest in the hotel. There was a note waiting for him, on the single table set for breakfast on the lawn, in an actressy hand. 'Bye-bye,' it said. 'I suddenly felt like moving on. It was awfully nice yesterday and meeting you. I do hope we'll somehow meet again. And please enjoy the orange! C.'

An incomprehensible joke. She was a girl to whom incomprehensible jokes came easily. But, after all, she meant exactly what she said. Perhaps people mostly did. Because here, across the lawn, came the waiter in his green velvet jacket and his silk cravat, solicitously bearing a single orange, glowing like a jewel. The waiter had one courtly hand behind his back. But when had she bought it? The waiter placed it on the table and smiled. Fred peeled it and ate it. It was dry and old and full of pips, as he had told her it would be.

'Very good,' he said finally, attempting a smile.

'Another?' the waiter said, and brought his other hand from behind his back, bearing another orange. Fred took it. As if choreographed, the manager of the hotel, the two cooks, the kitchen boy and three other men, old and bent, whom he didn't recognize at all, came in ragged procession from the door of the hotel. Each of them carried an orange in each hand. There was no mockery on their faces, no sign that it was anything but rational to request sixteen oranges. They piled up the fruit in front of him in a perfect pyramid. He felt some hostility in the gesture, which was not Carrie's but indifferent India's; a gift, like the hotels' garlands, to show that it was time for their solitary guest to go. He had been inspected and shown that he had brought nothing. It was going to take him weeks and months to discover what they so lucidly saw, and what it was that he had been given to take back with him.

Under the Canopy

He tried to have something ready to tell her when she came home: something about his day. It was not so easy. The little that happened had, generally, to be ruled out as something to be retold. He would not tell her anything he had seen on the television; he would not tell her anything about the simple progress of his illness.

Today, he had gone to see the doctor, however, and had something interesting to tell her. It had not been a regular appointment. They had decided the day before that he should turn up and ask to be seen. For that, you had to arrive at the surgery in Clapham Manor Street at eight a.m. at the latest. Toby had to look after himself; Sonia was leaving home for the office at six thirty, these days. He had wrapped himself warmly, and the minicab had been ordered for seven forty, to allow for delays and confusion. (And the inevitable irritated argument, the exaggerated performance of illness when the driver discovered that he had been given a job that meant driving only eight hundred yards.) He arrived; he paid the driver; he got into the ill-sorted queue under the canopy outside the still-locked surgery. Then he saw something interesting, and as he watched it unfolding, he thought: I must tell Sonia about this, when she comes home.

Toby told her what he had seen. She hunched over her bowl of brown soup, lifting it to her mouth with pale concentration, vulnerable and exhausted. She might have been the invalid, but it was just a long day at work. The rain of the morning had cleared. Through the window the garden looked rinsed, photogenic, spring-like, and the camellias' vulgar splash of red was shining. There were new beginnings going on down there.

'You didn't have to wait long in the rain,' Sonia said, in the end.

'No, it was only a few minutes,' Toby said. 'I was fine.'

'And the doctor?' Sonia said. 'Did you see Molly?'

'It's such a lottery, those on-the-day appointments,' Toby said. 'I had to see Dr Lady Whitaker.'

'I thought you weren't going to see Dr Lady Whitaker any more.'

Dr Lady Whitaker was a GP; they had discovered quite by chance that her husband, also a Whitaker, had been knighted for services to the Conservative Party, or making money in the City, or something. She did not use her title in the surgery: Toby and Sonia did, sometimes speculating what she would be called if the government made her a dame. Dr Dame Lady, perhaps.

'That was all there was,' Toby said. 'She was fine, really. They all have exactly the same information in front of them.'

Then he started coughing. He had to cover his mouth with a towel; it was disgusting to produce sputum while

Sonia was eating. When he came back from his efforts, hunched over with the effort of coughing, she had finished her soup and had drawn herself upright. She was doing that thing with her tongue on her teeth, cleaning a leaf of suspected spinach off.

'But it was fine,' Sonia said in the end.

'Yes,' he said, determined that what he had to tell her would not be what the doctor had said to him in the surgery, a story at the beginning of managed decline. 'Yes, they're very pleased with me.'

What he had seen was a story of distinction and shame, and it had amused him. Perhaps he had not told it well enough. It had been raining, quite heavily, when the tetchy taxi driver had dropped him off. There was a huddle of patients standing underneath the canopy waiting for the surgery to open. He had joined that huddle, in which a queue was somehow manifest, like a hierarchy in a chicken pen. One person waiting was not underneath the canopy, however, but sitting on the wall three metres away, in the full force of the rain. She was getting soaked underneath a plastic rain hood, and was smoking a cigarette substitute with determination.

'I just couldn't understand,' Toby said. 'I couldn't see— Why would someone wait in the rain when there was plenty of room under the canopy with everyone else?'

'That must have seemed odd,' Sonia said, but she seemed distracted, picking at a dried piece of food on the tray.

'Then I saw,' Toby said. The thing was that next to the surgery there was a pharmacy where prescriptions could be collected. It opened at half past eight in the morning, some time after the surgery itself. The woman waiting in the rain, sitting on a wall smoking a substitute cigarette, she wasn't a patient waiting to see a doctor. She was a junior assistant in the pharmacy, and was waiting for someone senior enough to be entrusted with keys to come and open up.

'Well, of course, it's important,' Sonia said, rattling it off a little impatiently. 'They can't give keys to a pharmacy to just anyone, probably only to people with some seniority. There's any number of things in the back there, heroin, even.'

'But the thing was,' Toby said, 'she just wasn't going to wait with patients. She really wanted to make it clear that she was much more important, or something, so she had to wait in the rain, ten feet away.'

'That's funny,' Sonia said. 'And then they unlocked the door and let you in, and only when all the patients had been let in, then she got up and stood by herself under the canopy.'

'Yes,' Toby said. 'She could have come in and sat in the warm in the waiting room, but then— Sonia?'

'It wasn't this morning,' Sonia said, as the door to the bedroom opened.

A figure came in, standing there, just as Toby started saying, 'Have I told you all this?' It was a girl, nineteen or twenty, her shoulders rounded in her green mackintosh, her blonde hair falling to both sides equally from a severe parting, dead on the centre of her skull. Toby recalled: her name was Lucy. She came every day.

'It happened weeks ago,' Sonia said, her head turning a little in the direction of the girl called Lucy, but not acknowledging her in any other way. 'I'm sorry, Toby. You're just a bit confused. It was the morning you first went to the doctor, the morning they diagnosed you. It's the medication, it makes you not clear in your mind. Anyway. Are you tired? Lie down. I'll rearrange the pillows and put the light out. Lucy's going now.'

And then it did seem to him that he had been confused, because it came to him in a moment of understanding that he was, after all, in bed, and Sonia, his wife, was sitting in a chair by the side of him, finishing a bowl of soup after her long day. He didn't know why he'd thought anything else. The girl called Lucy raised her hand in an upright gesture, unpractised and unfamiliar and embarrassed, a gesture from a political movement, or one made at first greeting or a first farewell, from one uncommitted to friendship and uncertain that any of this might happen again. He watched it with interest.

Maybe it was the next day that Lucy came into his room and said to him—

No, it was not like that. He was dressed and in his chair downstairs. But the chair had been moved and was now facing the mirror in the sitting room. Who would put a chair like that? It made reading so difficult, to look up between paragraphs and see that that was what you looked like, these days, and what you were made to wear by someone who thought you were old and might benefit from putting on your best clothes. (Cardigan, cravat.)

It was like that. Lucy came into the room and said to him, 'I've forgotten my shoes.'

'I'm always forgetting things,' he said. But she was wearing shoes.

'I'm such an idiot,' Lucy said. 'I'm going out straight away after this. When Sonia comes home, I'm going straight into Soho. I've got a date. I can't be turning up with these on. I need my good shoes and I've forgotten to bring them to change into.'

'Is he nice?' Toby said. He looked at her shoes again. They were flat, practical, scuffed, the shoes of a carer with miles of corridors to walk. She was wearing a green tweedy dress with pockets in front, and black opaque tights: she looked charming, he said to himself, relishing the octogenarian expression.

'Well, I don't know yet, do I?' Lucy said. 'I've made a date on Tim' – that was what she seemed to say – 'and I'm meeting him for the first time tonight. He sounds really nice but the things I said about myself – you know – the things I said about myself, I can't be turning up with these on. I'm going to have to—'

Somewhere about Lucy a harp twanged. She was surrounded with haloes of annunciatory noises, the harp twanging regularly as if in joy or celebration. He knew now what it was: her mobile phone announcing a text message, but Lucy never answered it in front of him, and it was as if nothing had sounded at all. She ignored the invisible harp now, sounding a chord. She assessed him with a long up-and-down gaze. He couldn't think what he had to do with Lucy's tasks, her schedule.

'I like your shoes,' Toby said. 'If I was meeting you for the first time, your shoes wouldn't be the first thing I'd notice about you.'

'I don't know what to do,' Lucy said, going to the window and peering out – up at the sky, down at the dry earth. 'I don't know what to do. How are you feeling today?'

'I'm not so bad,' Toby said, wondering. Had he had his lunch yet? There were no plates about with the lunch congealing on it. Lucy, he remembered, sometimes left his lunch there for an hour or two before she got round to clearing it up. His afternoon cup of tea, on the other hand, she usually took away quite quickly, washing it up with the lunchtime things so as to do everything at the same time. So, he thought with firm direction, he had probably not had his lunch yet. Then he remembered that he could have looked at the clock on the mantelpiece and he looked at the clock on the mantelpiece and it said that it was half past ten. 'I don't feel so bad today,' Toby said again.

'The shoes are at my sister's,' Lucy said. 'It's not so far away. I lent them to her two days ago. She had a do to go to, she's a PA in the City, she had a do to go to with her boss. I know where they'll be – she'll have kicked them off under her bed. She lives in Clapham, it's only a mile from here. I've got my little car, I'd be there and back in twenty minutes if I can find a space to park in.'

She came over from the window and, delicately, as if a part of her own personal grooming, she straightened his cardigan. It hung loose over his shoulders nowadays, this blue one. He must remember to wear the brown one tomorrow. That was a better fit.

'I was going to say,' Lucy said. 'You don't mind being left for half an hour, do you? I was going to say that, but you're feeling a bit better today than you were, aren't you? Don't tell Sonia, but I don't see why you shouldn't put on a coat and get in the car and come out with me. It'll be good for you to get some air. And then you won't be on your own, not for a minute. That sounds better, doesn't it?'

'I don't know when I went out,' Toby said. 'It was some days ago, I know.'

Lucy peered at him, as if at a shy beast in an overgrown burrow, not quite sure that she could see him there at all. She might have been trying to read the phrase that was now coming to the front of his mind: *total rest*. Was it for him to make up his mind? It was all coming at him backwards, and sorting it all out was too much. Lucy was going to take him out now: she would put him in his coat and scarf and put him in the car and drive him to the place where she wanted to go and then she would bring him back and everything would be just as it had been before. It was all decided. But who was Lucy?

He asked her as she was dressing him, in a grey tweed coat that belonged to someone else, someone much larger whose possessions flapped about him in a warmly annoying way, as she was placing a woolly hat on his head, and she told him quite quickly. She had been with him for three months now. She was the daughter of Sue, who was in Caroline's book club – Caroline who worked with Sonia his wife? (He knew who Sonia was, bridling a little.) She had finished at college and was looking for a job, had been looking for a job for eight months now without much luck. Remember? (He might have remembered.) It was a job in journalism she was after, in the fashion world, she loved that, but it was all sewn up, daughters of friends getting everything, she didn't think they read what she sent them. So it was this, this was to fill a gap, coming in to sit with Toby during the day so he wouldn't be on his own while

Sonia was at work, doing, Lucy said, whatever it is I do for you. But Sonia doesn't want you to be alone in the house for a moment. I can understand that, Lucy said. But don't tell her what we're doing today, Lucy said. And then the door was open and Toby was in the outside world.

They had lived in this street for nearly twenty years – had bought the house at the stretch of their incomes, had renovated it, then done nothing more. The street had risen about them; the pub that had been at the end, an old Irishmen's drinking den, had been utterly transformed into a chichi cottage with a sage-coloured front door and suggestions of tongue-and-groove through the frosted downstairs glass. The pub that had been at the other end was now a gastropub, with floorboards, that served shin of beef and took bookings. The street was altered, he knew that, but no alteration was like the one that had taken place in the weeks or months since he'd gone outside. He knew it had been weeks or months from the alteration. There was a lightness and a delirium about the air. The houses were luminous, weightless, drawn clearly against the purity of the air's colour. He felt if he touched anything in this street it would have no more substance than a Ladybird illustration of a happy suburb: that, dislodged by his pained touch, it would most likely float away into the blue sky. Lucy was here as his guide. It did not matter that his eyes, until just now, had not been asked to look at anything more than fifteen feet away, that looking down a long street or upwards into nothing at all, they sang and resonated with the effort. She lived in the world, stepped outside and inside without thinking about it. That was what she was hired to do, and now as she opened the door of the black

Mini that was parked at the bottom of the steps, she was talking about something else entirely.

'She's not at work today,' Lucy was saying. 'She's only got two weeks to go before she's off permanently on maternity leave. Well, I say permanently – it's only six months. It's not much. She was wondering whether she should be wearing the heels to the do last night at all, whether she'd be better advised to go in flatties. But she's like me, she wants to be glamorous. She should be in work today, but I know she's not. She was planning to call in sick today, she said they'd not care, it only being two weeks before she's off anyway. Are you all right there? Tuck you in. Do you want a blanket? It's not cold, but if you want one, I'll get you one.

'And off we go,' Lucy said. For the first time he could remember, she plucked out the mobile phone from one of her pockets, and stabbed at it with both thumbs. She sighed, put it back, and started the car. 'It's been a while since you've been out. Do you fancy going anywhere? Not to get out, just to have a look as we drive through.'

Toby thought, but nothing came to mind. The high street was astounding, full of people. What were they doing? What did their lives contain, so separated from Toby's long days in his interior? He must have seen them so many times before, been part of them, walked among them with no sense of detachment or ecstasy, never been overcome by the shimmer and flash of life reflected in the polished glass of the front of Sainsbury's shop; never seen with a full view the promise and meaning of people, animals, properties going between the long history of buildings and the lives they contained and still would contain. The dizzy quality of light held all of these for him as, with an invalid's eyes, he reflected on the unconscious world of the healthy. Could they see him? Driven by Lucy, he was not sure. And after a pause at the traffic lights, the rich openings of the high street proved to be only a preface, because in a moment of splendour the forgotten possibilities of the Common were before them, the shining round of the pond, the tall outlined possibilities of the white noble church, and beyond that, the green and brown atmospheres piling up in the radiant clarities of the Common itself. He had not thought there were such spaces in London, any more.

'I think I'd like to go to the butcher's shop,' he said eventually. 'The posh one over there.'

'We'll go on the way back,' Lucy said reassuringly. 'If that's what you'd like. We'll get something nice for your tea, if you feel up to it. She's in South Clapham – well, she says Battersea, actually, but it's hardly even South Clapham, it's more like Balham borders. I don't really know where these things begin and end. You're in Clapham proper. I wish she'd text me.'

'Look at that,' Toby said, meaning the boy running across the vast expanse of the Common, a kite high above his tipped-back head. To run like that!

'My sister's on at me to sort out my life,' Lucy was saying. 'She never shuts up. When I told her about this date tonight – the date I sorted out through Tim I was telling you about – she said, Oh, you mustn't do that, you don't know what they're like. But I've told her all about it, I've told you, I've told everyone, so I'm not going to get kidnapped or murdered or anything. It's quite safe, Tim.'

'I don't really know who Tim is,' Toby said.

'It's not a who,' Lucy was saying. 'It's a nap.' Or that's what he thought she said, but then she said, 'It's a dating app,' and he remembered what those were, or nearly. 'You put in your details, and he puts in his details, and you go on a little shopping expedition, and you chat a bit, and if he seems OK and you seem OK to him, then you might meet up. I've met some quite nice people through Tim. I'd tell you but I'd never tell my mum, and I don't know that it was a good idea to tell Katy either, the way she goes on about it. We can't all be like her with a steady boyfriend going to antenatal classes alongside.'

The glow and song and lightness of the world beyond the windows was gone now. Toby felt tired, or that phase of the body that he summed up by using those words – a tremor, a pressure, at the extremities of wrist and leg and a pressure on the part of the chest where you might breathe and even eat. The world seemed to be going past too quickly now. He closed his eyes and it was gone. When he opened them again he did not know where he was. The car had stopped and it was in a street with large houses set back from the road, mature trees to either side. He was in the passenger seat of a car, parked to the side of the road. He felt shaky: his hand when he held it out had a tremor in it, and when he pulled down the mirror in the sunshade against the windscreen, the face in it was white and frightened. A woman in her sixties, a well-dressed woman in a brilliant yellow coat and a headscarf, was standing across the road inspecting him. In a moment, she crossed the road, her polished handbag swinging with purpose, and rapped on the window of the car. Toby wound the window down.

'I don't think you can sleep here,' she said; her voice was patrician but regretful, kindly. 'You've been asleep for half an hour at least. I think you're going to have to move on, I'm afraid.'

'I'm waiting for someone, actually,' Toby said.

'You're lucky that the traffic wardens haven't been along,' the woman said. 'They're a holy terror in St Bartholomew's Avenue, patrolling up and down like soldiers on an exercise. Are you all right? You look rather unwell.'

'I should be all right,' Toby said. He tried to remember how it was that he'd come here, and in a moment he remembered that he had been driven. If he could just stay here for a few minutes then the person who drove him would drive him back safely, and then everything would be quite all right. 'I live in Clapham,' Toby said.

'Well, you're not so very far from home,' the woman said. 'But I don't think you can sit here all day. People might think you were casing the joint, you know.'

He did not know what to say to that and, quite at once, he felt extremely ill. The head he seemed to be in was expanding and yet stony, inflexible, and great invisible rocks were inflating within his mouth. He could not breathe. Soon it would be time to go home but how he was to find his way home he did not know. The woman standing outside the car might help him. He was in a car and he did not know how he had got into the car and how he had been taken to this place. The word *Lucy* came into his mind. He opened his eyes, not being quite aware that he had shut them, and although he did not feel quite as good as he should, the pitch and toss of the world had subsided.

In darkness it could be anywhere and he could be anywhere. He opened his eyes again in experiment and the street was as it had been. The woman who had spoken to him from outside the car had gone. A different woman was opening the car door and getting in.

'I don't feel all that well, Lucy,' Toby said.

'Did you want Lucy?' the woman said, and now Toby looked at her and found that she was not someone he had ever seen before. 'You're Toby, aren't you? I'm Lucy's sister's flatmate – I'm Minnie. She was lucky – it was my day off. I was just lazing about the flat. I'm so sorry. I wanted to come and bring you in, it was all taking so long, but we came out and you were fast asleep. You looked so peaceful Lucy said to leave you be. It's quite a performance. The famous shoes – they're not here. It took us twenty-five minutes to establish that elementary fact, and now it turns out that Charlotte, Lucy's sister, she left them at her friend Giuseppe's last night. How she came home and in what condition, I really don't know. Shoeless.'

'Is Lucy …' Toby said. He felt there was a question he needed to ask.

'She's all right, but it's all proving a touch more complicated than she thought. She's gone to Giuseppe's, he's only round the corner. I thought she'd driven there but she just sent me a message, can you believe it, saying she came out of the house and was so focused on the shoes and how to get to Giuseppe's that she totally forgot she had you sitting outside at all. She says she walked but I don't see how she can have done. She must have taken a taxi. So she says can I drive you home and she'll come back very shortly and she'll get another taxi, just once she's got her shoes from

Giuseppe. She shouldn't be more than an hour all in all.
I'm so sorry about all of this.'

Toby shut his eyes again.

'You're ill, aren't you?'

'Yes,' Toby said. 'I'm very ill. I should be at home.'

'What is it?'

'It doesn't matter,' Toby said. 'I haven't been outside for
weeks.'

'You shouldn't be outside now,' the woman said. 'Shall
I drive you home?'

'I don't have the keys,' Toby said.

'House keys or car keys, do you mean?' the woman said.
'Because she's actually left the car keys in the ignition,
look. Very unlike her, planning ahead.'

'I don't have either,' Toby said.

'And no one at home to let you in, I suppose. And no
key under the doormat, I hope. Right,' the woman said.

It struck him that in that other world, where he once had
lived, men like him had left the house with a number of
important props for their future convenience. There was
the car key, and there was the house key, neither of which
he now had. He would be taken from place to place and
deposited like luggage. And there was the wallet, which
contained money for any important purpose and the cards
that went with money. He felt in his pockets, but there did
not seem to be any wallet there. There was a hard rectangular lump, but that was not his wallet. He remembered
that he was hoping to go to the butcher's shop later, that he
really wanted to go to the butcher's shop, but now he did
not know whether he could. He fetched out the hard
rectangular lump, and that was the other thing that people

took out with them, that he had taken out with him: a mobile phone. He did not know the last time he had used or answered it, and placed it quietly on his lap.

'Do you want to call Lucy?' the woman said. 'Was that what you wanted?'

Toby was not sure. Outside, the other woman was standing at her gatepost. Now she had a small white dog in her arms, a terrier of some sort, and with its right paw she was imitating a sort of wave, a wave hello or goodbye.

'There's loony Georgina,' the woman in the car said. 'She's always bringing her awful dog out to say hello to the street. Pay no attention. Shall we call Lucy? I know where she's gone, it's not far. We could just drive round there.'

'I really wanted to go to the butcher's shop,' Toby said. 'But I think it might be too late now.'

The woman whose name was Minnie gave him a sideways look as she started the car. 'It's not late,' she said. 'It's not lunchtime yet. Is it the butcher's in Clapham you want to go to? They're open until seven today, I happen to know. Is it all a bit much?'

They began to drive off. When Toby opened his eyes again, they were on a dual carriageway, and the woman Minnie was explaining something.

'It's cruel, really,' she said. 'My sympathies are with you. My boyfriend's looked into it a lot, and I must say, when it comes to my turn, I'm absolutely clear – I don't want to drag on for months and years becoming a … just getting iller and iller. Just a quiet little pill and that's the end of it, and everyone can remember you how you were. It's simply tragic, though, you can't do that, it's against the law. My boyfriend says that by the time it comes to it – I'm only thirty-two – the law's going to turn a blind eye. I don't know. I think we're going to have to confront it sooner or later. I've told him that he can just grind up the pill in my food if I can't talk or move or anything, but he says he'll just do it anyway, anyone would. I'm sorry. I don't mean to go on like this. I'm like that, I just say what's on my mind – it just comes out even if it's a bit tactless. I don't mean to offend. Are you all right there? Little bit comfy? Not far now.'

'I'm tired,' Toby said. He wanted to say that he felt ill, that he had to go home. But he knew that you did not say that to a stranger who was being very kind and driving you about. There were the first days of his getting to know Sonia – oh, years before. He did not know why he was thinking of them now. They were sitting on the steps in the concrete forum at the university, the little square surrounded by buildings where talk echoed and shouted so. They had been in the same class together; the girl with ginger hair piled up carelessly anyhow, sometimes with a pencil stuck in it, but they hadn't spoken to each other until a couple of days ago. It had been in the queue at the canteen: he had been next to her and had said something, and she had noticed him. How would she summarize him – the ill man in the cardigan too big for him? No – that was now. The boy in the brown duffel coat his mum had thought was good for students, the boy with the bicycle that wasn't quite like other people's bicycles, the boy with a knack of jiggling his leg when listening to lectures? (He'd been told off about that, he remembered.) And now it was some days later. They'd met in the meantime; they'd talked, and now it was getting dark. It might even be a bit cold to be sitting there on the concrete steps, after eight, but he didn't want to be the first to suggest going inside. They'd had their dinner, ages ago. They were talking about Italy: she'd been, the summer before, he'd always wanted to, he knew all about what he wanted to see in Rome, and she was laughing at him with amazement. She didn't know half what he knew; she only knew a brilliant place just by the Tiber where the ice-cream was probably the best in the world, she'd gone back there twice a day all week, and once three times. She just didn't know Rome as well as he did. She laughed and laughed. And then it struck him that he didn't want to suggest going inside, and neither did she. It was like a projection into the thoughts of another human being, for the very first time in his life, and as silence fell she made a gesture: a gesture not suggesting that she was cold, but performing the sort of thing that a very cold person would do. It was an invitation, and in a moment he moved closer to her and did something in response. That was the beginning of everything and now he was dying and he was going to die.

He did not know how far they had gone. He was woken by the twang of harps, somewhere close by, and opened his eyes at a sound he knew was familiar. Outside the car, three women and a man, a dark unkempt young man, were standing. He knew one of them: Lucy. It was her that was making the twanging noise, the sound of her mobile telephone receiving a message.

'... told you about waiting outside the doctor's in the rain, and the woman who sat on the wall?' Lucy was saying.

'No, actually,' one of the other women said. 'He was very sweet. I think he needs to go home, though.'

'He's back with us,' the other woman said – she looked very much like Lucy, and now Toby remembered that they were visiting Lucy's sister. She was round, swollen, gross in appearance, but like Lucy in the face. Was there something wrong with her? Then he understood that she was pregnant.

'Got everything you need,' the man said, bending down and giving Toby a wave through the windscreen with an immense, white and insincere smile. He tried to smile back.

Lucy patted the supermarket plastic bag she held under her arm, leaned forward and kissed the girl who must be her sister. 'Hope they do the trick,' she said. 'Minnie – you want a lift?'

The other woman shook her head. 'Take him straight home and put him to bed,' she said. 'You shouldn't have brought him out. I'll be all right.'

Lucy smiled brightly, and for a moment it seemed to Toby that they were all just about the same person, that it hardly mattered whether Lucy or her sister or the other woman, whose name was Minnie, stepped into the car to be bright and cheerful and talk to him about ways in which death might strike, how death might be invited in and welcomed, how life might cease painlessly and with minimal inconvenience to anyone else. They seemed replaceable, well-balanced, differently aged but essentially the same. He wondered about the dark man. But then it was not Minnie or Lucy's sister, whose name he did not know and whom he had not met, who opened the car and got in, tossing the shoes onto the back seat and giving him a broad open smile. It was Lucy herself.

'Home then,' she said. 'Sorry it's been such a palaver. You're OK? I think we need to get you back into bed, mister.'

'Can we do something first?' Toby said.

'No, no, nothing first,' Lucy said, starting the car. A harp twanged about her person. 'I bet that's Sonia. God, I hope she hasn't been phoning at home.'

'I just wanted to do one tiny thing,' Toby said.

'Man, what are you like?'

'Just to go to the butcher's,' Toby said. 'Just to get a chicken for dinner. I really want to.'

'It's on the way?'

Toby shut his lips tight, nodded. He thought it was on the way. He wasn't quite sure. He definitely wanted to go to the butcher's. He knew that Sonia liked to eat, and he wanted to present her with a gift, a surprise, a chicken.

Much later in the evening, he was sitting in bed, feeling quite exhausted, and his wife was raging about the room. She had sacked the girl who had driven him about all day, had told her to go away and never come back. It was really quite impressive, like a scene from a detective drama, the things she had said. Sonia had tried to telephone, on the landline and then on his mobile, but had no response; she had tried many times. His mobile was out of batteries – he had no idea of the last time he had used it, or charged it. In the end she had come home, fearing that – well, she had just come home because that had seemed easier. And then she had waltzed in with him! What on earth did she think she was doing? There was some story about a pair of shoes, for Heaven's sake, and they seemed to have pushed poor Toby out of the house and driven him about London. She had no idea if this was the first time it had happened, even. The girl must be mad. Lucy had gone. He hoped her date went well with the man called Tim, though he really thought that, however nice her shoes were, she now wouldn't be in the mood to flirt, to put herself out and be attractive to the opposite sex. Toby wouldn't say this to Sonia, when she got off the phone to whichever one of her friends she was now talking to, so exhaustingly. It was lucky that Sonia only had to find someone else to come in and sit with him on Monday, because it turned out that tomorrow was Friday and Sonia could work from home, and then it was the weekend when she was just at home. Phone calls to friends complaining about Lucy had been alternating with phone calls to agencies, acquaintances, leads of all sorts, trying to find a stand-in.

He was very sorry that he'd put Sonia to so much trouble and rage. They had entered the house with a beautiful gift for Sonia, a beautiful big chicken, offered because he loved his wife so much and never did anything for her, these days. He had taken her to Rome once: it had been their honeymoon. And today he had given her a chicken but had been greeted with trouble and rage. It had been nice of Lucy, really, though the after-effects weren't so very pleasant. And she had in the end agreed to his one request, to a visit to the butcher's shop in Clapham. It was a lovely shop. He'd always enjoyed going there. It was tiled and polished, and heaped high with glowing flesh, neatly carved and displayed in its pinks and browns, piles of sausages, of steaks, of inner organs and a shelf of well-thumbed cookbooks to give their waiting customers ideas. He was only sorry that he didn't feel at all hungry. It looked so pretty. And the idea he'd had! A chicken! He had eaten it in the past, with his wife, just the two of them. He was sure that he had. He had seen it in his mind's eye with a red ruffle round its neck, and white frills on its little upward-pointing legs, and to be honest, the chicken was almost as picturesque, the chicken that the butcher, red in his twenty-something face and with a shock of white-blond hair above the blue-and-white-striped apron presented to them on a square of greaseproof brown paper. It was a lovely thing to do. He would have to arrange for Lucy to be paid back. She had forgotten to mention it to Sonia when they had arrived home and she had been standing impatiently at the door, and Sonia had hardly given her an opportunity to speak before bundling Toby into his nightclothes and back into bed. But that was only justice. He had seen the butcher's shop once more; its gleam and purpose, its use and its riches. It was more than anyone could ever eat in the rest of their eating lives, all that flesh, and Toby was both glad to have seen it once more, and hoped that at some point before he died, as he knew he would, he would be allowed to leave the house to walk the few hundred yards and see it all again.

The Day I Saw
the Snake

Their lives went in different directions, and quite quickly. Not all of them stayed in touch, but when the ones who met up did meet up, their conversation could be stiff and unsure after the first happy embraces. In the kitchens of their parents across the suburbs, the same kitchens but the parents now old and frail, they would cry out; would mention a spouse or the children, left behind or despatched on a Boxing Day walk; would smile inarticulately. Then silence would threaten to fall like a curtain between them, thick, velvet, satisfied and smothering. They had known each other so well in those single weeks in the 1980s. Sooner or later, on those afternoons during the Christmas holidays, someone would say, 'Do you remember – that afternoon when Stephen Cameron found the snake?' And that would cue them in. They all remembered the afternoon when Stephen Cameron had run up the lawn and across the terraces shouting out, and everyone could add something different. It was like a communal story that everyone knew. The one thing that everybody remembered was Albert, coming across the lawn still playing his bassoon. He liked to play the opening phrase of *The Rite of Spring* in the open air, in the spring afternoon light. (It wasn't the Easter holidays, but the summer week, they all agreed.) So he came across the lawn playing the opening phrase of *The Rite of Spring*, and finished it before taking the bassoon out of his mouth and saying a very Albert-ish thing. 'Very sage beasts, snakes,' he said. 'But they don't stick around to be gawped at. Lead me to it.'

They didn't all remember what Albert said in exactly the same words, but they all remembered the word 'sage'. And Stephen Cameron had led Albert and Sally and Patrick and Katie down past the lake to the woods. They were all there, all the sextet, apart from Alan and Sam Thomas, who played the piano. They were off somewhere, they agreed. (Sam Thomas and Alan had stayed in touch. At those Christmas gatherings, they could add details from the second half of the story, the disconsolate and amused return.) Stephen Cameron led them to the exact place where he had seen the snake. Albert moved steadily, just behind Stephen Cameron. It was still there, Stephen Cameron said, pointing. Albert relaxed, his shoulders dropping, and said another very Albert-ish thing: he said, 'I expect you'll find, on investigation, that you've discovered the end of a rubber hose.' And it was hard to see how even Stephen Cameron could have thought of it as a snake: it was the bright green that plastic hoses were. A gardener must have abandoned it at the end of the summer before.

The story ended there, or it ended with them coming back up to the house. In the story – in their mind's eye – they drifted up, carrying picnic rugs trailing on the grass, ankle-deep in the untrimmed wildness below the lawn. In their hands were their instruments: a flute for Patrick, a clarinet for Sally, and a bassoon slung over Albert's shoulder, dashingly, perkily. They clambered onto the stone terrace, and with a sad smile back at the lovely afternoons of their eighteenth or nineteenth July, they stood at the open french windows of the house. That was what memory supplied. It was a substantial Edwardian manor house in the country, used for conferences and training weeks by the local authorities, and the doors stood constantly open. There was always some noise on the lawn to tempt people out, and Sam Thomas and Alan, who had been inside somewhere, came out as the rest of the sextet and Stephen Cameron came trudging up the hill, laughing. A couple of the littlies were there, too. They were standing with Susie Westerhagen, the strings' tutor; she was smoking, as always. 'What are you up to?' Susie Westerhagen said, drawling in her amused and detached way, like a remote house with a beautiful view. She had some kind of supervisory role; pastoral, she said, like a shepherd with a colossal crook; and her pastoral role consisted of asking people what they were up to from time to time.

'Stephen Cameron thought he had seen a snake,' Katie said. 'So we went to have a look at it.'

'Oh, for God's sake,' Susie Westerhagen said, just as Albert was pointing out that there hadn't been a snake, that it had been something else, a plastic hose or something.

And that would have been that, except that one of the littlies just then dropped to her knees and was violently sick on the lawn. It was a viola player from the fifth desk wearing a skirt that only her mother could have made and a Festival of Youth Orchestras T-shirt from earlier that year; they recognized the blonde and scrubby top of her head, bent in rehearsals in studious terror in case she be picked on, bent over now in nausea. 'Oh, God,' Susie Westerhagen said. 'Someone take her inside. That'll be the sunstroke. It's hotter than you think, out here.'

Who was it, they always said, retelling this story years later, in the kitchen of one of the sextet? It was a fifth-desk viola player, they knew, but no one could think what her name was. Susie Westerhagen knew her name: she would have said, 'Oh, for God's sake, take Diana' – or Mandy or Polly – 'inside and make her lie down in the dark for an hour.' She would have known her name. That was her job. And phoning for a doctor from Ardlesford, she had done that. But what was the viola-playing littlie called? No one could remember any longer, and once a year, Albert could be relied upon to say at this point, 'It wasn't Karen Whitaker's little sister, was it?' and they would say, 'No, Albert, Karen Whitaker's little sister was very sensible, she's a dentist in Crosspool nowadays.' Because when the doctor emerged from the darkened room, he had a sharp couple of words with Susie Westerhagen, who had failed to notice not only that the littlie string players had got hold of a bottle of vodka but were sipping it in the afternoons in glasses of orange squash. Susie Westerhagen knew their names, but she couldn't recognize drunkenness in children until they were sick, literally sick, on her shoes.

'My God,' Katie might say at this point, years later. 'That orchestra – it would be closed down by the authorities nowadays. Letting thirteen-year-olds go off on their own to discover vodka and heavy petting.'

'Heavy petting!' Sam Thomas would say. 'Heavy petting!'

'That's what we always used to call it,' Katie would say. 'That was the phrase for it, back then.'

'For what?' Sam Thomas said. 'Does it just mean not quite having sex? I never knew.'

'Oh, a bit of finger fun, I dare say,' Albert said, who had somehow discovered his own funniness in the thirty years since the afternoon when he had discounted the snake. 'No more than that. It was always warned against, though – you never described what you were doing as heavy petting.'

'I don't think I ever did it,' Katie said. 'Never, ever, ever. Of course I was terribly fat, right up until I went to Africa.'

'Your relationship was with your oboe,' Sam Thomas said. 'And with your A-level grades, of course. You weren't fat. Not in the way teenagers are fat now.'

'I could have petted a little,' Katie said. 'Perhaps not very heavily. In between all the fretting. Fretting, fretting, fretting, then petting. It wouldn't have done any harm.'

They were at that moment when music was like a great door flung open onto the wide lawns out there, radiant and glowing, like an outlined cartoon of a landscape. The orchestra was assembled for a week's residence and rehearsal there, in that house in the country. In the morning was the second symphony of Brahms and the third piano concerto of Beethoven and an overture by Shostakovich; in the evening was the same. Each of them went so deeply into every note, not skating over it, not merely producing it, but trying to think of every aspect of every note, how it should be produced, with what swelling depth of tone, trying to hear everything around them. Even the littlies did this, and they dreamt of D major. For the rest of their lives, sometimes a doctor or a solicitor who had once played the cello in the municipality youth orchestra would find themselves thinking with terror of the F sharp from nothing that began the slow movement of Brahms 2, and wondering once again what exactly Brahms meant by asking for *poco forte*. The days had that strength of purpose in them.

In the afternoons they could do what they chose. Some sections met up for extra practice, especially the strings; others found a corner and prepared pieces of their own. Others went for walks in the countryside or, like the littlies, drank vodka and learnt how to smoke under the benignly oblivious nose of Susie Westerhagen, the strings' tutor. Sally and Katie and Patrick and Albert had been in the orchestra for three years, since its founding; they all knew each other well from sectional rehearsals, and from sitting next to each other. That year, Katie and Patrick had both independently learnt a Poulenc sonata – the flute sonata, the oboe sonata – and before they knew it, the woodwind section was Poulenc-mad, everyone learning the horn *Elegy* (Alan), the bassoon sonata (Albert), the clarinet sonata (Sally). It was Patrick who mentioned the sextet for piano and wind. No one could think of another piece for quite that combination. Everyone liked Sam Thomas, who was a good pianist as well as playing the double bass, and they played it through. The long hot lazy cadences of the slow movement stole through the open windows of the music room, like perfume; they were crazy about it. The clocks all through the house moved in unison; they were called slave clocks, all tied to a central mechanism, which now, a hundred years on, was not quite right.

'I wish I could play that now,' Sam Thomas said. 'I'm so out of practice. But what year was that?'

It must have been 1983, the summer of 1983, because Sally had had her first year at Oxford, and had come back full of sophistication and human observation. She was a year older than the others, and able to advise them. Patrick and Albert were going to music college – they were going to make a fist of it – but the others had all got into Oxford or Cambridge. Katie had got into medical school, and was taking a year out to volunteer in Africa; Sam Thomas was going to do English at Oxford – there was always a book in his hand to deposit on the piano before he yawned and started on the fast scale, almost a savage glissando, that began the Poulenc sextet. That week it was *Bleak House* – he had stopped after the first movement at one rehearsal and just said, in a lowering voice, 'Hope, joy, youth, peace, rest, life, dust, ashes, waste, want, ruin, despair, madness, death, cunning, folly, words, wigs, rags, sheepskin, plunder, precedent, jargon, gammon and spinach.' Then he had given that nod that the pianist gave, and they started on the second movement, not getting very far before they laughspluttered to a halt. And Alan had got into Cambridge to read music. They were all doing well, and the windows, open to the summer day, sent the long, lazy serenade of twining winds out into the elm-shaded gardens where birdsong responded.

There was another person in the room, often. Stephen Cameron had been there for ever. He sat brightly listening, his hands to the side of his chair, gripping. He played the violin; he was on the third desk of the second violins, and he tried so hard. Katie went to the same school as him, the one with the portico, named after George V where they had never got over no longer being a grammar school. He gazed at them; he listened; he was a vicar's son; he was good at maths; he said afterwards that he found this modern music a struggle – you didn't know what note was going to come next, it could be anything at all. He meant the Poulenc sextet. Sam Thomas, who had played the Webern variations in public and was struggling with the Stockhausen *Klavierstücke* and the Berio *Sequenza* in private, looked at him with amusement when he said this. But it turned out that Stephen Cameron was not really good at maths: that was just the air he had, of scholarly lack of attention to appearance. His clothes! (That was what Sam Thomas thought.) He wore the same clothes all year round, a patterned jumper, frayed brown cords. He had the air of someone permanently puzzled by the weather. He had applied for and been turned down by all five of his UCCA choices. He would have to wait until after his A-level results, then apply again, perhaps going to a university that was like playing on the third desk of the second violins in an orchestra. But he sat in his mother-knitted sweater and his brown, balding corduroys, and he listened with open puzzlement to the Poulenc sextet, his hands gripping the side of the chair. His gaze was on Katie, as it always was.

The day they saw the snake was also the day that Sam Thomas agreed with himself that he was going to tell someone else he was gay. And after that it would always be easier. He had thought about it for years, and it was now clear to him that he had handled it in the wrong way, in ways that would lead to nothing. He had sat in the kitchens of sympathetic girls, and had hung his head and muttered about how difficult it all was, what he had to say, and had stuck there for so long that in the end, patient but exasperated, they had always said it for him. And they had been kind and supportive, but that was a fat lot of good. It was like playing the Berio *Sequenza* to Stephen Cameron. They wouldn't know what to do with the experience or the knowledge. And then, twice now, he had met a boy in irregular circumstances. His mum had made him go to a law weekend for sixth-formers at Cambridge, and he had stayed at Gonville and Caius. ('Keys': he had found that out just in time.) There had been a boy there who came from Sheffield, too. His name was Alexander. They had sat up late, talking about law. Alexander was absurd, he saw that now: he had put up his hand after a lecture and begun a question 'I put it to you,' and the whole lecture theatre had laughed. But then he had loved Alexander. Two weeks after they had returned to Sheffield and the third time they had met up, Sam Thomas had said to him in his bedroom, 'I think I love you,' and that had been that. Alexander had written him a letter, an absurd letter beginning 'Sir', which would have hurt him, but for that absurdity. Afterwards Sam Thomas had known very well what to do with that experience and knowledge.

So the day they had gone to see the snake was the first day that Sam Thomas had decided that the thing he must, must do was to tell the fact to a friend of long standing, a male friend, in a neutral way, not declaring love or anything of that sort. And he had done so. After lunch he had found himself walking with Alan up the driveway towards the main road; Alan wanted to go to the village a mile away to get a packet of ten cigarettes, Benson & Hedges. Before they had reached the gatehouse, Sam Thomas had just said, 'I like men,' to Alan, and then again, 'I like men, I mean in the way most people like girls,' and had looked up at the trees because he knew he hadn't meant to say 'people' but 'men' or 'males' or 'people of our sex' or something.

Alan had said, 'Oh, I see,' and then, 'I thought you were keen on—' and had cut himself short. They had walked on in silence for a while, but a companionable silence, Sam Thomas thought. In any case Alan had not called him 'Sir', like a dog, or turned round and walked away. When they started to talk again it was about Brahms. Brahms had played the French horn and his father had played the double bass; Sam Thomas and Alan had had this conversation before, and they believed that Brahms, because of this, had a special affinity with and understanding of how these two instruments were played.

'It just feels exactly right,' Sam Thomas said. They were walking into Ardlesford; a woman was standing, irate, outside the Cross Keys waving at a rapidly departing yellow Cortina as if trying to attract the driver's attention. 'Those passages at the end, it's like an exercise in your tutor, how the hands fall exactly at the right point, just exactly as they're meant to fall. He knows, I reckon. He knows what your hands want to do.'

'Not like Berlioz,' Alan said, and they both burst out laughing, shaking their heads like veterans of last summer's epic struggle with the *Fantastique*.

What had they wanted to buy in the village? Sam had forgotten when Alan went into the village shop and asked for ten Benson & Hedges; he picked up a copy of *Private Eye* and showed it to Sam. On the cover was the prime minister and four of her colleagues, and she was saying something about hanging, how she was in favour of it but wouldn't bring it back. 'That's clever,' Sam said, knowing that was the sort of thing you said about *Private Eye*. Alan read it every fortnight, he said. You needed to read it every issue or you wouldn't get the jokes. For instance ... He opened the issue and started flicking towards the back—

'We're not a library,' the man behind the counter said, a fat man with no neck, red over the face and bare scalp. 'You want to read the magazines wi'out buying them, I've no doubt you can find 'em in Sheffield library service.'

'I am going to buy it,' Alan said, aggrieved. 'I've not seen this issue yet,' he added, turning to Sam Thomas.

'You'll be popular,' the man said. 'We get it in for vicar, one copy and just one, he's the only one as reads it.'

'Well, that's just hard cheese on the vicar,' Alan said, and bought the cigarettes and the magazine. Barely outside, he lit up, offering one to Sam Thomas. 'What a dreadful, dreadful person,' he went on. 'You don't suppose he knew, do you?'

'Knew what?' Sam Thomas said.

'Knew that you were – *a homosexual*,' Alan said, hissing the words in a way that would project rather than suppress them. In his burst of laughter, Sam realized that the words were strange but now would be familiar; that he had avoided them but they were true, that he had not said anything about a passing feeling but had definitely described, almost with an absence of feeling, a scientific category into which a specimen could now be placed. It was funny, it was; but in the memory afterwards of what was called a coming out, Sam Thomas would always recall not the sentence he had spoken, something about finding the same sex appealing, or some other euphemism, but Alan saying outside the scruffy village shop, with dead flies on the plastic children's toys in the window, that the owner had been dreadful, that he must have known that Sam Thomas was *a homosexual*. That was it.

Their rehearsals of the Poulenc sextet in the afternoon had set off all sorts of impromptu chamber investigations and rehearsals. The percussionists had abandoned their instruments altogether and were getting some spoken-word piece into shape. It was a sort of fugue that was nothing but shouted names of places. They were practising it now, the timpanist and the three others. They must be down by the big sundial, and someone was shouting, 'Trinidad … and the big Mississippi and the …' There was the Lake Titicaca, too, Sam Thomas knew, and Popacatapetl, which was not in Canada, rather in Mexico.

'God, that is driving me up the wall,' Sam Thomas said.

'The town Honolulu,' Alan said. 'I thought it was an island.'

'It's the Lake Titicaca I hate,' Sam said. 'It must be fun to do, though.'

And that seemed to be a cue, because Alan then plucked at Sam Thomas's sleeve, first impatiently then hard, pulling him, and in a second Sam Thomas found he was kissing – no, being kissed by – Alan. It was the first time he had been kissed by a man, not initiated the action. He was not likely to forget the feeling of the bark of the tree against the back of his head, the sensation of Alan's thin and forceful mouth against his own, the familiar taste, made strange with the push of the tongue that brought it, of cigarettes. Trinidad. In a moment it stopped, and Alan bent to pick up the copy of *Private Eye* where it had fallen onto the wood's layer of mulch. Sam Thomas followed him up the path, asking himself whether now was the moment to take his hand, whether any of that would now make sense. He wondered who Alan had thought he was keen on.

That was the year Katie lost all that weight. She never put it on again. There was something in her mind about going to Africa – she was volunteering in the north of Kenya, in a health centre that served hundreds of miles around. It was ridiculous, it made no sense, but she didn't want to turn up and start saying she could be of help to all these people when she had obviously had far too much to eat all her life. She told nobody, only her mother. At the end of March, almost as soon as it was feasible, she went with her mother to Halfords and bought a bicycle – she hadn't had one since she was seven, a fairy bicycle in pink. She rode down the hill, at first terrified at the velocity, then determined to enjoy it, then all the way down the Manchester road as far as the Rivelin dam. For the first day that was perfectly all right. One day soon she would get as far as Ladybower.

Nobody knew about it, apart from Stephen Cameron. He saw her one day. She was hurtling along the Manchester road, her usual morning outing. What was he doing there? He was standing against a dry stone wall, staring into space, a mile from the nearest house. Stephen Cameron was often alone, but alone in crowds. He didn't need to walk a mile into the moors to stand and relish aloneness. He could find aloneness on a crowded bus, in a classroom, at a party. She saw him approaching as she pedalled furiously; it was a June day of bright winds, the clouds scudding as if thrown across the blue. He saw her approaching, too. You could see him gripping himself, tensely, preparing for Katie. It was as if he knew that she took this route in exercise, four days a week, and had positioned himself exactly there in order to greet her. But how could he know? She had told nobody except her mother, and her mother had told nobody, she was sure. The thing that could not be allowed to happen was for her cycle route to become, like the maths set and the physics set and orchestral practice, an opportunity for Stephen Cameron to gaze at her sorrowfully. She stared straight ahead in concentration. Five yards away from Stephen Cameron, she allowed herself to look at him, to give him a bright wave to acknowledge his own long-raised hand and worried expression, to cycle straight on without slowing. The next time she went out on the bicycle, she started by going up the hill, not down, along the top of the golf course and through Lodge Moor. He wouldn't have known where to stand, even if he had known where to go.

A year went by, before the next time they met. They were at Patrick's: he had suggested that they get together to see each other before the orchestral week in July. Sally had agreed; she'd left the orchestra now that she was going into her last year at university, and Katie, too, thought this was going to be her last one. She was calculating the loss of time for her oboe practice once the rote learning of joints and bones and organs started, all that slicing into her allotted corpse, and she didn't think it was fair to cling to things if you didn't really have time for them. She was going to call her corpse Wendy, she'd decided. It was all right for Patrick and Albert: they did nothing but play the flute and the bassoon all day long at music college. Medicine wasn't going to allow much time for keeping on top of things musically, she knew.

She had come to Patrick's parents' door, and gratifyingly, he had just stared at her. She had always found their house entrancing: his mother had done it beautifully inside, with lovely elegant white rooms, just shaded with pale blues and purples, and always a bowl of flowers in just the right colours. She could have stared at it for hours before noticing the one strange thing about it, that there was never a book to be seen in it. Staring at Patrick, too, she had been: for years in the woodwind section she had let her eyes fall on him, and had never quite reconciled herself to the beauty of his dark-curled head, the fine features nodding with solid dedication over the sumptuous sound of a flute played by a man. Until now, she had loved Patrick's masculinity in its unexpected places; loved a man so confident he could play the flute without any raising of eyebrows, loved his dark presence, heaped up with motherlove in that most feminine of houses. But that had been last summer, when she had been fat. She had seen so much since then: had seen a child die in her hands, and let an American doctor, a qualified adult, roam confidently over her new thin body in the room in the white-plastered residency. She felt almost too old in experience to think of starting university in October. She had done all that. She had stared once, so long ago, at Patrick and at Patrick's mother's beautiful house, and now she was thin, and it was Patrick's turn to stare at her. 'My God, Katie,' he said. 'I hardly recognized you. You look— Come in.'

'She looks amazing,' Sally said in the hallway, but dismissively, almost ironically, as if 'amazing' were all that could be expected of her. 'We want to hear all about it.'

'Oh, it's just what you would expect,' Katie said. 'It was very hard work, to be honest, and very uncomfortable. Where's Sam Thomas? I thought Sam Thomas was coming.'

'I'm feeling guilty,' Sally said, taking her arm and leading her through. 'The truth of it is – I haven't seen Sam Thomas at all, all year. It's ridiculous. His college is only five hundred yards away, and I've hardly seen him, really not at all. The thing is,' Sally said to Katie, sitting down, 'there just isn't time to sit around with people and chat all afternoon. *You'll see*. Just because you're at the same university – my God, the terms at Oxford, they're only eight weeks long. I don't know how we fit anything in. You just don't have time – I hate to say it, but you're going to find it's completely true – you don't have time to be kind to people from home. I'm sorry, but there it is.'

'He was probably just as busy, really,' Katie said.

'Sam Thomas?' Sally said, although it was Sam Thomas they were talking about. 'Oh, I'm sure he was absolutely fine. But it was awful that he kept sending me notes, four or five, suggesting that we meet up for a coffee or something. I saw him in passing in orchestras, you know, but only that, a quick wave. I'm sure he was fine. It takes some people time to find their feet.'

'What are you talking about?' Patrick said, coming in. 'Africa? You've got to have so much to tell us.'

Sally had the grace to smile, and say, 'I want to hear *all about it*,' but that only made Katie feel that she wouldn't waste her time beginning to tell. What was the point of starting to tell when it was so immense an alteration, and to tell it would mean another year of telling to follow the year of doing? She said something bright about probably waiting until the others were here, but Patrick said that there were no others coming, only perhaps Sam Thomas. Albert was teaching this morning – he had taken on some eleven-year olds from his teacher, and was being paid for it – and Patrick hadn't heard back from Alan. He thought he might be away.

Katie asked about Stephen Cameron, but that surprised Patrick, you could see. Sally knew about him.

In a way, Stephen Cameron's appearance and presentation had been a matter of the most perfect genius. He had persuaded almost everyone that he was one of the clever kids; a vicar's son, he had the handed-down and mildly frayed, clean look that you would expect. They had taken one look at him, his hobbies and his glasses and his side parting, and they had put him into the top maths set. But Stephen Cameron was not one of the clever kids. The school had written off his O-level results as a strange off-day, and had taken him into the sixth form. He loved maths, he said, and was in the further maths set. But he couldn't do it. You saw him puzzling over a page of figures, letters, equations, pencil scribblings in the corner of the common room, between halves of the rehearsal as if it was all he wanted to get back to. Then a flourish of the pencil, a clearing of the brow, a bright wide smile, a series of scribbles. Katie had seen those triumphant scribbles: they were usually wrong or not to the point at all. Like the cerulean hand-knitted Aran sweater with patches at the elbows, Stephen Cameron's maths performance was all theatre in the wrong setting. And still the teacher had persuaded himself, somehow, that Stephen was a natural, a gifted mathematician who saw the result, or saw another result, or saw something else entirely, and leapt to that conclusion where it wasn't helpful. He went to pieces in tests, always, the teacher used to say, fondly cudgelling Stephen Cameron's head. But it would be all right on the night. He gave a cursory glance at Katie's work. It was correct, and he went on.

The admissions tutors at the different universities had not seen Stephen Cameron; they only knew what they had read about him in the tutor's report; so they went on thinking that he was a gifted mathematician until they saw his interim reports, or the paper that he did for his Cambridge exam. Then they did not offer him a place. It was just where everyone else had applied, to Cambridge, because it was the best, then to a good London college, then a traditional place for second-choice after Cambridge, then two good old red-bricks. They all refused him, except one, which failed to answer at all. The refusals came in steadily, one after another, and Stephen Cameron had said that it was just bad luck, he was up against stiff competition, he knew, he just fell to pieces in exams, that was the trouble. Then Katie got her place to read medicine at Cambridge. The teacher bumped into her in the second-floor corridor between lessons, the Monday after she'd heard. He waved his hand with a dismissive cheerfulness, said, 'I knew *you* would be all right.' She looked out of the window, burning, as he walked away. She felt she had always taken for granted that the teachers' job was to concentrate on those who needed help and support. They had taken her for granted in return. Just once, she would like to be told that she had done well. It was as if she had inherited her ability, unfairly, from an aunt she had never met, who ought to have left her abilities to Stephen Cameron. And Stephen Cameron went in the end to a polytechnic in Dundee to study maths and computing. He went by train.

It must have been in March, towards the end of the spring term – the Hilary Term, Sally went on calling it – that Katie had a letter from Sally in Oxford. It was Sally's last year in Oxford, and before the dreaded job market struck, Sally said, she really wanted to go to a final summer ball. It was Trinity, she said – not her college, but a beautiful one. She was going to ask Patrick, too, and Sam Thomas was coming. It wasn't his final year, but he was thrilled to be coming. Finals!!!! Sally wrote, and then a despairing little figure, its head in its hands and question marks exploding from its wild hair.

So they went to the Trinity summer ball. It was a hot day when Katie got off the coach from Cambridge, her dress in a plastic hanging bag, just as she had brought it from Sheffield at the end of the Easter vac. It was her mum's dress – she really didn't want to spend three hundred pounds on a dress she was only going to wear once before sidling back into last year's size – and she thought it would do. It had hung from the luggage rack all the way. There were three other big luggage bags hanging in the same way;

the coach was the only way to get from Cambridge to Oxford, and there was a fair amount of movement between the two. One boy, obstinately reading a chemistry text book, had got on the bus already wearing his black tie. An older man had got on at the stop outside Cambridge – perhaps a don of some sort, he looked so distinguished with his shining white whiskers – and had surveyed the half-full coach before deciding on the seat next to Katie's. It had worked then, if only on older men, possibly dons. But no – he was not a don, he was a porter at Churchill, had been there since it was founded, almost. His son was at Oxford, was going to see him. He expected Katie was going across to see her young man. His son – how he got the same sort of job as his dad but at the other place – that was a story. He was still telling it, leisurely, practised, passing the time as the coach was rolling into Oxford. He could have been innocent and paternal, but for the way his large hands kept running down his thighs as if to smooth out his trousers' wrinkles, and incidentally against Katie's legs in their white summer skirt.

'Do you mind?' Katie had said once, and he had seemed not to hear, but had stopped for five minutes before his hand, like a nervous feeding animal, had fallen back to its unsupervised to and fro. And now they were arriving. There was Sally at the side of the bus station, peering into the coach, not having seen her yet; she was trim, precise as an ant, shining and clipped and small, and next to her was Patrick, dark, smiling and beautiful, but somehow meaningless. 'Here we are,' Katie said dismissively, getting up and pushing past, walking towards the front of the coach before it had even properly stopped, and the groping porter was behind her for ever. Patrick had just said something to Sally, and Sally laughed brilliantly, head back, her white teeth bared. When Katie looked at Patrick, waving in a cheerful, sexless way, she looked first of all at what seemed to be missing, his flute in his other hand, ready to be raised to play. His masculinity seemed incomplete, without a point or purpose, without the surprise of femininity the flute proposed.

They were to go back to Sally's room in college. Katie and she were in the same position, or nearly; she reflected that Sally was, after all, on the other side of a divide. In Cambridge, the final-year students were friendly, remote, jarred by a long and testing experience. Katie was walking not with her friend from the youth orchestra but with someone who had experienced the future. All the time, walking up the wide street, divided between white museums and flushed red colleges, Patrick was talking in his unchanged way about music, about the day they thought they had seen the snake, about the Boulez sonatina his tutor was making him learn with a pianist called Sue. Frank was the name of his tutor; he and Sue had become characters in the narrative without Katie or Sally knowing them at all. 'At first I hated it – it just had nothing to hang on to, and it's one of those pieces that you wonder whether the composer just hates you. Frank said I would wonder whether it was written for the flute or against the flute before I was done. But then it's weird – something happened – Sue said the same thing – I found myself thinking about the tunes one day. There aren't any tunes! But I was thinking about them. It's really got inside me, now. Do you know what I mean?'

They went into Sally's college, and Patrick was talking, reaching out to them from his old life. He was so beautiful still, and generous, smiling, and nothing had happened to him but the Boulez sonatina. It had not occurred to Katie that anything had happened to her in particular, but when people who had known her for years had said to her, 'Is that you? What have you done? You look …' they seemed lost for words, as if they were trying to explain not the trivial daily undertakings on the bicycle, but the things she had seen in Kenya, the understanding of the body she had reached in the last year, handling the innards and preserved organs of a corpse that had once been a woman. She had not named her corpse Wendy; she had only thought she would, before she had met her in all her sullen nude horizontal dignity.

Patrick was despatched off to change, smiling, happy, and Katie and Sally went into Sally's room. The clarinet case was on top of her little bookcase: a photograph of her mum and dad in a silver frame; a pencil drawing of Chatsworth, was it, above the bed where Katie had an RSC poster of a production of *Hamlet*? 'Let me see,' Sally said, and Katie brought her mum's dress out. She had seen it before, in fact. Katie had sent her two photographs. Her mum had bought two versions of the same dress, a long chiffon floral print, and a short chiffon floral print. Her mum had thought of the knee-length version as an ordinary summer dress, the long one as a dressy version, but Sally had written back promptly to advise the short one, definitely – and Katie had brought that. She wondered. She was not very clothes-minded, and though Sally applauded delightedly from the bed when she saw it, she then dashed to the oak wardrobe and pulled out a dark green taffeta fantasy, a proper ballgown down to the floor, creaking and rustling and hugely billowing, like a ship at anchor rolling in the wind.

'Oh, that's amazing,' Katie said politely. 'It must have cost a fortune.'

Sally pouted, pleased. 'It's only the once,' she said. 'I can't imagine not making a big thing about it. You know – you'll see.'

'I know,' Katie said. She was, after all, at Cambridge. They had balls there, too. If she was ever going to come to see to the point of buying a huge taffeta ballgown, it would have happened by now. She knew she would be the only woman there in a chiffon dress, and the only one whose knees would be showing. She didn't curse Sally; she cursed herself for being so easy for Sally to manipulate. Really, she had thought about her dress for about seven minutes, all in all, and now she was going to have to wear what Sally had decided, to allow herself to be outshone, all night long.

'You smell gorgeous,' Katie said. 'What is it?'

'It's Fahrenheit,' Sally said. 'I love it. People here know when I've walked down a corridor in front of them. Someone told me it was my signature scent. Do you want to borrow some?'

'I couldn't,' Katie said, to please Sally. 'I just couldn't – I couldn't live up to it.'

'It's going to be beautiful,' Sally said, looking out of the window. 'Look – here's Sam Thomas in his dinner jacket, and look – he's got some flowers for you – he's got a whole bouquet – look, look – adorable. He doesn't know you're supposed to give something that the girl can carry – oh, how sweet of him, though …'

And he was there, coming round the quad in exactly the same dinner suit that he wore to play concerts in, the old one with the double-breasted jacket, a serious expression, a new sort of haircut. The size of the bouquet was absurd, and no one seeing him walk through the college quadrangle could doubt for a moment that here was someone with no interest in women. No doubt, either, when he came through the door and looked from one to the other, smiling but focused elsewhere. He might as well have opened his mouth and said, 'Where's Patrick?' It was for Sally to make the best of it and, in her mode as hostess, to welcome someone she'd spent two years ignoring, and to say soothingly, 'This is going to be fabulous – I'm so excited.' Then he came over and kissed Katie, kissed Sally. It was a new gesture. They had never laid cheek to cheek.

Sam Thomas was off work the day that Sally phoned. He hadn't heard from her for years. Afterwards, he wondered why she had called on a Wednesday morning when he almost definitely wouldn't be in. She had probably wanted to leave a phone message, to give him the chance of deciding whether to call back or not. But he had answered and, strangely, she hadn't sounded disconcerted: she seemed happy to be able to speak to him. He had a dreadful cold, one that almost qualified as proper flu. It had been going since Friday afternoon. His awful boss had sounded sceptical on the telephone on Monday morning, but they would manage, he supposed. His flatmate had come and gone, not offering to go out for Lemsip and soup, even. He was at a low point when Sally phoned. She bet he didn't know who this was.

'It's Sally,' Sam said. 'I knew exactly.'

'I can't believe it,' Sally said. 'I haven't seen you since – God, I was trying to work it out – I was just finishing at Oxford. It was the Trinity ball, wasn't it?'

'No, there was that time afterwards – you know, I came round later that summer, don't you remember?'

'Oh, God, yes,' Sally said. 'Oh, God, I'd obliterated that.' Because when the degree results had come through, Sally had done really very badly: she had gone to Oxford in glory, the pride of her school, and left with a third. Her tutor had told her, Sam remembered, that she was lucky to be given a degree at all. 'That was awful and you were so sweet. I got your number from your mum – we had quite a chat about you, and what you're up to. Listen.'

'I'm listening,' Sam said, amused.

'There's someone I really want you to meet,' Sally said. 'I know it's been years, and I know we're living probably about a mile from each other, but I'd really like you to meet someone. Does that sound …'

'Lovely,' Sam said. 'I'm not going anywhere at the moment. What's his name?'

'Richard,' Sally said. 'Well, I don't know whether this could work, but actually, we're not going to be far from you tonight. Can we maybe pop in?'

'Oh, that would be so nice,' Sam Thomas said, almost moved. It was so like Sally, after all – to move on, to have no time for them, to busy herself, but at the end, when something important like this happened, a serious

191

Tales of Persuasion

boyfriend, a fiancé, even perhaps a husband, to make the effort and to phone up and say that there was someone she wanted them to meet. 'Do you ever see any of that old lot? Katie and Stephen Cameron and Patrick? I saw Albert last Christmas. He came round and we went to the pub. He's exactly the same.'

'Katie's a doctor in York,' Sally said. 'I know that much. Listen, let's talk later. It would be so nice to see you. Around six? I've got your address. Rostrevor Road?'

Years later, when they all met up, Katie and Alan and Albert and Sam Thomas and sometimes Patrick, too, someone would mention the day they thought they had seen a snake.

'That was the year you lost all that weight,' Alan would say kindly to Katie. Alan had failed his degree: with him, it hadn't seemed to matter. He'd opened a business, had made a fortune, or so he said, but in any case he lived in a stone house with his girlfriend and their three children, paid the mortgage from the second-hand record shop. 'I came across a photo of you before. I couldn't think who that was.'

'Oh, you're always fat in your mind if you're fat when you're seventeen,' Katie said.

'And then that littlie was sick on the lawn,' Albert said. 'Do you remember? And Susie Westerhagen …'

Was it the Easter holiday, or was it the week in the summer, the time somebody thought they had seen a snake? They couldn't decide. The manor house that had belonged to the council for that sort of thing, it was privately owned now. Someone lived in it as if it were just a house. There had been forty bedrooms in the tacked-on dormitory – they must have demolished that. Sam Thomas

192

had been at school with the girl who had bought it. God knew how she'd made all that money. And what had they been rehearsing? Brahms 2, they all remembered, but there was an overture, as well – was it *Candide* or had that been the year before? They remembered the Poulenc sextet: Sam Thomas said modestly that he couldn't play the piano part now, not in a million years. He was so out of practice. Patrick played in the LSO now; Albert was a professor of bassoon; they smiled, as if the question were going to arise. And, remember, all those Poulenc afternoons, there had been poor Stephen Cameron, sitting in the corner of the room, gazing at Katie. (He had been killed in those bombings in London, the day after the Olympics had been announced, on 7/7, as people were starting to say.) Poor Stephen Cameron, going to work on an ordinary tube train, and twenty years before he had been sitting in a corner of a room, being bad at maths, loving Katie when she was fat, loving her when she was thin, not really noticing anything when it changed, not being very good at anything, puzzled by the weather, by the Webern piano variations, by maths.

'That was sad,' Sam Thomas said. And then they would talk about the last time they had all seen Sally. It had been the same for all of them, except Albert. She hadn't been able to track him down, maybe. Sally, over the phone, had someone she would like them to meet. They had all thought the same thing: that Sally was engaged and wanted to introduce her fiancé to her old friends in the orchestra. They thought she was doing the rounds. It must have been the same for Katie and Albert and Patrick and perhaps even for Stephen Cameron – who knew?

Sam Thomas answered the door, and there was Sally exactly as she had been: tight, clipped, tidy, neat, and next to her a man with a huge briefcase, a man maybe ten years older than them, with a heavy five o'clock shadow. Oddly, Sally asked if they could come in. Sam led them upstairs. They sat down in the kitchen. Sally immediately started reminiscing about the days in the orchestra – do you remember, do you remember, and Susie Westerhagen, and the day that – and Sam made them a pot of tea. She had launched into it, not found herself in the middle of it, and Sam joined in dutifully rather than with pleasure. The man, whose name was Richard, Sam remembered, sat back and looked with calculating interest at the kitchen – the cupboards, oven, fridge, the sink. The kitchen was filled with an outrageous, peppery, puddingy scent. He remembered the smell. Sally came to the end of what she had practised. She had taken four minutes, not counting Sam's contributions.

'Do you ever buy bottled water, Sam?' the man said.

'Sometimes,' Sam said. 'I like San Pellegrino.'

'Have you ever wondered, Sam, how much bottled water costs you, annually?'

Sally was sitting forward in her chair, smiling in an unfocused, embarrassed, determined way. She knew how bad this was going to be.

'And yet, Sam, we don't like to drink tap water, especially here in London, do we? Look, Sam …'

He lifted off the lid of the teapot in which the tea was stewing. He indicated some sort of film on the surface of the tea. 'That's the impurities and mineral deposits – harmful mineral deposits – that come with the water that comes out of your tap, Sam. Now, if I can show you something ...'

'This is so exciting, Sam,' Sally said, as the man lifted his heavy case onto the table. He wondered if she had ever brought out his name like that, back when they were friends.

It was some sort of device they were selling. You attached it to the tap in your sink, and it purified your water. It cost two hundred pounds and had a filter, costing much the same, which you had to replace once a year. Sally had been going through her address book. She was trying to make money out of people she'd once known, people she'd played Brahms 2 with, people she'd been to a summer ball with and danced with, people who thought they'd once seen a snake in the long grass, years ago, on a hot afternoon in Yorkshire.

'I went along with it,' Katie said, much later, when they were meeting up. 'After half an hour they were explaining to me how you could recruit your friends and how much money you made out of them. It was incredible.'

'I sat down and did the calculations,' Alan said. 'I worked out how much it would cost to buy a bottle of water every two days compared to the cost of this bloody contraption. There wasn't much in it.'

'I took it off them,' Sam Thomas said. 'I said I'd try it out for a week or two. Do you think they were going out with each other?'

They couldn't agree; they all thought that this man Richard was her puppet-master in the sinister cult of water-filters, had probably recruited her. But they couldn't make up their minds whether the relationship between the two had a boyfriend-girlfriend feeling, or whether it was just control and agent.

'Did you keep it, Sam?' Katie said. 'The two-hundred-pound filter?'

He had tried for about a minute to attach it to the tap, then given up and put it back in its box. Sally had come back a week later, this time on her own. He had seen her coming, had gone down to the front door with the box already packed. She had been ready to come in. He had handed it back on the doorstep, saying briefly that he didn't think it would suit him. Her face fell; they said goodbye. Afterwards, they would always say that it was a strange summer, the summer that contained the day that contained Stephen Cameron claiming to have seen a snake. But it wasn't strange. It was the last normal summer and perhaps the only normal summer. Afterwards, it was the rest of their summers that were strange, that didn't go the way summers should. Sam Thomas, from the first-floor window of his rented flat, watched Sally, with her neat, clipped walk, trot down towards the Fulham Road. The box was bulky, and causing her problems. There was a terrible pathos in the woman, so professionally dressed, her confident odour of Fahrenheit, being condemned to lug heavy boxes around. He imagined her going onwards, walking through back-streets and calm pavements, shadowed with plane trees, uninterrupted by duty or worry or obligation, until she reached the river. Like many women of London before, she would kick off her tight shoes, and in holed and laddered tights clamber up onto the embankment with her useless and expensive box in her arms, and, like many women of London, fall with a heavy lack of grace into the thick waters of the river. Sam Thomas watched her go with her clear-edged determination. It was a handsome evening: the sun was at the hour of aperitif, and was painting London in the tangible golden promise that it normally only possessed when glimpsed from long leagues away. His flu had kept him off work for nearly two weeks now, but he was feeling a little better. He thought he would phone Nick, that boy he'd met for the first time three weeks ago at the Daisy Chain, and ask him over.

The Pierian Spring

Once, an ill-intentioned acquaintance in the London Library had remarked in passing that Pentel were discontinuing those nice green roll-tip pens. Those ones you always use, Sam. She had noticed Sam writing, day after day, in the same turquoise-backed notebook with the same pen. It was one of a long series dating back to middle-childhood. She was observant, that ill-intentioned acquaintance, and the same day Sam had gone out to Paperchase and bought seventy-two of the green Pentel roller balls – twenty-four packs of three – to see him, or what passed for his inspiration, out.

There had been no truth in it: the Pentel roller balls were still, five years on, being produced, but Sam proposed to take no risks in the matter. He had always written with the same style of pen in the same style of notebook. He did not know whether he would be able to write at all, if the pen that fitted into his hand like an extra finger, never to be thought about, were to disappear overnight.

The reliance on habit had got worse, not better, with the event of his Success. He had written two novels, which had been reviewed. The first was described as clever and elegant; the second, elegant and clever. The third, on the other hand, had won a prize, and had sold. Incredulously, Sam found himself turning down an offer to transform the book into a film, and observing the incredulous looks on the faces of what could only be called executives on the other side of a boardroom table. Nobody – Sam, his agent Barbara, his editors at Meersbrook and Edgeworth in the UK or Muffin Parker in the States, Helena or Peter, who was anyway too young to know really what his father did for a living – none of them had ever expected such a thing. All it had been was two hundred pages about an old woman meeting an estranged daughter in a seaside town without a single adverb from beginning to end. It was devastating, heart-rending, exquisite, and made seven separate reviewers in three different continents weep on public transport, or so they claimed. That year, it constituted three million last-minute Christmas presents to less-regarded family members from Peru to Japan, and Sam, Helena and Peter moved from two bedrooms on the second floor in Kentish Town to a Georgian town house in Clapham Old Town. His new study on the second floor had a view over the Clapham roof-tops.

The Success hit Sam like a tidal wave, which outlined the crossroads of his newly soaring career – no metaphor was too grotesquely mixed to render so bizarre and terrifying an event. The transformation could only make Sam regard the daily properties of his luck in an analytical spirit. It was then that the observation about the Pentels had been made by the library acquaintance. After his mass acquisition of the pen that made him able to write in the first place, a similar mass acquisition of Ordning & Reda turquoise A4 notebooks had taken place. The study on the second floor, on the other hand, was quite new. He gave up reviewing for those little magazines at three hundred pounds a time, quitting regretfully over three polite lunches with three openly envious but gracious editors; he took his son to school in the mornings, returned and ascended to the white-painted, book-lined study, opened the notebook and stared out of the window at the roofs, dark and wet and open as the underside of a gull's wings.

A contract had been signed for a fourth novel in, it seemed, every country in the world, and for months Sam sat at the desk, and stared out, and wrote nothing. 'How did it go?' Helena said, returning each day from her job administering the NHS, and he said, 'Oh, fine,' allowing her to talk about what, after all, was much more interesting, the various loonies, halfwits, Asperger's cases and, frankly, trollops who made up the mass of her colleagues. It was not the pen; it was not the notebook that made him incapable of getting on with it. It was the study. It made him, horribly, feel like Henry James.

In reality, he had written every single page of those three novels in a pub in Kentish Town – the reissued two early miniatures and the horrible Success, extended before his eyes over two entire shelves in forty-three languages, of *The Journey To Handsmouth*, the lot. That setting had abundantly suited him. Four half-pints of Staropramen between two and four in the afternoon, and after every other completed paragraph, a cigarette. He had been going there pretty well every weekday afternoon for five years. The barmen had come and gone. In the hopeless human circus of Kentish Town, a shabby man in his early thirties in a succession of tweed jackets and corduroy trousers, writing in a turquoise notebook with a green pen, breaking off every twenty-five minutes for a cigarette and every forty minutes for another half of lager had attracted no curiosity.

The boy had asthma. He could never be more than ten feet away from his inhaler, and never was. It was agreed between them that Sam would only ever smoke outside the house, not more than five a day, and not smoke at all within three hours of seeing the boy, in case of fumes on his clothes.

Not one of those barmen had ever given any sign of recognizing him, not because he was famous, of course, but he was surely their most regular customer; only one had ever engaged him in conversation in order to remark that he, too, could take to writing to, what, write a novel, the things he'd seen. And that had been one of the few who was English, rather than from Eastern Europe. As it happened, he had not lasted long.

In the new and unfamiliar opulence of Clapham Old Town, Sam investigated his circumstances. It might be the Success that had stopped his ability to write – Sam had read Freud, and knew all about that danger. Or it might be a single change in his habits. Guiltily, he left his pristine notebook where it lay and, one afternoon, went out to a pub on Clapham High Street. It had no distinction what-soever; it was one of a chain. Perhaps once it had had an English name, unchanged for decades, but what had once been a Queen's Head was now a Monkey and Merkin. It felt like a return. Sam sat in the front of the quiet pub. A

cricket match played on the suspended forty-inch television, the upper registers of the commentator's tessitura
getting a real work-out; the two barmen wiped glasses and
gossiped; a pensioner in a frayed grey coat systematically
drained three pints of yellow beer, staring at the charity
muggers in the dirty spring sunshine outside. By his third
half, Sam was considering the specific verbal terms in
which Eve might leave her lover, Simon, the father of her
two-year-old, Hettie, and thereby kick off his novel with a
scene like a hook in a chorus. And the next day he returned
to the quiet little pub with a notebook, two pens, a packet
of Marlboro Lights, and from two to four, wrote solidly.
The cigarettes and the half-pints of beer festooned his
undisturbedly creative afternoon like bunting. 'Going
well?' Helena said.

'Yes,' Sam said. 'I had quite a good day, actually.'

The fourth novel came out, and was a great success,
though not, this time, a Success. Meersbrook and
Edgeworth had sucked their teeth at the notion of a party
to launch his previous books, but this time they shelled out
for a Regency members' club in Fitzrovia, with canapés on
silvered plates, each thumbnail nibble recapitulating quite
substantial dinners in miniature, moving serenely through
the crowd, like destroyers on the high-held hands of
dazzlingly shirted waiters. Standing at the front door with
a dozen other smokers, Sam greeted two Nobel Prize
winners, half a dozen beautifully sustained actresses, and
three bold-haired rock stars he had never even heard of,
but who made quite a stir in the party's outer depths. He
felt blessed, and Peter, in his white fedora, showed off
horribly. Only at one point did his composure falter, as

Helena, towards the end, joined him. In a bronze cloud of Mitsouko and a black pleated Issey Miyake gown, her confidence was high. 'It's a nice house,' she observed to a group of agent, publisher and two journalists. 'We had the room at the top gutted and reshaped for a study for Sam. God knows why. He writes in the pub in the afternoon just as he always used to.' There was a ripple of laughter.

'I didn't know you knew,' Sam said stupidly.

'Of course I know,' Helena said. 'It's the talk of the school gate – Sam Clark, who writes in the window of the Monkey and whatever it's called. What is it called?'

'Merkin,' Sam said.

'What?' his editor said.

'The Monkey and Merkin,' Sam said.

'How very peculiar,' his agent said, attempting to laugh.

'It's the most awful dump,' Helena said.

It was two months after that that Sam went into his pub and set himself up, as usual, at a quiet corner table, well away from the front window. The Polish barman was frowning over a red-top paper; there was nobody else in at all. It was two o'clock on a Monday. Sam collected a half of Staropramen from the bar, took it to his table, opened his notebook and cracked his knuckles. There was something missing on the table, and Sam looked at the tables around him. He went back to the bar.

'Excuse me,' he said. The barman looked over his paper. 'Could I have an ashtray?'

'An ashtray?' the barman said.

'Yes,' Sam said, enunciating more clearly. 'An ashtray.'

'There's no smoking permitted in here,' the barman said. 'Haven't you heard? The smoking ban started on Saturday.

There's no smoking in pubs any more. The government here has banned it.'

'There's no one else in here,' Sam said. He never read a newspaper beyond reviews and interviews, never watched the television news, hardly ever listened to topical conversation, even. 'I'll stop if anyone comes in and objects.'

'You must be joking with me,' the barman said. 'The landlord could lose his licence for allowing that. And I am working here, and I do not smoke. I welcome that I do not now suffer from passive smoking in my job.'

Sam was not an I-know-my-rights type of smoker, but he thought of pointing out that when the barman had taken the job, he must have known he would have to work around smokers. If he had objected so much in the first place, he should have taken a job in Woolworths.

'There is a table outside, on the pavement, where you are welcome to smoke,' the barman said. But Sam had not got to the point where he could write a novel on the street, as Helena's acquaintances wandered by, taking an interest. He envisaged the passers-by of Clapham peering over his shoulder at his forming paragraphs, as holidaymakers always peered at the work of *plein-air* watercolourists before a view. He went back to his table.

The novel had been left in the middle of a sentence. Sam completed that sentence, took a sip of beer, and wrote another sentence. In fifteen minutes, he had written a paragraph. His pen somehow drifted up to his mouth; he set it down, and after five minutes, he saw that he was drumming on the cigarette box with the cigarette lighter. He wrote the words 'Quite suddenly', and then stopped. Quite suddenly what? They could do anything. They could do nothing.

When he left the pub an hour later, the words were still there, their sentence uncompleted.

He tried everything: he tried leaving the pub to have a cigarette, coming back refreshed with nicotine, but it wasn't the same. The key point was to smoke while looking at the paragraphs you'd just written, in contemplation, so he took the book outside with him. 'Hello, Sam,' some unplaceable woman said, going past with a quizzical look and a bag from the butcher's; he must look pretty odd, balancing his own work on one forearm and using the other hand to smoke.

'I can see you're a creature of habit,' his friend and near-neighbour Anish said. He wrote think-pieces for the *Watchman* of varying quality, under a ten-year-old photograph of his phizzog, as he put it; he was one of those people who never quite knew whether the readers recognized his name or did not, and it showed. Helena called him the Fifth Columnist, since four more eminent names always preceded his views and sometimes pre-empted them, more informedly. He had heard it and was delighted; Sam wondered whether he caught Helena's acid implication of the unnecessary, the suggestion that he would be the first to be sacked when the paper started to make its next round of cuts.

'Well, I am,' Sam said. They were driving to the theatre; Anish was reviewing a new Chekhov at the National for a critics' programme on Radio 4, and Sam could be, Anish said, his date. 'Most writers are, I think. You need to be comfortable with your little routines.'

'We all know your little routines,' Anish said. 'They're famous.'

'Oh, yes?'

'Absolutely. When we play poker—'

'I always lose.'

'Yes, you do,' Anish said. 'But do you know why you always lose? Whenever you've got a hand you're not bluffing over, you always – I mean always – take a sip of whisky. When you're trying to bluff, you always go quite unnaturally still. You might as well have a neon sign over your head.'

'I had no idea,' Sam said, aghast.

'And when you lie – I mean, that time two years ago when you were having an affair with—'

'Please, not that,' Sam said. 'Don't start telling me what a middle-aged novelist does when he's sneaking around after publicity girls. I don't think I could bear that much information. I'm self-conscious enough as it is.'

'It's rather charming,' Anish said. 'That thing you do. It really is.'

For three weeks, Sam wrote nothing; he sat in his study all morning and read *Martin Chuzzlewit*, and went out for a walk on the Common and down the high street, manfully boycotting the Monkey and Merkin. One day, he needed to pick up a prescription for Peter's asthma, and went down the side-street towards the doctor's surgery. On his way back, he took an indirect route, through post-war estates and little knotted alleyways. He thought of himself as having a good sense of direction, but was soon lost. He turned a corner, and there, wedged between two rows of three-million-dollar terraced houses, was an old pub. It was called the Duke of Clarence; its sign, an incredible likeness of an ermined fool, painted by someone's cousin's best mate fifty years ago for thirty shillings, was gnawed about the edges by wind and rain. The windows had not been painted in an age; the net curtains were yellow and a single azalea in the window near death; outside, a propped-up blackboard promised Dart's, TV, Home Cooked-Food.

A fat man in a bulging Aran cardigan outside observed Sam suspiciously. He took out a cigarette, and lit it – London's pubs were now sentried by such smokers, like guardsmen at the Palace. Then, incredibly, without putting it out, he turned and went back into the pub.

Sam crossed the road, entranced, and followed him in. There was a faint aroma of last-night's fags, overlaid with this lunchtime's fags, exactly as pubs had smelt until two weeks ago. The man was behind the bar, as Sam had fore-seen, puffing away. There was nobody else in the pub. Sam ordered a drink – a pint of inelegant international lager. He would not ask, but he placed his Marlboros and his cheap plastic lighter on the table in front of him. And in a few minutes the landlord, hardly seeming to take any notice of him, called out, 'You can smoke if you want to. I don't give a rat's arse.' Sam took out a cigarette, lit it with trembling hands, and drank a great big consoling cloud. Soon he would know exactly what was going to happen in his book, what was going to happen all of a sudden.

Ted had done everything you could imagine. He'd never got on, in a manner of speaking, with school. His old man had lived, still did, off the Abbeville Road, the other side of the Common. You wouldn't believe what houses were fetching there nowadays. It made you laugh. He'd always lived in London – no, come to think of it, he'd had that stretch in Devon with his ex-wife. He'd prefer not to think of it. How had he met her? That took him back. Him, he was forty-eight, and who was asking? Well, the truth was that in the, what, 1970s, you went onto the assembly line at one of those factories in Wandsworth or you went into the Armed Forces. (The Armed Forces: Ted, despite his frayed appearance and frayed-edge pub, spoke the words with something approaching reverence.) His elder sister had gone to work for Bedwynne's in Wandsworth: they'd made metal pushcars for children. If you worked for Bedwynne's, you were known as a dirty Arab – Bedwynne, Bedouin, you see? All gone now. Nothing but New York Style Loft Apartments where people used to make things that might have been a bit of use to someone. But Ted, he had gone into the Armed Forces – into the Royal Engineers. Went all over the world. Northern Ireland, mostly, though.

Met his wife there, didn't he? Girl called Sue. Gym instructor in the army. Tough girl – could shin up a rope like a monkey. Thought that was a recommendation at the time – big, beefy girl. His old dad's eyes were out on stalks when he took her home that first Christmas. Then they married and he looked at her one day and he couldn't remember why he'd married Desperate Dan. Her family, her mum and dad, two brothers, cousins, aunts, the lot, they called her Crusher. They all lived in the same valley in Devon. Sheep farmers, her dad had a pub. Like something off a biscuit tin, with roses round the front door. They'd got her number, though, calling her Crusher. She'd crushed him, in the end, too. First off, when Ted met her – gym instructor in the army, hair like Tom Cruise playing a Marine, biceps like grapefruit – naturally anyone would have thought she was a Lezzer. He'd taken his fair share of stick over Big Gym Sue from the NCOs. Then he'd married her and they'd stopped it, the frolicsome banter. But then they'd started it again and, to cut a long story short, they were right: she was a minge-jockey. Lives in Bideford, these days, with a pre-operative FTM transsexual called Ken, used to be Wendy, makes goat's cheese, he wouldn't be surprised. FTM? Female-to-male. You get to pick up the jargon, the technical information in the old Lesbian game. They'd met in that same valley in Devon, or Devonshire, whichever you like to call it, Sue and Ken, used to be Wendy, pair of great big buggers, like lumberjacks. Nobody's fault, just a bit of wrong wiring somewhere.

Sam listened over a series of afternoons between two and four, and three pints of an industrially bland lager – his consumption was upgraded with the transfer to the Duke of Clarence. He didn't think he could actually say the words 'A half, please,' to Ted. For two days, Ted had let him be, watching him with a benevolent air, as Sam wrote in his turquoise notebook with his Pentel pen, taking a break every so often for a sip, every other paragraph for a cigarette and a judicious going-over. On the third day – there never seemed to be anyone in the pub in the afternoon – Ted greeted him and introduced himself, after a lengthy and involved and head-shaking and actually rather one-sided conversation about a government minister's emerging financial disgrace. Ted had never heard of Sam – it took a direct question for him to find out that he was a writer at all. But once the information had lodged in Ted's brain (it took him two successive afternoons of the same run of questions to remember it), it led unstoppably to the traditional observation 'If I had the time, I could write a novel, the things I've seen.'

It was hard for Sam to understand it. No one could be less prepossessing than Ted. He wore the same thing, day after day, and his hair never seemed to be washed, falling in a solid shining cowlick across a grey-white forehead. From him, and from the members of his family who very occasionally dropped in, leaving a teenage son to play the one-armed bandit or some bags of shopping, a marshy odour arose. He and his pub had no charm, good looks, money, good taste, likeability or a toilet you could venture into with confidence. And yet he had something. He had ignored the smoking ban. So Sam listened to his stories with absorption and pleasure.

After the first week or so, Sam had hardly pretended to open his notebook and begin to write. He had just turned up, bought a beer, lit up and waited on the bar stool for Ted to start his telling. On the bar, like a token of what they had in common, was the notebook, which remained unopened. But Sam didn't feel that writing had, once again, been taken away from him in yet another pub. Rather, he had plugged into a purer, more wonderful source of narrative than any he had ever known, and the day would come, soon, when it was up to him to start writing again. He could feel his batteries recharging as he listened. And one day, Ted told him about his neighbour in Devon.

'His mum and dad had died when he was nineteen, on the roads. Those old Devon farmers, they go out of a night, get pissed, get in the car, drive back thinking nothing of it. They don't think of drink-driving like normal people. Met another pissed Devon farmer coming down a narrow lane at forty miles an hour. Ka-boom. Green lanes of England. Left this poor bloke with a farm and two hundred acres, a farmhouse, a great big barn, a dairy herd and not much idea what to do with any of it. He was twenty years older than Crusher. That had all happened years before, before she was born or before I ever came to the valley.

'When the pair of us got out of the army, we didn't have anywhere to go or any idea of what to do. So we went back to live with her old man in his pub. I'd help him to run it, she'd get a job teaching PE in Exeter or somewhere. That's how I got to know this bloke. He was fifty and he looked seventy. The dairy herd had long gone, and the two hundred acres, sold. God knows what he was living on.

'Some alcoholics drink in the pub, and some of them drink at home where no one can see them. He was a home drinker. You'd have thought he'd know better than to drink at all, with his parents and that, but he knew just about enough to drive out sober and drive back sober, but with four bottles of white wine on the back seat. Every day, that was. Crusher's dad's pub was only a mile from his farmhouse, on the sunny side of the valley. The next place was fifteen miles away, in Bideford. He wouldn't have trusted himself to drive that distance back without a stop in a lay-by. We knew to a bottle how much he drank, and how much he spent on it. Would have been about twenty-five quid a day, quite a lot then, four bottles. As I say, in this business you get to know the types of alcoholic.'

Sam looked at the inch and a half of whisky in Ted's hand, clearly not the first of the day at half past two. Ted raised it to him, laughed, drank it in one. Sam smiled. In a moment Ted went to the back of the bar. Sam lit a cigarette and smoked it in a calm, leisurely way, and in five minutes extinguished it. He picked up his pen. He began to write.

'You don't write short stories,' Helena said, five months later.

'I know,' Sam said. 'I thought I'd write this one, though. I don't know where it came from.'

'You don't know where it came from?'

'Well, I just made it up, I suppose.'

Helena looked again at the pages she had just read, suspiciously. She flipped back to the front of the story, then to the back, then to the title page of the magazine, as if there might be some acknowledgement or explanation she had missed.

'You never make anything up,' she said. 'That's the one thing you can't do. It's always something that Anish told you, or something that nearly happened to your aunty Sylvia, or something someone told you about in the news, like that girl who was kidnapped you put into *The Twelfth Girl*. You just don't.'

'Well, I might have heard something like it,' Sam said.

'If that's all there is to it, I should write a novel,' Helena said. 'I see a lot more stuff than you ever hear about.'

'Well, maybe you should,' Sam said. 'No one's stopping you.'

'But this one you just heard somewhere.'

And then there was one of Helena's awful silences. Sam remembered what Anish had said, how open he was when undertaking any kind of deception; he did not think that his own wife was any less likely than Anish to detect his behaviour when mounting a lie. So in the interests of marital sweetness, he told her the whole story: about the unused study and the pub; about the ritual cigarette at the end of every other paragraph and the smoking ban; about the Duke of Clarence and Ted's story. He would have told her about the ecstasy of the writing, the paragraphs between the quiet cigarettes, if the words existed between them to explain it. Sam finished.

'He should be prosecuted,' Helena said.

'What?'

'He's breaking the law, and he's putting his staff and customers at risk. That's the plain truth.'

For Sam, it had been a story about how he had got his inspiration back; she had heard a different story altogether. 'He doesn't have any staff, as far as I know. There's only ever Ted there and sometimes his brother, and he smokes as much as Ted does.'

'It's against the law. If you saw the effects of smoking as much as I do – not that you ever take much interest in my work – if you saw the effects, I tell you, you might take this a bit more seriously.'

'The effects of smoking—' Sam was about to go on to say that the effects of smoking, after all, had paid for the house they were living in, but he saw that wouldn't do, and he hadn't seen it like that at the time.

'Somebody ought to say something,' Helena said, a dangerous glint in her eye. 'Somebody ought to tell the police. They can shut a pub down for breaking the law like that.'

'Be reasonable, Helena,' Sam said. 'It's not harming anyone. If people don't like it, they can turn round and go out again. And I'm writing really well, these days. I've found somewhere I can write.'

'Maybe you should find somewhere you can write in a healthier atmosphere,' Helena said.

'I can't. I've tried.'

'Well, it's not the end of the world, is it? You've made enough money now. You don't have to go on writing at all if it's as hard as all that – if other people have to die of lung cancer just so that you can write another one of your little books. It seems quite a high price to pay. It's called the Duke of Clarence, is it? I know someone who would be really very interested to discover—'

'I don't think—' Sam said, but just then the kitchen door opened, and it was Peter; he was wheezing horribly.

'Mummy—' he said, getting it out between heavy-laden breaths.

'Oh, God, Peter – have you tried your inhaler? Come on, I'll get it. You see,' she said, bundling Peter off and giving Sam the evils as she left, 'sometimes there are more important things, and I really think—'

Sam sat and waited for the recrimination, which hardly needed to be voiced. He never smoked in the house; he had no idea where Peter's asthma came from. In his pocket, the hard potentiality of a box of Marlboro Lights. In time, the dreadful wheezing from the next room, like the basso of a much-punctured vacuum cleaner, began to subside. He considered. He had never thought about the way in which their lives rested on something so small; how Helena's sustaining contempt for him as well as his capacity to write relied on the habit, acquired in his late adolescence, of no more than seven cigarettes a day. He heard, from the now quiet sitting room next door, the tiny clatter of the telephone being picked up, and sat gazing out of the window at the bare trees and densely parked cars. It had been a cold, dry day, and in a few moments, soundlessly, snow began to fall on the street, empty of people.

The Whitsun
Snoggings

That Whitsun, they were nearly late getting away. It was Miles's fault. Sally and Mum had drilled it into him that he had to be ready to leave the house by eight thirty. They had packed their suitcases, all three of them, the night before, and Sally and Miles had each had a bath before bedtime so they didn't need to wash very much the next morning. Miles was always late for everything. Before last summer, when they were all together, Mum used to say, 'He takes after his dad.' But she didn't say that any more, and his lateness was all his own, these days.

It was their Whitsun treat, to go to London to stay with Mum's friend Katy. 'It'll make a nice break for all of us,' Mum said. She had known Katy for ever, since they were at college together. Going to London was a break from Sally's new school, which was horrible, and also from the divorce, which was going on for ever, in Sally's opinion. There were plenty of things to look forward to in London, and plenty of activities to keep them busy, Mum said.

But on the morning when they were supposed to go to London, Sally was woken up by the sound of her brother unpacking his suitcase, next door. The thuds from his bedroom were huge boys' noises. 'Oh, *no*,' her brother was saying to himself. 'I *can't* believe it.' Sally got up and went next door. Miles was standing by an empty suitcase, the contents spread all over the floor – they had been carefully packed and folded last night.

'Mum's going to kill you if you don't put it all back, right now,' Sally said.

'I thought I'd packed my red shorts and my blue cap from Whipsnade and my new best boots *and* I haven't put any of them in.'

'We're only going for five days,' Sally said. 'You'll just have to manage without.'

'I can't manage without my new best boots and my blue cap and – and – and my red shorts, I can't.'

Then Mum came upstairs, holding the phone. She was in her dressing-gown. 'Miles,' she said. 'Oh, God' – she was speaking to whoever it was on the telephone – 'I'm going to have to call you back.' She hung up.

'You said I could take my shorts and my cap and my new best boots,' Miles said. 'And I know I put them in but they're not there now.'

'We went through this,' Mum said. 'Last night we talked about all of this and we agreed what you would put in and what you'd leave out. Oh, God, Miles, I really don't want to deal with any of this now. Just put everything back into the suitcase just as it was, and we are going to leave the house, ready or not, at half past eight.'

She walked downstairs, dialling the number again. 'Katy?' she said. 'No, nothing. The kids being …' and then the kitchen door closed behind her.

Sally knew that the kind of threats that mums made had become serious in the last year or so. Since last summer. Before then, the sort of threats that mums made, and actually dads, too, were threats that never really happened. They would say, 'If you don't pipe down there isn't going to *be* any supper,' or 'I'm only taking you to buy new shoes if you promise to behave yourself,' and there would be no piping down, and no promise to behave, and yet the supper and the shoe-buying would somehow go ahead. But after last summer those threats had become strange and real. One day Mum had said, to Miles, 'Honestly, Miles, if you don't stop whining about Sally breaking your things' – and it wasn't true, anyway, Miles had broken his Action Man Bungee Jump all on his own by trying to use it to hang the hamster – 'then I'm not going to take you to Max's birthday party.' And Miles had carried on whining about her breaking the Bungee Jump, and quite soon Mum had picked up the phone and told Max's mum that Miles couldn't come because he couldn't behave himself. Then she had gone to sit in the armchair and lit a cigarette. They had been astounded.

So when she said, 'We're leaving the house, ready or not, at eight thirty,' Sally knew that she meant it. Mum walked past their rooms, ignoring them, and went between the bathroom and her bedroom, getting herself ready, singing her cheerful-morning song. Somehow, Sally and Miles put everything back into the suitcase, and somehow found his blue cap and his red shorts. The boots would just have to be left behind.

After breakfast, Mum sent them upstairs for their bags and to clean their teeth, and at eight thirty, Miles and Sally and Mum were just about to leave the house, exactly on time, when Miles said, 'I know. I'm not going to pack my boots. I can wear them, can't I?'

'No, Miles,' Mum said. 'You're going just as you are. You'll have to manage.'

'I'll only be a moment,' Miles said, and he darted upstairs.

'Oh, for Heaven's sake,' Mum said. 'We'll miss the train.'

'He'll only be a moment,' Sally said.

'Miles,' mum called. 'We're going. NOW. We're leaving you behind. There's some food in the fridge. Have fun. You can call Dad if you run out of everything. Go and stay with him. He'll look after you. Him and Joanna. Bye, then.'

And then Mum actually opened the door, her suitcase in one hand, Sally's hand in the other, and started down the garden path. She hadn't checked that they had everything; hadn't asked them if they'd brought a book to read; hadn't made sure that they both had their mobiles because London was a big place and it would be horrible to get lost in it. She had said none of that as she opened the door and started down the garden path. Miles, too, knew that these terrible threats could turn into promises these days, that those promised punishments could materialize. He hurled himself down the stairs behind them. He had his butter-yellow Timberland boots on, but they were unlaced; he could easily have tripped over them. 'Ready?' Mum said, unconcerned. 'Let's go.'

* * *

220

Dad had been coming and going for months on end, before the 'going' finally turned into 'went'. He first went straight after Christmas. Mum afterwards told them that he would be spending some time on his own. But they'd heard her telling him on Christmas Day to go and live somewhere else. He'd come back after New Year, but then the same thing had happened in February, and then in April. And then in the summer, after he'd come back for three months and they'd all tried to make everything work and had made everything worse, Mum had found some messages between him and Joanna on Facebook where everyone could see them and she'd told him to leave and not come back. Mum wasn't on Facebook. She said it was stupid when you could see your real friends or pick up the phone and talk to them.

They had heard of Joanna, and glimpsed her once, at the very beginning, when she had come to their house for dinner. But they didn't meet her until the summer, after the awful holiday in Wales where everyone was crying or shouting or alternatively taking them on canoeing trips to cheer everyone up. Sally knew that she was someone Dad worked with. For six weeks after Dad had moved out for what turned out to be the last time, he didn't come to see them or phone them. That was though both Sally and Miles now had their own mobiles, in case of being abducted or lost, and he needn't have had to speak to Mum first if that was what he was worried about.

But then after six weeks he did phone, on the landline, and spoke to Sally, then Miles. He said he'd like to take them out for a day, because there was someone he'd like them to meet. He sounded very cheerful; there was somebody shouting and laughing in the background, a woman's voice. From time to time, Dad said 'For Pete's sake,' and Sally realized he wasn't talking to her. At that time, Mum was crying a lot, even in the mornings, and Miles afterwards said that he didn't want to go. Mum told him not to be stupid, that of course he wanted to see his dad. Miles said that he didn't want to see either of them, and Mum told him that wasn't very polite.

There was a lot of telephoning to arrange the outing, which was for a week on Saturday. In the end, it was to a stately home nearby, one that Sally had gone to loads of times with the school and with the Guides and with Granny Hopkins, too. 'It was Joanna's idea,' Mum said quite firmly. 'Apparently she wants to see as many stately homes as she possibly can, while she's in this country. That's nice, don't you think? That she's taking an interest?'

It was the end of August, and because of the end-of-summer rains, there was some talk about it being put off. But in the end the forecast was good. They met Dad and Joanna at the car park outside the Bovey Tracey crafts centre. It was on the way to the stately home, and near where Joanna lived, in a small village with one pub and a post office. When they arrived, there was only one car in the car park, and Dad stepped out of the driving seat. He was wearing a new suit in a strange colour, a vivid, shiny green, and some very pointed black and shiny shoes. They could see that there was someone else in the car, facing front. Mum asked them if they'd like to have a cup of coffee before setting off, but Dad said it was better to get on, because there was plenty to see. Mum said goodbye, and Sally and Miles got into the back of the unfamiliar car.

'Hello,' Joanna said. 'You must be—'

'Hello,' Miles said.

'Hello,' Sally said.

'These are the kids,' Dad said. 'Miles and Sally.'

'Hello,' Joanna said. 'You're right – they do look like you. Right.'

She had a loud, accented voice. Afterwards, they found out that she came from New Zealand. She had black, cropped hair around a big bony skull. Her nails were painted black, and her lipstick, which she immediately started to renew, was purple.

'My God,' she went on, 'I thought those friends of yours would never leave.'

'Who's that?' Miles said; he'd thought she might be speaking to him.

'Those friends last night, Tom, sweety,' Joanna said, not exactly ignoring Miles, but sweeping over him. 'My God. They just sat there and sat there, and there was not one thing to be done but get slaughtered on whisky. Jeeze, I feel fucking rough this morning. You've got some fucking dull friends, Tom, I'll tell you that for nothing.'

'All right, kids?' Dad said.

'They're at school, still, right?' Joanna said.

'Yes, of course they're at school,' Dad said, trying to laugh. 'One's nine, and the other's twelve.'

'Wow,' Joanna said. 'You really take education fucking seriously in this country. Still learning at twelve. Which is which? No, don't tell me. I'll only forget. Just not a children person, that's me. So, what about this stately home, then? I'll tell you – it's got to be something to be as great as Blenheim. Wow, that was what I call a house. What's this fucking place called?'

'Chorley Bagwood,' Dad said. 'It's not like Blenheim.'

'Oh, I get it,' Joanna said. 'It'll do for an outing with the kids. Divorced-dad type place. Social awkwardness, a herb garden and some fucking linenfold panelling.'

'I'm not going to comment,' Dad said, chuckling. Joanna reached across, put her arm round his neck, and whispered something in his ear. It went on for some time. When she had finished, as she slid back into her position in the front passenger seat, she turned her head, and for the first time assessed Sally with her gaze, assessed Miles in the same thorough way, head to foot, glaring.

Later, Mum put down the phone and said, earnestly to them, 'Dad wants you to know that he's sorry it didn't go that well today. Joanna's a nice person, he says, but some people, they're just not a children person, that's what he says.' Sally could see that Mum was doing her best.

'I never want to go to that place ever again,' Miles said. 'I hate that Chorley Bagwood. It's really fucking shit.'

'That's what that Joanna said,' Sally said, making an excuse. 'She said fucking all the time. Like literally every sentence.'

'Did you get to go down to the end of the garden?' Mum said.

'It was really muddy,' Sally said.

'Well, it would be after all that rain,' Mum said. 'Was Dad all right in his new clothes?'

'He said his trousers were completely ruined,' Sally said. 'It was because he was messing about at the top of a slope and then he fell and slid right down. All up one leg there was mud. And that lady said it was his own fault for wanting to come to a stupid – a stupid stately home.'

'Oh dear,' Mum said, but she seemed quite cheerful about it. 'Don't say fucking, Miles. No one wants to hear it.'

Plenty of people had never been to London. Even at Sally's last school, there were people who hadn't been. At her new school, she wouldn't want to raise it. Everyone was friends at her last school, and if you had done something different from everyone else, or hadn't done something that everyone else had done, that was all right. You could say, 'We're going to London,' or 'I sent a poem to the newspaper and they gave it a prize.' Or you could have said, 'My mum and dad are getting divorced,' probably. And no one would have thought anything of it, because you had all known each other for ever. But something went wrong in the last year of small school and probably Dad forgot to send in the form in time, and Sally ended up going to Treetops School, where no one she knew would have wanted to go. It had been her fourth choice on the form. She didn't know anyone there, and now she was there, she certainly wasn't going to say, 'We're going to London,' or 'I sent a poem to the newspaper and they gave it a prize.' She started to think that maybe she wouldn't send any more poems to anyone now, because if you said it, or Jack Ballard or Sophie Okonwe or Chloe Macdonald or any of that tough lot found out, that would basically be the end of your life. Anything quite small, anything that made you a bit more obvious, that would do it for you.

But Sally had been to London quite a lot. She had been to visit Aunty Susanna and Uncle Boyd in their pretty house in Fulham. And they had been to visit Mum's old friend Katy. And once as a really special birthday treat they had all gone up to see *The Lion King*, which had been fantastic, and had lunch at Joe Allen's first, too. And there had been days out with museums, and once, her and Mum, just the two of them, they had gone up on the train and had a day at the sales and they had bought shoes and both had their nails done in Selfridges, Mum having zebra stripes and Sally a real rainbow on every finger, and Mum had said that she wasn't to tell Dad about any of it. And then in year six when they'd all had to have a penpal and Ulrike came to stay with them for a week, Mum had thought there wouldn't be enough to show her in Devon, so they'd had a day up in London, all of them, with the Natural History Museum and the London Eye and Nelson's Column and the Houses of Parliament (from outside), and Ulrike hadn't been at all impressed, which was ironic since when Sally went to Bonn in a return visit there was nothing to see except Beethoven's boring house, and Ulrike's mother had made no effort at all, except for creating endless salads covered with that horrible stuff called dill.

So Sally had been to London quite a lot.

They got to the station in plenty of time. Mum had been stressing that they had to get the nine-fifty-seven because that was the train they had tickets for. If they missed that one then they would have to get three new tickets, and they couldn't afford that. 'Why couldn't we just tell them that we missed the train and they could find us places on the next one?' Sally had wanted to know. Mum said that the train company didn't allow that, for reasons best known to itself.

But they got there in plenty of time. Mum paid the taxi driver and they each got their suitcase out of the boot. 'Everyone ready?' Mum said. 'This is exciting, right?' And then at the barriers, she fumbled for the tickets – they were somewhere in her big green purse with lots of old tickets and receipts and people's phone numbers. The guard held the big gates open for them, and told them that the train would leave from platform five. And then they all lugged their suitcases up the stairs, and over the bridge where you could see the trains standing underneath your feet, and down the staircase again, where it said not to run because seven people had been seriously injured falling downstairs at this station last year. The seven was in a different lettering, like this – 7 – so that the station could change it if anyone fell over and died this year. Then Mum checked on the board – the train to London was the third one to arrive. There was plenty of time, after all, and Mum needn't have worried.

'Is Dad coming to London, too?' Miles asked.

Further down the platform, in a different new suit, this time brown and pinstriped, Dad was standing. He was with Joanna. Next to them were two suitcases – new, dark brown and leather, and matching. Joanna was wearing a man's black vest and a long purple floor-length skirt in a sort of attempt at fashion; with her little head she looked rather like a Dalek, Sally thought.

'Is Dad coming to London?' Miles said. 'Is that the surprise?'

'No,' Mum said, and that was stupid of Miles. He some-times said these things he didn't believe and couldn't have thought, because he thought it was cute to be stupid and pretend not to know things. He always went on pretending to believe in magical things at Christmas and the dentist's years after everyone else, if he thought there was some advantage to be got out of it. No one could have thought that Dad and Joanna were coming with them to London as a lovely surprise. 'No, they must be getting a train somewhere else.'

'I don't think they're going to go anywhere together,' Sally said. Dad and Joanna were in the middle of a really loud argument. Joanna had reached that point where she had placed a hand on either hip, was leaning forward right into Dad's face and was shouting, really shouting, into his face. 'Only a fucking ignorant fucking moron …' she was shouting. Everyone, not just on their platform but on the platform opposite and even further away, across two lines of tracks was staring at them. Dad was shouting back, but he was making no sentences, just shouting, 'Don't you – don't you—' His face was dark red, and Sally matched it with satisfaction to a new word she had found out that week: *puce*, she said to herself.

'I tell you what,' Mum said, and she looked a little puce in the face, too, 'let's go and sit in the café and wait. It's still another half an hour.' She fiddled with the strap of her handbag: she pushed both wings of hair back behind her ears in the way she had.

It seemed like a small gesture Mum had made, that movement with strap and the stroke of her hair, but it was enough. Sally knew that, when you were in the schoolyard, you didn't need to do or say a conspicuous wrong thing in front of Sophie Okonwe or Chloe Macdonald or any of that tough lot. They would jump on your back and start beating you up if you made just a small movement, said just one thing, put on your coat when no one else was. It only took a small movement, one that drew attention to you.

Mum putting her hair back in place and adjusting the strap of her handbag was one of those small movements. They were things that she did all the time: they were things that were very much like her, like the particular neat clack of her heels on lino when she was coming towards you. People would only have to meet Mum three times to remember that she was someone who smoothed her hair back behind her ears with both hands at once, and then adjusted the strap of her handbag. Though Joanna was sixty yards away, she must have seen someone making the gesture out of the corner of her eye. It must have said something familiar to her. She looked properly. She saw them – Sally saw her seeing them, her eyes going over Sally and Miles and Mum. She didn't say anything to Dad, who still hadn't seen them, but she immediately stopped shouting. She looked back at Dad. Then, almost jumping at him, she threw herself at his face, and started snogging him furiously. Dad hadn't expected that. His arms flew backwards, and he almost stumbled. Joanna's arms were round his neck, and she was pulling him towards her. Dad's arms went round Joanna's back. At first he patted her on the back, that pat, like you give an animal, saying, 'No, that's enough now,' but Joanna carried on, clutching him to her and pulling his face down towards hers. It was a real snog. You could see she was pushing her tongue right into his mouth, and he was pushing his tongue right back into hers, pushing as hard as they could. Sally had seen Joanna look at them before she started. On the platform opposite, three students were standing. They were watching Dad and Joanna, and were laughing. On this platform, two old ladies had picked up their bags and were coming this way. They hadn't minded the shouting, but they didn't want to watch the snogging.

'Let's go in the café,' Mum said. 'Let's get some breakfast.'

'We had breakfast,' Miles said. 'We had breakfast at home.'

'Well, we'll have another one,' Mum said. 'Our train's not coming for half an hour.'

In the Pumpkin Café, they also sold magazines and some books, and Mum said they should get a puzzle book to do on the train. They could choose one each. Sally liked the hidden words ones, where you knew there were forty names of plants, or pop stars, or countries secreted in a big grid of letters, like this: DFILKUNADANACHQPX. And all you had to do was find CANADA written backwards and put a big ring round it. Miles liked the logic puzzles, ever since Granny Hopkins had shown him how to do them. But he still wasn't very good at them. After ten minutes of frowning and crossing things out and putting Xs in boxes and reading out the clues that went 'JOHN is the only shopper who doesn't have any vegetables in his trolley' and 'The boy who rides the bicycle does not play chess', Miles would always turn secretly to the back, and start putting Xs in all the boxes as if he had worked it out himself. So they bought one of each of those, and a cup of tea for Mum, and went to sit down at a table inside.

'What's your number one plan for when we get to London?' Mum said.

'I want to go to the Marantine Museum,' Miles said – that was what he called the Maritime Museum, insisting that that was how it was pronounced. 'I want to see that ship again.'

Outside, on the other platform, two uncle-types, in bold checks and striped ties, gave a big shout in unison; a cheerful, upwards gesture with their arms. One of them shouted something smutty. They had cards dangling from strings in their lapels; on the way to the races, they were enjoying whatever it was that Dad and Joanna were doing on platform five.

'I want to go to the London Eye,' Sally said. 'That was brilliant.'

'You've been on the London Eye,' Mum said. She looked a little bit more cheerful now. 'We can go anywhere you want. Don't you want to go on a boat this time?'

'Oh, yes,' Sally said gratefully. She hadn't thought very hard about what she really wanted to do. The boat or the London Eye or another museum or just staying inside with Katy. And when they finished talking about all of that and the train came, Dad and Joanna would have got on another train, going somewhere else.

'Katy said that if the weather's not too bad, then we could probably go up to Hampstead Heath one day and have a picnic,' Mum said. 'That would be really nice.'

'I don't know about that,' Sally said. 'It's been raining for days and days and days. I expect we could go up on Hampstead Heath anyway. But it might be too muddy to sit on the ground, I expect perhaps.'

'Well, you never know,' Mum said.

'Oh, God, not a picnic,' Miles said. They looked at him, surprised. 'Picnics are fucking awful.'

'Stop it at once,' Mum said. 'Or we won't be going anywhere.'

Outside, a train came, and the passengers got off and on, and the guard blew a whistle, and it moved off. You could never see the moment at which a train started to move; at one moment it was absolutely still and then, before you could tell, it was sliding into movement and then, by the time the last carriage left the station, it was moving too quickly for you to see anyone's face inside the train. Ten minutes later, they were still sitting inside the café when another train came. Mum had finished her tea. She didn't say anything; she might almost have forgotten that they were there. She stared ahead of her, through the window. Sally thought, not for the first time, how pretty Mum was, especially with her special parrot earrings on. All at once she remembered that Mum had bought those parrot earrings at Covent Garden market in London, one day last year when Katy had come out with them to go shopping to give Mum a bit of a boost, as Katy had said. That was the day she had bought them, and Sally had been allowed to choose them for Mum, once it got down to a choice between the parrot earrings and another pair – Sally couldn't remember what the other earrings had been like. And today she and Mum and Miles were going to see Katy and were going to stay with her. So of course Mum had put her special earrings on.

'Isn't that our train?' Miles said, but Mum said that it wasn't, it was a train for Edinburgh that went through

Birmingham and Sheffield. Miles offered to go outside and make sure, but Mum said, quite sharply, that he should stay where he was. She didn't want any of them to go out on the platform until they had to.

The guard looked up and down the platform, like a spectator at tennis; he raised his little yellow flag; he blew his whistle. He did this hundreds of times a day, you could see. The train began to move, so smoothly that you thought it was silent. 'Good,' Mum said, and she gave them a smile, one each. 'Let's go out, shall we?'

Mum had made a mistake. As soon as the train had cleared the station, the two fat uncle-types on the opposite platform gave out a great cheer. They, like Mum, had thought that Dad and Joanna were going to get on this train, that their entertainment was going to be taken away from them. But they were delighted to discover that the huge and farcical Punch and Judy show was still going on. 'Go on, my son,' one of the race-going uncles shouted.

It was too late for Mum to turn back, and say, 'We'll wait in the café, after all.' She hesitated with her suitcase in the doorway. She made a decision. 'Come on,' she said. 'Let's go and say hello to Dad and Joanna.' Sally couldn't see how they could say hello to Dad and Joanna, as they were still trying to get each other's face in their mouths. But she and Miles followed Mum along the platform. It was interesting that, though the platform was quite crowded with people, a space had cleared around Dad and Joanna of about fifteen yards. It was as if they were a very bright light that you didn't want to get too near; that once you had gone far enough away, you were free to stop ignoring it and start staring directly at it. Mum broke through that invisible barrier and went straight up to Dad and Joanna.

'Hello, Tom,' she said. Her face was red, and her expression was almost cross, but determined. 'Hello, Joanna. How nice to see you.'

Dad broke away from Joanna. You could see that she would have gone on kissing him and ignored Mum. But Dad broke away and looked in a silly, embarrassed way at Mum. 'Hello!' he said, overdoing it, pretending that he hadn't seen them. His face was wet and slobbered over, his hair crumpled upwards. He looked as if he had been in a fight. Joanna pulled his face sideways towards hers. She looked at them without saying anything.

'Bye, then,' Mum said, and together they went back down the station platform. 'It'll be along in a minute,' Mum said. 'Now, I know we're in carriage H, but I don't know where that's going to be. Do you think carriage A is at the front, or at the back? I don't know where we should stand. You've got everything – Miles, you've got your logic magazine, haven't you? I think it's probably around the middle. If we stand here, we won't be too far out, anyway. What do you think?'

They didn't need to look; a cheer from the platform opposite, and, joining the uncles, three or four big boys. One shouted advice across the gap. Dad and Joanna had started up again, almost without a break. And then the train came in and they could get on it.

They had their own seats, three of them around a table. There weren't many tables on the train. Most of the seats were just in twos, facing the back of the seat in front, like seats in a bus. Mum had booked the train so long ago, almost two months ago, that she had been able to choose exactly the seats she wanted, and they had been much cheaper than if she had bought them on the day. Mum had explained all that, and why it was so important to get this exact train, and that Miles shouldn't make them late. But they weren't late, and they turned out to have been standing almost at the door to their carriage, H. 'This is us,' Mum said. They put their suitcases in the luggage rack at the end of the carriage – it was a squash, but they managed it. When they got to their table, there was a man sitting there, a man in a yellowish sports jacket, reading a book. You couldn't expect the train company to let them have the whole table, just for themselves. The man had his bag, a brown sort of satchel on one of their seats, but he had a kind face, and apologized as he got up and put his satchel in the luggage rack. 'Don't let me forget that,' he said. 'I'm always getting off trains and forgetting things I've put in the rack.'

'Oh, I'm just the same,' Mum said, as they all sat down. 'I've lost count of the number of umbrellas I've left on the train, just like that, putting them up on the luggage rack and then forgetting them when I get off.'

'I don't know what the trick is, to remember what you've put up there,' the man said.

'I heard,' Mum said, smiling and settling, 'that it helps if you just count how many things you put up there – one, two, coat, umbrella, three, like that. I don't know. Where are you getting off?'

'Me – oh, London,' the man said.

'We'll make sure you don't forget anything, won't we?' Mum said, including Sally and Miles.

The man had seemed quite friendly and pleased to be sharing his table with them. Perhaps, though, he didn't mind saying a couple of things to them, but he didn't want to have a long conversation with them, because sometimes people were like that. Because when she said they would all remind him about his satchel he smiled in a vaguer way, as if he had seen someone that he wasn't sure had seen him, over the top of everyone's head, it might have been, and went back to his book.

Mum had a book, too. It was called *The Line of Beauty* and had a photograph of two people on the cover – Mum had bought it in the charity shop last week to read on the train. She had only just opened it when Sally's phone made the noise it made when it had a message; it was a shriek of birdsong, like a parrot sounding the alarm in the jungle. The ringtone was called Amazon. Sally kept her phone in her pocket – once she had phoned her friend Martha without meaning to, just by leaning against the wall, and Martha had had to listen to the inside of her pocket rustling, and only after ten minutes Sally had noticed the tiny noise of Martha's voice from her pocket, shouting, 'It's me, it's me,' like a secret fairy she'd hidden in her clothes. Since then she had learnt how to lock the phone, but she still kept it in her pocket. Sally picked out the telephone.

'Who is it, Sal?' Mum said.

Sally looked. 'It's Dad, Mum.'

'Oh,' Mum said. 'What's he saying?'

'"Hello Sal," Sally read. '"Saw you were on the train. Want to come and say hello? I'm in carriage F." He's down there with that Joanna. I saw them.'

'He hasn't sent me one,' Miles said. 'Why doesn't he want me to come and see him?'

'Well, I'm sure he'd like both of you to go, but there's no point in sending two messages if he knows you're with Sally.'

'Why does he say only "Hello Sal"?' Miles said. 'Why doesn't he say "Hello Sally and Miles"? It's not fair.'

'He means both of you,' Mum said.

'But if he means both of us why wouldn't he say—' Miles said, his voice rising.

'Oh, for Heaven's sake,' Mum said. 'I really haven't the faintest idea why your father would do anything at all. Are you going to see him in carriage F, Sally?'

'Do I have to?'

'Well, it seems like a very long walk, and if you don't feel like it, I don't think you have to.'

The man at their table, who had started to read his book, didn't seem to be reading his book any more.

Sally texted with one thumb, two letters. 'No,' she texted, and then sent it.

'That was a short text,' Mum said.

The train stopped at Taunton before it would go straight on to Reading and then London Paddington. They had settled into their puzzle books, and Mum into her book, when a pink-faced lady came bustling up the aisle, some time after Taunton. 'Disgusting,' she was saying, to nobody in particular, and immediately Sally knew that she must be talking about her dad and Joanna. What were they doing – were they snogging still, or were they arguing and saying 'fucking' at the top of their voices, or both? 'Disgusting,' the lady was saying, as she went past.

'Wasn't that Miss Jenkins?' Mum said. 'You know, Miles, the lady who was your form teacher at Kendall Primary?'

'That wasn't Miss Jenkins!' Miles said, almost howling. 'Miss Jenkins didn't look like that at all.'

'Miss Jenkins was Miles's favourite when he was an infant,' Sally said. 'He loved her. Didn't you, you baby?'

'That wasn't Miss Jenkins,' Miles said.

'It looked a bit like her, I thought,' Mum said. Ten minutes later, the lady who wasn't Miss Jenkins came back down the aisle of the train, followed by the train guard, in uniform, the one who was checking everyone's tickets. The train was crowded, and you could hear him going 'Pardon me – pardon me – pardon me,' as he pushed past the people standing at the end of the carriage, or sitting on their luggage.

'Something's up,' the man at their table said, watching them go past.

'You see,' the lady was saying, 'I don't mind asking someone politely in those circumstances, but people of that sort – you know, I'm very sorry to have to—'

'The man who owns the greengrocer,' Miles said slowly, 'is not the man who rides a red motorcycle.'

The lady who wasn't Miss Jenkins and the train guard passed into the next carriage. The people at the end of the carriage, and some of the people in the seats craned their heads after them. Sally lowered her head over her puzzle book. This one was famous composers. There was one called Borodin, but Sally just couldn't find it. Usually, when you couldn't find a name, it was diagonally hidden, forwards or backwards. She just couldn't see it. She went on looking. And in fifteen minutes, the guard came back, having sorted out whatever the problem had been. Sally wanted to say 'whatever the problem had been' but she knew it was her dad and that Joanna. They had been snogging and saying 'fucking' and everything. The lady who had come down the carriage saying that she didn't mind asking someone politely in those circumstances had been talking about her father.

When the divorce had started coming, it had approached from a very long way away. Of course Sally knew about divorce. But she hadn't thought about it in relation to Mum and Dad. The first argument she hadn't been meant to hear. It had happened downstairs after she had gone to bed. She had only heard it because she had stayed up reading her book and hadn't gone to sleep; it was Mum shouting, though you couldn't hear what she was saying, and then Dad's voice mumbling. What was it about? It was over too quickly to find out, and the next day she wondered whether she had imagined it all. But then a few days later, the same thing happened. Perhaps she was listening out for it this time. And the shouting went on for longer, and Dad raised his voice, too. 'That's your problem,' he was shouting. 'It's all in your mind.' But it wasn't in Sally's mind. She could hear them downstairs.

Quite soon, the mood in the house stopped being bad in the evenings. You would get up in the morning and they wouldn't be speaking to each other. They would go off to work separately without saying goodbye, and when they came in in the evening, they wouldn't say hello to each other. Dad went upstairs as soon as he had finished dinner, into his study. He spent the whole evening on the computer. He said, as he went upstairs, that he had work to do. But really he spent the evening on Facebook. Mum would open a bottle of wine and switch the telly on, watching the whole of an evening's programmes, one after another. Then, after Sally and Miles had gone to bed, Dad would come downstairs and they would have an argument. It was worse at weekends and it was very bad at Christmas, after which Dad had left for the first time. It was on Christmas Day that Mum first mentioned the name of Joanna in front of Sally and Miles.

'This is nice,' Mum said.

'What?' Dad said.

'Oh, I was just saying something,' Mum said. 'To keep the party atmosphere going. It's nice to sit here with your children on Christmas Day with a glass of wine and the turkey finished and over with.'

'Did you like your presents, kids?' Dad said.

'Have you phoned your mother?' Mum said.

'I phoned her first thing,' Dad said.

'I'd have liked to say hello,' Mum said. 'You could have said.'

'You were busy in the kitchen,' Dad said. 'I was up in my study.'

'Yes, I could hear you making your phone calls,' Mum said. 'I didn't want to disturb you.'

'You can phone her again now,' Dad said.

'How's Joanna?' Mum said.

'Joanna?' Dad said.

'You know, Joanna you work with,' Mum said. 'I thought you were phoning her this morning.'

'This morning?' Dad said. 'No, I was phoning my mum. Why would I be phoning Joanna?'

'I don't know,' Mum said. 'It was just that you were making about five phone calls, one after another. I could hear when you were putting the phone down, it rings down here, and you were laughing a lot over one phone call. It didn't sound like your mum you were laughing with, if I'm honest. And I'm down here putting the stuffing in the turkey and making an X on the bottom of every Brussels sprout, and there's the man I married, laughing away with someone called Joanna who only six months ago you said, Oh, let's have her for dinner, and she came for dinner and she asked if the kids could be sent to bed. Remember? We asked Pete as well. You thought that a single woman like that, in Devon, she'd be glad of meeting a single man, they'd do for each other, you said. And she got drunk and obnoxious and Pete said he had stuff to do. Remember? And then you never mentioned her again because I thought the dinner had been a disaster, and because she'd been so rude, sending the kids off like that because "I'm jist not mach of a children persin", that's what she said, and getting drunk like that. I thought you thought of her what I thought of her, so why would we be mentioning her? I'm so stupid. Not knowing what not mentioning her meant. And now it's Christmas Day and I'm stuck inside with you and you spent most of the morning on the phone to bloody Joanna.'

Sally hadn't known the name for the colour then, but if she could have named the colour of Dad's face, she would have called it puce.

'I don't know what you're talking about.'

241

'Just get out,' Mum said.

'She's on her own,' Dad said. 'It can't be nice, spending Christmas Day on your own in a foreign country.'

'My heart bleeds,' Mum said. 'But it seems to me that it wasn't loneliness that was her problem in your office three weeks ago, after lunch.'

'I don't know what you're talking about.'

'Catherine told me. Your colleague Catherine. Do you know how Catherine knew about it? Joanna told her. Boasting about it, Catherine said. She thought I should know. She was probably right.'

'Do you think—' Dad said. He made a face towards Sally and Miles. They had been sitting at the kitchen table. Ten minutes ago, they had been trying to solve a wooden puzzle, a globe in pieces. It had been a stocking filler. They had stopped trying to do that some minutes ago.

'No, I don't think,' Mum said. 'I've done enough shielding and protecting and telling lies on your behalf and pretending nothing's going on, to you, to me, myself, to the kids, to my mum and dad. So you can get out, tonight.'

There was more crying to get through, and more shouting in the other room. And then it seemed to be all right. At least, Dad said so. But it couldn't have been because the next morning he drove away after breakfast and didn't come back that night.

When the train got to London, it turned out that Mum had got three Oyster cards for them. They were brilliant. You just held your card up to an electronic pad at the gates at the Underground and the gates opened. They had known how to deduct some money from the Oyster card. How did the money get onto the Oyster card? Mum said that she'd asked Katy and Katy had sorted it all out and sent the cards by post, which was really nice of Katy. Miles's card meant he didn't have to pay anything, but Sally was over eleven, and she paid half fare, and Mum, of course, paid the full fare. Sally had been on the Underground before, but she always found it confusing, with its tunnels and signposts saying if you wanted to go WEST, when she didn't know what direction they wanted to go in. Once she heard a man's voice from behind that might have been Dad's, shouting, 'Wait, wait,' but the three of them just went on walking.

Katy lived near Waterloo, and Mum explained this meant they went on the Bakerloo Line, which would take them all the way there. But a horrible thing happened. Sally had thought that she had heard Dad calling from behind them, but she must have been wrong. Because when they got to the platform for the Bakerloo Line, there were Dad and Joanna, and they were standing on the platform with their bags in front of them. 'Let's go this way,' Mum said. She had seen them too. And Joanna saw them – you could see her seeing them. She turned round and took Dad's face and starting kissing it. Her tongue was all the way out and pushing into his mouth. They were right there in the Underground, where the air was so dusty and dirty, and snogging and snogging. All the people around looked, or pretended not to look, or started paying attention to their newspapers. And Joanna and Dad were just feeling each other all over. The train was due in four minutes. Now they had their hands in each other's hair, and Joanna's face was pushed sideways. She had her eyes open. You could see that she was looking at them, even though her mouth was snogging Dad's mouth and she was feeling him all over.

'Have you seen that poster?' Mum said. 'Look, it's clever, isn't it?'

'I like that one, with the man up in the tree,' Sally said.

'Yes, I like that one, too,' Mum said. 'I'm really tired. As soon as you come to London, it tires you out.'

'It won't be long now,' Sally said. 'We'll be at Katy's and she'll make us a cup of tea and we can put our feet up for a bit, have a bit of an old chinwag.' That was what Granny Hopkins often said, and she said it as a sort of joke. But Mum didn't seem to notice that she was joking. She was trembling, looking in the other direction, the direction from which the trains came. Sally remembered the whoosh and the roar and the hot wind when a train came. It always frightened her a little bit. Mum was holding tight to both their hands.

'I hate that,' Miles said. 'I'm never going to do that, never, never, never.'

'What, Miles?' Mum said.

'That snogging,' Miles said. 'It looks horrible. I never want to do that. As long as I live, I don't want to. I'm never, ever going to do anything like that.'

'You don't have to look,' Mum said. 'Let's just not look. Pay no attention.'

The train came, its hot wind and roar carrying torn papers up from the black, dusty bed of the tracks. Mum had closed her eyes. Her mouth was tight shut. Only when the doors opened did she look again. They picked up their suitcases, one, two, three, and stepped into the train. But here came Dad and Joanna; she was pulling at him, and pulling him towards the carriage they were in. Joanna had a mean, determined face on; she was looking at them but not looking at them in a way that meant to be looked back at. The doors shut, and Dad and Joanna were at one end of the carriage, and they were at the other. And instantly, Joanna dropped the bag she was holding, and there, in the dirty and half-full carriage, full of strangers reading and trying to work out the tube map and twiddling with their iPhones, she began to snog their father again. Sally knew that if they stepped out at the next station to wait for the next train, Joanna would pull their father out, too; if they moved to the next carriage, she would follow them. Joanna and their father would snog and snog until Joanna decided that it was time for them to step out, and leave his wife and children, and she would leave them with a backwards glance and a look of snogged triumph, saying loudly as she went that she supposed she was just not a fucking children sort of person.

And then Mum was there with a hankie. 'Please don't cry, Sal,' she said. 'There's no reason to cry, is there? We're going to have a fantastic time in London. They'll be gone soon. We don't need to look at them if we don't want to. They don't matter if we don't look at them. They're not enjoying it, much, either. They look so stupid, don't they?' But Mum was crying now, too, and Miles was clinging to her, in terror at what he might one day have to do. 'If you don't think about them,' Mum was saying, 'then they don't exist. We'll be at Katy's, soon, and we can all sit down and have a nice cup of tea.'

What Mum said seemed to be true. Because at the next stop, as people drew away from Dad and Joanna, they pulled away from each other, and got out. Joanna went with a backwards glance and a look of snogged triumph in their direction. Sally could not help but look. She seemed to be saying something to their dad as she went. Where they were going she didn't know. They had got out at – she looked – Piccadilly Circus. And, in time, Mum brightened up, and Sally's crying had stopped. They came to Waterloo Station. It was big and complicated, and they kept having to stop and make sure they were going in the right direction. Mum said she would have phoned Katy to find out the right exit, but of course mobiles wouldn't work down here, underground. Miles kept saying he knew where to go, he'd take them to Katy's house, he knew how to get there, but that was just his way. Mum said she hoped it hadn't started raining outside. You wouldn't know down here. Somewhere out there, on the surface, the rain might be coming down in buckets. In the end they found the right exit, and the rain was really nothing at all. The station was only a few hundred yards from Katy's house – it was a pretty house, with a yellow door and a brass number and, Sally remembered, red flowers in the window-boxes. Sometimes she got details like that wrong, but not this time. When they turned into the street, they could see the yellow door and the red flowers in the window-boxes, exactly as she had remembered it. As they came up to number eleven, there was Katy herself, Mum's oldest friend, her pretty round freckled face and piled-up ginger hair, there in the window, poking aside the flowered curtains. She was looking out for them, and an expression of pure delight now came over her face.

The Painter's Sons

(i.m. D.H.L.)

Thorpe Lindley was the foreign painter on Antidauros. The houses on this small Greek island had been uniform, cubed, white since long before memory. They were clustered around the circular harbour, and began to climb the steep white rocky hill behind. The landscape was bleached by the summer heat, the scrubby grass and rocks remaining drained of colour even in winter. The people of the island had always gone with their sweethearts up the hill to sit among briars and wildflowers, to embrace and to notice the view. When they had married their sweethearts, their use for a view came to an end, and they rarely climbed the hill.

But some time in the early 1970s, new houses started to be built on the island. Rich men from Athens discovered it and, finding it unspoilt, decided to begin the work of spoiling it. They built four or five luxurious villas with fine views of the harbour and the sea, from far above. When they arrived, they first agreed to be transported up the hill by the villagers' donkeys, but in time roads were built, and a taxi firm with one driver started to find it worth his while in the summer months, when he was not working as a waiter in the taverna. After the rich Athenian men, the locals began to build new houses for the tourists who would come. They discovered that houses, if lived in but left unfinished, were not taxable. So the tourists, when they came, had to look harder for the island as it had been, unspoilt. Much of the hillside came to be covered with ugly brown square blocks, iron rods stiffly poking into the sky and rusting from the square-topped surface of the roof.

To suit the sense of the picturesque that the tourists sought, first coming from Greece, then from France, Germany and England, it was necessary to encourage a painter, a foreign one. A painter might become rich quickly on more established islands, but here that was all in the future. The painter who came was there for the peace, and money, perhaps, might come much later on. The studio and school of art was a large single-room building, finished and painted white, surrounded by purple-flowering oleander bushes on the edge of the island's single town, and in spring by wildflowers. The painter had tried to plant ivy against the toilet that stood behind the building, perhaps to hide it, or maybe to remind people of where he came from – it looked very strange on that Greek island, and was much discussed when it started to grow and cover the little kiosk. A hundred metres away was the house that the painter and his family lived in: square, bulky, white, but without rusting metal rods shooting up from the roof.

Thorpe Lindley had come to Antidauros at the age of twenty-seven. He had been a painter in London, taking occasional work teaching for schools and trying to make his name as a painter. His wife believed in him: she worked as the personal assistant to the editor of a political journal, and they managed to live on what they made. She was confident that things would work out for them, as the daughter of a prosperous estate agent who had turned against all that materialistic shit. He was the son of an office cleaner and a clerk in an undertaker's office, who were awed by their clever son making it through grammar school, and were no more worried when he went to art school to become a painter than if he had gone to law school to become a solicitor. He was not confident that things would work out for them. His art had been pencil studies of nudes, then Graham Sutherland, then Bacon, then Jackson Pollock, and now it had been simplified into blocks of floating colour, given texture on the canvas. He had become fascinated by Mark Rothko, with whom his wife said he was in a dialogue. Sometimes he sold a painting, but in London, he had no dealer. They talked the matter through and came to Antidauros to live more cheaply, more honestly, and to introduce the innocent people of the island and those who visited to new currents in art.

The people of the island and almost all of the holiday-makers showed no interest in Thorpe Lindley's paintings. Few of them could see why anyone should set up in front of a handsome Cycladic view and then paint a vast canvas, three feet by nine, consisting of a black rectangle floating over a very dark green ground, and nothing else. They lived for a year on Mrs Lindley's parents. Then they talked the matter over, and Thorpe Lindley worked for two or three months in the spring, before the holidaymakers came, on neat, careful, well-executed paintings of the harbour.

Bundles of moulded frames arrived for the painter, and sheets of hardboard matting. He had already learnt how to stretch canvas over wooden supports. With the help of the ironmonger in the back-streets by the harbour, he now learnt to frame his own pictures. The picturesque views of Antidauros harbour, brightly coloured and firmly outlined with a touch of English pop art, sold well. He despised what he did, but continued to do it. Towards the end of the summer, he found himself teaching two Greek ladies on holiday, widows of Thessaloniki merchants. They struggled through his Greek and their English to suggest to him that he might place an advert, early in the spring, in the Greek national newspaper, and one of them kindly wrote the correct wording in a language he was only slowly learning. He placed an advert there, and also in an English newspaper, with similar wording. It was good that only after all this happened did Thorpe learn that the two Greek ladies were supporters of the Colonels, and he kept this information from his wife. The next year there were plenty of students, and he painted his large abstract slowly, in the interim times.

His wife accepted the position that nobody, yet, wanted anything to do with advanced thinking about art. She went about the village pale, intense, furious, explaining to anyone that her husband's art was not to be identified with the little paintings he sold to make money. He was at work on a great project, she explained to the old fishermen of the town and the rich visitors from Athens, making no distinction between them. The old fishermen had no interest in different schools of art and the rich visitors from Athens knew and mostly ridiculed abstract painting, so she grew angry. After some months, she learnt that it was better to confine her anger to the family house, and not to vent it in front of strangers, who would first be shocked, then laugh at her loss of dignity. She had too little to do, and raged in misery and disgust, only ever saying at the end of it that it would all be so much worse in England, horrible and stupid as the Greeks were, or could be.

The children were conspicuous on the island. They were English, and could be nothing else. They had shocks of blond hair, white-blond, like the first stab of the sun in the morning, and quickly their skin grew dark in the summer until their eyes and hair and lips were paler than their cheeks. Still they did not look healthy, but thin-faced, uncertain, withdrawn. They were more at home with each other than with the other children of the island, who were entered into and withdrawn from the school according to how much their fathers needed them in the family business, on board a fishing boat, to help out at a taverna or unloading a ferry's wares. The Lindley children never missed a day, and walked down the hill to the little school in procession, splash of white-blond after splash of white-blond, their hair cut by their mother to save money. For a long time, there was another Lindley child every two or three years, until there were six. Then it stopped. The two eldest were boys. Oak Lindley was short and pugnacious, with a look of a fight about to start and a wrong about to be put right. Thyme Lindley, the second boy, was fearful-looking, fretting as he walked, his fingers fluttering about his bag, opening and shutting it as he checked that the books he needed were still there. The others walked behind them, silent or murmuring. It was cause for comment in the village how very quiet the English children were. But whether it was a Lindley quiet or an English quiet, it was a quiet that had no calm in it, only some sort of fear, and it was felt to be unnatural that children all their days made no scream or yell to break the morning.

After the passage of some years, Oak Lindley returned to the island and set up in a small office mending broken computers, under the business name of OKIT, and an internet café with six computers, his father's unsold pictures on the walls and offering English cakes, with sultanas and carrots, made by his mother. He lived in a small flat upstairs. His café, which was popular with tourists in the summer and had steady unemployed regulars most of the winter, had a sign outside reading δρυς. 'Drys' was his name in Greek, but few people knew that; they thought of him as O-uark, a sound and not a meaning word. There were no oak trees on the island and the islanders thought of the name of his café as ordinarily fanciful. Thyme, who still lived in the bedroom he had shared with Oak, made a little money teaching yoga to tourists and to students at his father's painting school. He charged 250 drachmas a lesson. Yoga was a skill he had learnt from a visiting teacher who, in addition to yoga, taught *tai chi* and meditation. She had spent the summer on Antidauros, ten years before. Thyme dreaded a customer who was already experienced in the art.

One day in late May, Thorpe shut up the studio and walked down through the town towards the harbour. He passed his son Oak's internet café. Oak was sitting inside, talking to his brother Thyme, two blond boys of different shape and size, their family resemblance seeming only to be made by their shared colouring. They were twenty-three and twenty years old. They did not see their father go past. Thorpe had seen the ship approaching from far away. It was the weekly cargo ship, and he was sure that it would be bringing him a supply of canvas, paper, stretchers and framing material, as well as paint, brushes and other important stuff, for himself and for the pupils who would start arriving in June. An assistant was arriving in two weeks from England, a rich boy who would pay him for the privilege of painting around him all summer, and of learning how to stretch canvas and mount frames. It was a biannual delivery, sent by the suppliers in Thessaloniki, that had once filled him with delight and anticipation, and now gave him feelings of dread and age. He knew as he walked towards the docking ship that he would feel, on opening the ordered cargo, the coagulating presence of a hundred inept views of the same stretch of land and sky from his pupils, the same ten pop-art-flavoured views of the island that he would paint this month and sell, and not the masterpiece that he had known he had in him and still heard his wife urge him towards. He painted somewhat in the manner of Willem de Kooning, these days. Even people he had spent time with had sometimes observed that his art of that sort was like the art on the side of subway trains, was influenced by graffiti. But it did not sell.

At the dockyard, he signed for the tea-chest-sized cargo, and asked Marina if her son could drive it up to the studio that afternoon. It was the best time of year. The wildflowers on the island were still rich and abundant, and the sea was fresh. When he had first come to the island, he had found the abundant spread, up on the hill, of flowering broom, of purple borage, nasturtiums, anemones, daisies, wild irises among the smell of sage, rosemary and lavender, intoxicating. Now he liked this time of year because it was warm, but there were few tourists yet, and the town had painted itself. It presented itself fresh and brilliant, white and blue, to the arriving visitor, preparing to make a go of it.

His name was called, an unfamiliar voice, not Greek or English. He shaded his eyes and looked on the terrace of the harbour-side café, Leonidas, and saw a waving female figure, ruddy and plump. He recognized her. She was a Swiss woman, a German speaker, a regular visitor at this time of year. She had been coming to Antidauros for at least twenty years, and greeted Thorpe as if he were an old friend. Next to her was a frail, gaunt man, shrunk into his grey flesh. Thorpe remembered that she came every year with her husband; she looked much as she had for the last year or two, but this man, surely, looked very much older and frailer than he had. Thorpe greeted them heartily enough, not remembering their names or anything about them. He did remember, however, that they had a son who was perhaps in his early twenties.

'It is so pleasant to come back to Antidauros,' the woman said. 'We look forward to our holiday almost as soon as Christmas is over and done with. We always have. Herbert, my husband, he always says to me, Maria, Maria, it will be here before you know it and over before you know it.'

It was tactful of the woman to mention their names so casually. Thorpe did not believe that he would have remembered them unassisted. He had never liked or admired this pair, any more than any of the other regular visitors to the island. They came every year, but their clothes were exactly as they had been twenty years ago, the clothes of a comfortable Swiss-German pair of shopkeepers on a Sunday trip to the lake. The woman's bright floral dress in orange and red, her vividly artificial tights and white slingback shoes corseted an abundant flesh that would be wobbling red and sore, her shoulders streaked with yogurt by the end of the holiday. The old man's blue shorts and cheerful Hawaiian shirt were loose on him; his white socks and brown sandals, polished to a shine, were those of any other descending Teuton this year or any other. Thorpe reminded himself that these people kept the island going, and it was his responsibility to be pleasant to them, as much as any other resident of Antidauros.

'I hope your painting is going well,' the woman confided, leaning forward. 'I was so looking forward to seeing you before much longer. You see,' she patted her husband's hand, 'you see, I wanted to ask you if you could do one thing for me. It is, if you like, a commission.'

'Well, that's always a welcome suggestion,' Thorpe said.

'My husband wants to have his portrait painted,' the woman said. 'And I said, let us ask Mr Lindley of Antidauros. I must explain.' She hurried on, seeing, perhaps, Thorpe's unwillingness in his eyes. He never painted portraits for exactly this reason. It required sitting in a room, facing another human being, and perhaps even engaging in conversation with them. Thorpe believed that if the suggestion ever arose, it would arise from the people he already spent enough time with, the rich holidaymakers, the wealthy of Hamburg and Lyon, here on the island for two weeks, and full of unreasonable demands. He started to shake his head. The woman could buy one of the landscapes he had left over from last year.

But she went on swiftly: 'It has never happened before, this desire to have Herbert painted,' she said. 'And now it is our last chance. You see, Mr Lindley, Herbert is ill, and is not expected to last until the end of the year.'

'I am so sorry to hear that,' Thorpe said. The old man, fleshless, sunken, now began almost to grin, to nod in a slow, satisfied manner. Thorpe could not remember if he understood English, or if this conversation was being carried out in the safe knowledge that anything could be said in front of him. He remembered nothing of this pair except their bold appearance, and that they had a son. 'It's an honour even to be asked,' he said in the end.

But there was something about that response that dissatisfied the woman, and she shook her head sharply. 'Money would be no object,' she said firmly. 'You could name your price, Mr Lindley.'

'And your son?' Thorpe said, revolted. 'Is he with you?'

'Florian is not with us this year,' she said. 'He has just started a new job and he found it impossible to ask for leave. He is the new junior manager of a branch of Starbucks in Solothurn, a beautiful city, not so very far from us, a hundred and fifty kilometres away, and he visits us every week. How kind of you to ask after him!'

'I see,' Thorpe said. In his mind he shrank from this family and its deeds. But he needed money: he perpetually needed money. And even the mother of a man who spread American filth and called it coffee could supply him with money for good deeds. He wondered how much he could charge for how little.

'Won't you join us,' the woman said. 'Join us in our morning drink. It is a little too late for breakfast, but we like to enjoy ourselves on holiday. It would be as our guest, of course,' she went on expansively. Thorpe had not noticed that the pair of them were drinking, as very old Greek men sometimes used to, glasses of ouzo, although it was only ten thirty in the morning. The father took up his glass, half empty, and in the vacant café, looking out over the sun and the sea, finished it in one gulp.

'That is kind of you,' Thorpe said, with some distaste. 'But I have some work I need to do before lunch. I would be happy to work on a portrait of your husband, and honoured. Perhaps he would like to come up to the studio tomorrow morning. Would that suit you?'

'What do you think of charging?' the woman said, her eyes wet and hungry.

Thorpe assessed her. She was probably not immensely rich; she was of the class of persons that had little reason to spend on ordinary things, and on the rare occasions, like a holiday, when opportunities arose, she must enjoy splashing around the small margins of her income. He thought about what he could get away with, and named a sum. She lowered her eyes to her ouzo, her handbag, clutched in her hands, red-varnished. It was more than she had thought. She had never dealt with a proper painter before, she confided. But then she gathered strength, and said that this was important, and she agreed. Her son would transfer the deposit from Solothurn. This would happen in the next day or two days.

He told the story to his wife and children, over lunch that day. His wife shook her head when she learnt that their son was the junior manager of a branch of Starbucks. 'Do they not have coffee of their own in Switzerland?' she said. 'I think it's rather well known to be extremely good. The Germans! They know all about coffee. And now the Americans, they come with their shops, selling slightly flavoured foaming milk, calling it coffee, and driving everyone who knows about coffee out of business. The minds of these people – their children working for scum like that. I would be ashamed to know anyone who worked for Starbucks, I truly would. My God, what does your son do – he's the junior manager of a branch of Starbucks. These people.'

'The son seemed reasonable,' Thorpe said. 'He had an odd name. He was called – he was called Florian. I think I remember him.'

'I remember a Swiss boy called Florian,' Thyme said. 'He was nice. He's been coming here for years. I remember him being our age.'

'The father is going to die, his wife said,' Thorpe said.

'One final trip,' Rose Lindley said. 'They are so deluded, these people. They think that they come to a place once a year for two weeks, even for twenty years, and they think anyone remembers them. It's only their lives that are so drab, back home, with their son working for Starbucks and— What did they do?'

'God knows,' Thorpe said. 'But they made some money at it. She's asked me to paint a portrait of her husband before he dies. He's not expected to last more than six months. This is their last chance.'

'Don't they have artists in – where was it? – Solothurn? No. That was just where their son was living. Where are they?'

'I forget. I'm the artist who came to mind. They've offered me a good sum of money. I'll paint what portrait I can in the next ten days, then they'll pay me five thousand euros. It isn't a bad deal.'

'You should have asked for ten,' Rose said. But she was pleased. Five thousand euros, and the guaranteed payment that the student painter was going to make for staying with them the whole summer. If they could only guarantee selling eight paintings to tourists this summer, and if nobody dropped out of the painting courses, they would be all right for the winter.

'Why didn't Florian come with them?' Oak said. 'He was nice. I don't care if he is the manager of Starbucks.'

'Junior manager,' Rose said. 'I think she must have meant deputy manager. He won't have been able to get holiday. They work them to the bone, those people, for nothing, just a degrading gruelling job for ten hours, having to smile at people constantly and going home with the stink of boiling milk in your nostrils.'

'Is it just the mother and the father, then?' Thyme said.

The next morning, the two Swiss arrived at the studio exactly at nine thirty, as Thorpe had asked. They came up the hill in the taxi driven by Marina's son, and Thorpe could hear them fussing about in a curious, yawping, golloping language outside. He had arranged the studio for a sitting, with an old armchair to one side where the light was good, and hung a tatty old purple shawl of Rose's against the wall behind the chair.

'Here we are,' he said heartily, as they came in. The old man was in a plain shirt today, and a thin red bow tie; his wife was still in her shiny, floral, polyester holiday garb. Thorpe explained where he should sit, and his plan to sketch today with charcoal and to get to work on the canvas tomorrow. He explained soberly that sitting for a portrait was much more tiring than might be imagined, and that he would not ask the old man to sit for more than an hour without a break, and not more than two hours a day in total.

'Should Herbert sit here now?' the wife said.

Thorpe suggested that the wife should go, and come back in two and a half hours. He liked the idea that he would not have to talk to his sitter at all. She hesitated, perhaps wondering how he would explain anything necessary to the sitter, but after a moment gurgled some explanation to him, and left with a little wave.

The sitter focused sharply. He had seemed vague, led about like a pet spaniel, unsure, but he had made his own life and had run everything in his house and business for decades. He had his own purpose. Now he sat and focused sharply on the man who was to paint him before he died. But he had not sat for a portrait before, and it was as if he were posing in front of a camera. He produced a strong grin, as big and stretched as he could manage. Thorpe looked. It was a terrifying grin. Under the thin stretched skin, the broad yellow Swiss teeth were pulled back as if in agony. The grin revealed the skull beneath. If there was any joy in this grin, it had disappeared years ago. But it was how a man pictured himself in his portrait. Today there was no need for the man to hold any facial expression at all.

Thorpe had painted few portraits in his life, but he knew that the thing you did was to block out the relationships of parts of the body, to form a structure, and only then to move on from charcoal on paper to the portrait on canvas. Then there would be time to discourage the grin.

The assistant from England arrived at the end of the following week. He was a boy called Charlie who had been on one of the painting courses, a year before. But he had proved himself too good to fit in with the ladies and amateurs who wanted to learn how to sketch on a Greek hillside. He was a student at an art college, and had taken Thorpe's course only because he wanted to get away, to paint in the sun. He had shown an interest in Thorpe's abstract painting; he had sat with Thorpe and Rose outside on the terrace, arguing about de Kooning and Twombly, late into the night. The painting school had not been the right place for him. He was limp, affected, timid in manner, Thyme said decisively, and he had seen how the people of the village stared after him as he walked through the town with his elaborate moustache, wearing a blue-and-white-striped Edwardian one-piece bathing costume and Roman sandals. But he scared off the women on the painting course that week with his work and his confidence with a brush. He was, it had emerged, rich. His father was something in the City, he said, with a flourish, and had provided Thorpe with a joke. 'Art schools,' he said, 'are the downwardly mobile section of higher education. Taking the sons of commodity brokers and introducing them to a way of life in which they'll find it impossible to make a living.'

Rose had laughed with the others – Charlie, too, had let out his feminine giggle, high-pitched and quickly covered with the back of his hand. She had said when they were alone that Charlie was the real thing, that he had, like Thorpe, a vocation. She felt, however, there was a way to use Charlie's trust fund, and go on using it. When he had written suggesting that what he needed was more than a week, Thorpe had invited him to come and stay as his apprentice – a word in inverted commas, an old-fashioned word that neither of them would feel they would have committed to – and learn through osmosis, by working alongside, by making frames and helping Rose out with the books.

Oak couldn't remember him. In his internet café, he paid little attention to his father's pupils. They were all middle-aged women. Sometimes, when things were quiet, Oak and Thyme would sit and discuss handsome men of the town, or handsome men who had come on holiday to the island. They had both told their parents that they preferred men to women, years ago. Rose had made a point of saying that it was a tragedy that both her sons, the eldest children, were gay. But she said it as a joke, raising the back of her hand to her forehead as she spoke, to parody the intense melodrama with which such things were responded to in the past. In reality she welcomed it. She felt that no man would take Oak or Thyme away from her, that a relationship with a man would always be a secondary thing. Oak had had a relationship lasting two years with a boy from the village, the son of the post office, a dark, glowering boy with an early moustache. They had been seventeen and eighteen, and it had been a secret from his parents, but not from Oak's, who had invited Nikolaos to supper whenever he wanted, and cherished him. After two years it had come to an end and Oak still came up the hill to eat supper with his mother. Thyme was more shy. If he had had a relationship, his mother did not know about it. She felt and said that he deserved to be happy.

Rose had half remembered the assistant called Charlie. She saw him getting off the ferry and waved energetically. She realized that she had remembered, above all, the moustache he had worn the summer before. She had hung on to that moustache when reading his letters; it was the moustache of a Victorian strong man in a circus, curled and immense, and she had constructed a strong man about him. The moustache was gone this year, and instead there was an apologetic small person, Greek-dark but as small as a fifteen-year-old, coming towards her with a valise and a suitcase on wheels. The Disappointment held out his hand, and Rose, making the best of it, embraced him. His narrow little chest, like a tubercular child's, inflated beneath her strong arms. He would do very well for Thyme, who had not done very well on his own behalf. She felt this with certainty, and with some amusement.

'Thorpe's busy still with a commission,' Rose said, as they dragged up the hill – Marina's son's taxi was only for students, not for apprentices, she had decided. 'It's a portrait.'

'That's a new development,' Charlie said. 'I don't remember him doing portraits before.'

'Oh, he's done portraits before,' Rose said. 'He painted one of me when we first met. He doesn't do them often. This one was supposed to be finished by now. It's a holidaymaker who just decided out of the blue that he wanted his portrait painted, and since he was here for two weeks, Thorpe said yes. And charged him five thousand euros,' she went on, deciding that the Disappointment might as well hear about everything, if he was hoping to learn about the life of a painter.

'When is he going?'

'Well, that's the thing,' Rose said. 'He was supposed to go last Friday, but announced that Thorpe shouldn't hurry, that he'd put his flight off for ten days, and could put it off for ten days more. It should have been done by now. But I think it's nearly finished. You might like to talk to Thorpe about it now the piece is nearly done.'

'I look forward to seeing Thorpe's new pieces,' Charlie said, pausing for a moment and letting his suitcase rest on the ground. He mopped his brow, speaking formally but breathlessly. He had caught that word, *piece*, from Thorpe last summer and had caught it again just now from Rose. It gave the products of painting a new dignity, an intellectual substance, a suggestion of white cube buildings in Mayfair, galleries of art, and not the white cubes rented out to holidaymakers on Antidauros. Rose used it again.

'Yes, I think it's a strong piece,' she said casually. What a Disappointment, she said to herself. But he would do for Thyme, this summer. She was proud of her generosity.

She took Charlie to the house first, where he could wash himself and change. His shirt was dark-stained. For a moment she thought that somehow water had been poured over him. He did not seem capable of doing anything as physical as sweating, and he gave off no odour. He would be living in Thyme's room this summer, Rose explained.

Thyme would move down to share his brother's flat over the internet café, but had not cleared out all of his stuff. Rose apologized for this as she showed Charlie the room, saying that Thyme was a lazy little sod, but a charmer, and he would get the rest of his stuff out later that day. She was pleased at this accident, or Thyme's lack of organization. She saw that it was a way to introduce Charlie and Thyme again to each other in intimate circumstances, and after that, they would easily move to the next stage. Charlie hardly looked around, although the drawers in Thyme's room were open, spilling clouds of the clean white underwear he hardly ever wore, and on the shelf were dusty trophies from inter-island chess matches, on the shelf the disco CDs she had encouraged him in and which he never played. It came to her that Charlie, last summer, had struck her as no kind of observer. Did a painter need to be a talented observer? She did not know, but Charlie was not one. His paintings might have been produced with his back to any kind of sight of interest, in a cell or before a blank wall. It was more than that: she remembered, and she thought now of how Charlie could be taken to see something of interest, and give the strong impression of boredom, of not seeing, of wanting only to project himself into the space and talk about what was already inside his head.

He was a bore with only the normal powers of perception, not an artist's perception. She remembered those long conversations at night that had engaged and interested Thorpe so much. Not her. They had been abstract, philosophical, nothing to do with the world. When he talked about the tactile, or about sensuous textures of paint, or about the quality of light in this part of the world, it was

265

with no engagement with facts, and was not the product of observation. She had listened to him moving little chess pieces of abstract values about the field of conversation, and for him the phrase 'quality of light' had the same abstract value as the word 'similitude' or 'ontology'. He could not say what colour the quality of light possessed, or endowed. And his body, his physical presence, in his clean, short-sleeved blue-checked shirt, bought after hardly a glance in a high-street emporium, his odourless and insubstantial, thin-calved, elbowing body, was barely present. No wonder she had only remembered the moustache and the high-pitched, feminine, apologetic and shameful giggle. He had never looked at the quality of light before bringing out the term; he had not inhabited, fully, his body before sponging it and placing it in different clothes. She allowed herself to think this. He was a Disappointment and he would do very well for Thyme. She allowed herself to think that the most concrete thing about Charlie might be his money, of which he had a lot.

They went over to the studio, where Thorpe was in the last stages of the portrait of the Swiss shopkeeper. Rose had not seen it: she preferred to keep out of Thorpe's way when he was working on a piece, and she did not especially want to see the result of this. A shopkeeper whose son was the deputy manager of a Starbucks. She opened the door of the studio, saying, 'Look, it's Charlie.' What struck her with alarm was not the painting, which she would not look at, but the expression on the face of the sitter. Why was he pulling his face back like that, to show his teeth? The look of strained terror in his face, the bones underneath the yellow skin, the sockets of bone holding the yellow bits of

jelly he had for eyes. Behind the easel the sitter's wife rose
up from her chair, smiling more gently to greet Rose; a fat
woman in a dress from six summers ago, surely hot in here
with her orange tan tights on. The sitter did not move.
Thorpe set his paintbrush down and shook Charlie's hand.
The sitter's wife offered hers to Rose, who, after a moment,
took it and shook.

'We are very pleased with the progress of the painting,'
the wife said. 'It looks so like Herbert. I wish we had done
this when Herbert was in good health, but this is so like
him.'

Rose looked. Thorpe had rendered with absolute accu-
racy the grin of a skull the sitter was performing; the yellow
eyes were blurred as if with terror and, with some careful
precision, the blotches and patches of the sitter's yellow
skin had been accounted for. Behind him the purple shawl
she had always loved and had missed only the other day
was rendered in great slashes of brush, and given a gory red
tinge. Blood had been pouring down the wall behind this
poor sitter, and the terror and rictus of his expression said
that he knew it.

But it was as if nobody else could see the painting for
what it was. Charlie had been led over by Thorpe, and after
they had stood there for a moment, Charlie said, 'It's a very
strong piece, Thorpe,' and started talking about the quality
of light.

'It should be finished tomorrow,' Thorpe said. 'I thought
I would leave the backdrop like that, those fat brush-
strokes. I like those painterly gestures.'

'It reminds me a little of Francis Bacon,' Rose said, out of
devilment. She knew that you did not say to a painter that

his work resembled the work of some other painter, particularly one whose work (she believed) had been grown out of. But Thorpe was not taking this commission seriously. It did not bear on his own, proper, work, which was nothing but pure Thorpe. She felt dizzy, alone, windswept, about to plunge into the depths without any kind of support, and that she must say what she meant before the abyss swallowed her. She would never see this man again, tight-pulled in his skull's grin, and the painting, too, would disappear onto the wall of a house in Switzerland where she would never go. Perhaps at some point the deputy manager of a Starbucks in a provincial Swiss town would look at it, and see that it was too strong a rendering of his father dying, and destroy it. These people were capable of anything.

When the taxi pulled up outside, Oak got out. He had caught a lift with Marina's son, knowing that he was ordered every day for twelve thirty, and handed the taxi over to a stiffly bowing sitter and his fat, smiling wife. His brother Thyme had forgotten, he explained, his toothbrush and razor, still sitting on his dressing-table in the bedroom. Did Charlie mind if he went to collect it?

'I don't know why Thyme couldn't come himself,' Rose said, filled with rage. Her purpose was being frustrated.

'He's looking after the café,' Oak said. 'And I thought I'd come up to say hello to Charlie.'

He smiled, not a rictus like Herbert, but a warm smile, the head tipped on one side, all pugnacity gone. For a moment Charlie did not smile back before remembering where he was, and who Oak was.

'I think I might have put a lot of stuff in a drawer,' Charlie said. 'I didn't know anyone was going to need it.

It might be easiest if I come up and help you find your brother's stuff.'

'Yes, go on, that would be quickest,' Rose said. 'And do you want to eat lunch up here or go down into the village? Thorpe won't need you to start work today. Go off and have a nice afternoon on the beach.'

That afternoon, Oak sat with Charlie on the terrace of the taverna on the corner beyond his café, Drys. He went with Charlie into the kitchen and, after discussing the food with Marina, selected lunch for his guest. Charlie pushed it round his plate, hardly eating anything. He said that he rarely ate anything at lunchtime. Oak persuaded him to drink a glass of wine, however. They made themselves conspicuous then, and afterwards, as they walked down through the village towards the chain of beaches that stretched out towards the southern tip of the island. At one point, as they were passing a house on the outskirts of the town, a Greek man stood on the upper terrace of a half-finished house and called down to them. Oak rattled back something, scowling. The man went inside, banging the shutters and laughing in a sour way. When Charlie asked what had passed between them, Oak said it was nothing, that he paid no attention to what these people said. The man had been one of the brothers of Nikolaos, one of the ones who had told him to stop bothering his brother. He kept the post office, a minor inconvenience. Nikolaos had a fiancée now. They would be very happy together.

All over the town, the villagers saw Oak walking to the beach with Charlie, or having lunch with him, or walking back from the beach, and afterwards they said to each other, 'That English boy, the faggot, he's got himself a boyfriend. You never saw such a little drip and a pansy as the boyfriend. They should be very happy together.'

But the next day, or the day after that, Oak and Charlie and Thorpe and Rose, all together, went down to the harbour, Thorpe in his one jacket and Rose in a clean ironed white dress with her hair up. Thorpe walked with his wife holding his arm, and in front of them, Oak and Charlie, also arm in arm. Thorpe and Rose said good evening to everyone, smiling and nodding. The villagers afterwards said it was the funniest thing they ever saw, the English painter and his wife treating her faggot son and his new pansy boyfriend like an engaged couple to be paraded. But they said good evening back, even complimenting the new pansy when he managed to say *kali spera*, and somebody afterwards said that the new pansy was a millionaire. That English boy knew what he was doing, and his mother, too. Somebody said that the person who had let it be known about the millions was the English boy's brother, who was supposed to be a faggot as well.

They had dinner after their walk along the harbour-side. Oak smiled tightly, as his father offered Charlie a glass from a bottle of the taverna's most expensive wine. Charlie accepted, but hardly drank, and when they suggested that they order some grilled octopus, Charlie said he would prefer something very plain.

'There's nothing plainer than ordinary grilled fish,' Oak said, astonished.

'It wouldn't suit me,' Charlie said. 'But order it and I'll eat some salad, and perhaps a little rice.'

'Are you having some problems?' Rose said. 'You shouldn't be drinking wine if you are.'

'No, nothing in particular,' Charlie said. 'I suffer from intestinal problems, though. I have to be careful what I eat. I don't think I can eat octopus.'

'Try a little,' Oak said. 'You never know until you try it. You don't want to be one of those English people, complaining about the food swimming in oil, asking for fish fingers for their kiddies.'

Rose saw that there was a little edge of contempt in the way Oak was addressing Charlie. It was early in their connection for this to make itself plain. She heard herself talking about the English people and their kiddies and the fish fingers, and reflected that if Oak could learn one way of talking from her, he could learn another, too. He should understand that the reason they were able to take Oak and Charlie out for dinner and pay for wine and octopus and some brandy afterwards was that Charlie was staying with them for sixteen weeks, all summer, and paying them twelve hundred euros a week all summer. Charlie was allowed to eat whatever he liked, and Oak should concentrate on being the fundamentally nice person that he probably was.

Towards the end of the summer, Charlie said to Oak, 'What is it like here, in the winter?'

They were on the beach. Charlie didn't like to lie in the sun all day; he grew brown easily, but he thought there was a risk of skin cancer for all northern Europeans. He was sitting under a borrowed sun umbrella, wrapped in a beach towel that had been inherited from one of the lady painters. *Paris Jolie*, it said in large art-nouveau letters, like the Paris Métro, and there were figures of the Eiffel Tower, a pierrot and a Piaf-like person playing the accordion under a starry sky. Oak was lying in the sun, six feet away from Charlie. He was naked; they were on the furthest beach, where no one ever came. By now, at the end of August, he was as brown as he ever got. Not only his hair, but his pubic hair and the hair on his legs were a vivid blond against his dark skin.

'It's nice,' Oak said. 'It can get very cold, and then you just wrap up warm and put the fire on. Some people shut up and go somewhere else. I like it. There's not many people around. You're not going to make very much money from the café, though. It's only kids from the school and a few grandmothers sending emails to their grand-children in America. I keep thinking about starting up a computer literacy course. It would be really popular. I'll be all right this year, though.'

'I don't think I want to go,' Charlie said. 'I'm supposed to go in three weeks' time.'

'It's two weeks,' Oak said. 'I was thinking about it the other day.'

'I'd have to check,' Charlie said. 'It suits me here.'

Oak made no reply. And in a moment Charlie started explaining, with all the foresight and care of the very rich in search of a project, that it would be perfectly possible for him to go on painting here, on this island, that he felt his painting had started to develop. And there were other possibilities. It was very cheap living here. Did Oak realize that, with his mother talking about the cost of living the whole time? You could buy a very nice house, a Venetian mansion, on the island for only three hundred thousand euros. It was nothing – it was a bargain. Of course it would need another hundred thousand spending on it – 'another hundred K,' Charlie casually said – to bring the bathrooms and the heating up to scratch, but compared to living in London!

'Where is this house?' Oak said casually.

'On the other side of the island,' Charlie said. 'That was what I was doing the other day, when you said I was being mysterious.'

So it was clear to Oak that Charlie would take him to the far side of the island, enough to take him away from Thorpe and Rose, enough to play the English squire. Charlie went on talking from his mummified position in the shade and, merely to amuse himself, Oak allowed himself to lie back, think of scenes from the past, and feel his cock engorge and rise, there on the beach. Charlie went on talking in practical terms, as if the stiff pointing member in its blond thicket was something that might happen to anyone, was hardly worth mentioning or responding to. And what about the internet café, Oak asked finally, strumming his cock, pulling it back and making it go *thwack* against his tight drum of a brown belly. You could keep that going, Charlie said. Or you could up sticks and start one in Hora. Or best of all you could ask Thyme to run it on a day-to-day basis, and you could just drop in once or twice a week. Pay him a salary. Put him on a regular footing. It's not the other side of the world. It's right you should have something to keep you going. Don't give everything up for my sake. Oak thought of the truffling and snuffling and complaints over the food; about the high-pitched giggle; about having to stop himself thinking of what people were calling after him and – a painful sensation – what would happen when Charlie had learnt enough Greek to understand what they were calling him, too. But it was clear that Oak had succeeded in keeping Charlie on the island, that by next spring they would be moving into a Venetian mansion, the old place in Hora, with what Charlie would call a wet room and what the villagers would wonder at, twenty windows replaced in one go without regard to the expense. When they told Rose, she said she looked forward to them being allowed to marry, once the law changed. She would wear a hat when it happened, she said, mildly laughing.

The next spring, and the year after that, it was clear that everything had changed. Thyme was regarded by everybody as having a job. He woke up in the flat above the internet café, and made himself a cup of coffee before walking down the road to the baker's to buy a roll. He came back and, before opening the café, went back upstairs and did any small household chores. The half an hour at the beginning of the day was the best time for doing this. There had been some suggestion that he might like to go on living at Rose and Thorpe's, so Oak could rent out the flat over the café to tourists. But Thyme had said that it would be best to be able to keep an eye on the computers downstairs, in case of burglary. Charlie said sarcastically that he was an expensive burglar alarm, keeping his brother from making money from the holiday trade, and occupying the little flat rent free. Oak had not insisted, however.

Today he went downstairs after sweeping the floor, and switched on all the computers. People would start to dribble in some time late in the morning. He ran the security scan on each of them. He turned on the coffee machine behind the desk. He pulled out the chair he liked to sit on and, sticking his buds in his ears, went to sit on the front pavement while listening to an old Jam record. It had been a violent winter: the storms, of which the summer visitors knew nothing, had torn at the island, battering away until roofs and shutters and tethered boats had been flung loose. All spring, the winds had flung clouds across the bright sky, and the whole island had worked at painting, at nailing down, at renovating and cleaning and making their houses and businesses white and blue and ready for the first visitors.

Oak and Charlie had finished the renovation of their house by the time the storms had come in January. Their house, solid and new-windowed, was a sealed nut against the storm, and they settled in with the luxury of open fires, burning ash logs and coal imported in sacks on the ferry, and the safe alternative of oil-fired central heating. In the summer, the air-conditioning would be powerful, but in January the pair of them sat in the warmth, as of an English suburban house, and listened to Charlie talk about his plans for the pair of them. Oak said it was just perfect, living there; he'd never been so happy, he said. He told his brother, sniggering a little behind his hand, that when the visitors started to come, in the summer, they would turn the Venetian house in Hora into a party house, in the centre of town. The swimming-pool in the back garden hadn't yet been begun; it was going to be done by the middle of June, Oak thought. He was just going to go and ask all the cute boys on the beach if they'd like to come over; he would select and choose, and the best-looking boys all summer would come and hang out there. It was going to be a blast, Oak said. It was Charlie's idea. When Thyme thought about Oak and Charlie, his face grew still with the rage he felt against them, against all of them. The shutters in his flat above the internet café rattled and banged all day and all night; he hunched over the single electric fan heater with two sweaters on. Thyme wondered about the power of Charlie, the power the little man had to compel things to happen to his own convenience and to suit his existence. He had had some power over Oak; that power had been enough to uproot him and yet to fix him for ever in the place he had grown up, to set a limit to what Oak could ever achieve or ever become. Oak had gone along with it, hardly thinking about the possibilities of a life without Charlie. Was that power nothing but money? Or was it the power of a will that had stretched out across nations and established itself here? Thyme hunched over his heater and thought, all winter, of how he would have brushed Charlie off indignantly, would have told him that he'd been refusing better offers since he was fourteen, would have told him to get out and put his trousers back on – his face trembled with a smile as he envisaged in detail the first scene between Charlie and Oak. Oak had not told him anything, as he had gone into detail about Nikolaos. Too much rested on Charlie. And Charlie had not come to him. He had come to Oak.

A barrier of efficiency and established relations had arisen between Thyme and his brother, and it was of Oak's making and Oak's choice. It was not just the arrangements between proprietor and employee that now existed, but the way a poor, plain brother with no future and no life must be required to look at the dream existence on the other side of the island with wet room and central heating, a Labrador puppy and a vast white leather sofa on which to lounge, barefoot. Oak must look away from so much in establishing this life as the way he wanted to live. Thyme had seen the way he made his gaze busy elsewhere when Charlie started talking about his painting, the festivals of regret and denigration that he could keep up for hours. It was as if he had married a painter even worse than his father, and Oak would look away from all of that, and at his father, looking smiling at a son-in-law who was just like him, but no threat whatsoever. Oak had got rid of his life, and he was glad of it. In the evenings sometimes, if someone was around, Charlie talked about the possibility these days of fathering a child, of fostering, of surrogacy and parenthood for people like them. This, Charlie said, would be an ideal place to bring kids up. Oak knew that he was talking about the island with the village school where they'd hardly learnt to read, where maths had dried up when they were twelve, with the textbooks sometimes thirty or forty years old and one computer, and he looked seraphically into the middle distance as his husband – his new word – talked.

Now Thyme was outside his brother's internet café, in the sun. The wind had died off completely in the last few days. The sea was still cold, and churning with sand and mud brought up in the past months; it would be June before it had its usual transparency. But the air was warm and still, and Thyme sat outside in the empty street. The very first visitors had been arriving in the last weeks, and soon he would be too busy with tourists writing their emails home to sit on a wooden chair and greet whoever it was walking by. He watched a couple approaching round the narrow bend of the street, looking carefully behind them in case a car might clip them. They came from a more orderly country than this, where the needs of pedestrians had been considered and pavements constructed. He watched them approach, having nothing else to do. They were oddly assorted: an old woman in an old-fashioned sun-dress, brilliant with greens and purples, plump in white patent slingbacks. She clung to the arm of what must be her son, a tall man, a little plump, in a pair of new white knee-length shorts, crisp and brilliant as whitewash, and a blue-checked shirt. To Thyme's surprise, the man waved at him before saying something to the old woman, who brightened, smiled, raised her own hand. He made a gesture in response. Friendliness towards forgotten holidaymakers meant nothing.

'I know who you are,' the woman said, in English with some kind of accent. 'Your father is Mr Lindley, the painter. I think there are only his children on the island who look as you do. You don't remember me.'

'I know I should,' Thyme said quickly.

'No, no, no reason,' the woman said. 'Your father painted my late husband, not last year but the year before. He was very ill and he wanted to come to Antidauros one last time, and I said to your father that I would like it if he would paint Herbert before he died. And he did and it is wonderful, a wonderful thing to have.'

'Yes,' Thyme said. He remembered something of the sort. The son, holding his mother's arm, looked at him; a gentle, penetrating face, a face that might have come from a time when there was nothing to do but look with mild interest at anything that was going on around it. He was on holiday, and his gesture towards his holiday was that he had not shaved today, or yesterday, or the day before that. It might, too, be too painful: his face was a brilliant red, as were his arms and legs.

'He was only fifty-five,' the mother said. 'That seems old to you, I expect, but fifty-five – it is nothing.'

'That looks bad,' Thyme said, pointing at the man's arms, as if the mother had said nothing. He hadn't known what to say: his embarrassment found something in the vicinity to offer sympathy with.

'Excuse me?' the man said, but politely, asking for an explanation rather than affronted.

'Your sunburn,' Thyme said. 'It must be a bit painful.'

'Only a little,' the man said. 'I went out on the beach yesterday and stayed too long. It was so nice. My mother was sleeping and I did not want to come back early and disturb her. I will give it a rest today and it will be fine tomorrow.'

'Yoghurt's the thing,' Thyme said. 'Just paint yourself with yoghurt and it should be fine.'

'Any sort of yoghurt?' the mother said. 'Ordinary yoghurt or Greek yoghurt? Which is best?'

Thyme wondered: he did not really know what yoghurt that was not Greek was like, and the yoghurt that could be bought on Antidauros was certainly Greek. He said he thought that anything would do. It was three years now since Florian – the son – had been to Antidauros, the mother went on to explain, but he corrected her and said it had been five years. The last time he had been eighteen, and had gone away with the friend he'd had then, with a backpack, like wander birds; the next year his father had said he would have to pay for himself and he could not pay for himself, so he had stayed at home; the year after he would have come, but he had just started working and he could not have time off; the year after that was last year, and his father had just died, and they had not come at all. 'For the first time in twenty-three years,' the mother said, wondering at this upheaval in rhythm, like Christmas being cancelled. 'For the first time we did not come to Antidauros for our holiday in the spring.' But now they had come and they would always come from now on. Florian smiled, a smile not quite meant for Thyme but one definitely not meant for his mother. She would be allowed to believe that for this year and perhaps next year too, but Florian was not going to go on holiday for ever with his mother. Thyme liked his kindness, and its limits. He remembered him.

'You work for Starbucks,' he said, making an effort to keep his tone neutral. He had probably never heard the name 'Starbucks' pronounced in a neutral way, and it needed some care.

'Yes,' Florian said. 'Yes, I do. But how did you know that? Oh, my mother must have told you or your father when they were here two years ago. But you remembered. Why should you remember? Do I seem like the sort of person who has to work for something like Starbucks? Well, I work for Starbucks, and it is a very good company. My mother, she should be proud of me, being a manager for Starbucks. But here I am in Greece, again. And today we are going to sit under the shade, in a café somewhere, and watch boats come and go and we will read our books, all day long.'

'Remember, yoghurt,' Thyme said, smiling. 'And tomorrow you can go back to the beach.'

They went on, down towards the harbour, each holding a book, the mother clutching her tall son's arm. There were no customers all morning; around noon, Oak telephoned to say that he would be over that evening. Charlie had things to do, so it would just be him. There was a bunch of Charlie's friends arriving on the ferry that got in at seven and he'd be driving them back, but he'd drop by first. 'I thought I should warn you,' Oak said, giggling, 'I just spoke to Ma and she's on her way down the hill, she's probably going to put in an appearance any second now. Just saying.'

Rose was coming down the road, looking cross and hot. 'She's here now,' Thyme said. 'Got to go. See you later.'

'You don't look busy,' Rose said, kissing him.

'Done nothing all morning,' Thyme said. 'Just chatting with whoever. Those Swiss people are back.'

'What Swiss people?'

'Those Swiss people. Pa painted his portrait. It was two years ago, he didn't think much of them.'

'Oh, yeah,' Rose said. 'I think I remember. Wasn't he supposed to be dying? What's he doing coming on holiday?'

'No, he died all right,' Thyme said. 'They were just saying. It was the wife and her son, they've come back. They were saying how much they liked and valued their beautiful portrait by Pa in his best vein.'

Thyme pulled what in the family was called a Clement Greenberg face, sanctimonious and art critical. 'It was a very good portrait,' Rose said. 'I remember them now. And the son. Didn't the son work for McDonald's? No. Starbucks. Why should I remember that? Useful brain cells are being occupied with that information. He worked for Starbucks. God save us.'

'He's nice, Ma,' Thyme said. 'He's called Florian.'

'I'm being naughty,' Rose said. 'We shouldn't sneer at the people who keep this place on the road. *Kali mera*,' she said, as the priest's wife came past; she nodded, unsmiling, at Rose, ignoring Thyme altogether. 'Are you coming up for dinner tonight? I think Oak's coming, and Charlie too.'

'It's tomorrow night, Ma,' Thyme said. 'Or the night after that.'

That afternoon, Thyme closed the internet café and, instead of sleeping, went down to the beach. He took his towel and a swimsuit, not expecting to use the swimsuit. He didn't think there would be anyone he knew around. It was too cold for the island boys to go swimming. He walked down through the town, an old pair of his brother's khaki shorts on, loose on him and needing a tight-cinched belt, and a stained and faded T-shirt advertising a Rolling Stones concert from ten years ago. He went barefoot; the soles of his feet had half an inch of hard, thick skin. If the people of the village looked out and saw him, they would say, 'There goes that English boy, the other one who's a faggot, the one who's not so good-looking.' He was young-looking, with a pointed chin and a little mouth. If he had to say what might be nice to look at about him, he would have to say his thick blond hair, or perhaps his blue eyes, commented on by every Greek. He was less good-looking than his well-knit, shorter, squarer brother, and yet he knew that his brother was not good-looking at all.

He was thinking of other matters, and his path took him towards the beaches without him thinking about it. The brilliant scarlet-flowered gardens of the town gave way to wildness, and the scattered debris and garbage around the roads was swallowed by wildflowers, great clouds of white and pale pink and palest blue he did not know the names for, and the scent of sage and rosemary and lavender on the hot air rising from the drying earth. The thick fistfuls of blossom – was that what it was, blossom? – were like snow on branches. He wondered what it was like for Florian to wake up in his Swiss winter, and look out of his little wooden window, and see heavy snow poised on the bare branches. Thyme had never seen snow settle, only on television, in films that the Greeks loved. He walked towards the beaches with a regret that surprised him, that Florian would not be there. He had said he would be sitting in the shade today, minding his sunburn with jealous and scrupulous care.

The road that circled the island veered away from the last of the beaches, and to reach them you had to cut across bare land where Pavlos the accountant rented grazing to goatherds. The goats were tearing now at the scrubby juniper bushes and the thyme for which he was named, leaping as Thyme went barefoot through the grass. There was a white chapel, no bigger than a shed, by the head of the last beach. It contained a single icon and could hold no more than two worshippers. It was never used, but somebody painted it yearly. A mulberry tree grew in its shade, staining that side of the chapel with heavy purple. The beach was long and narrow, curving like a bow. There was nobody there but, to Thyme's surprise, the Swiss woman, sitting underneath an umbrella in a folding chair. She must have brought them with her, along with the beach towel extended at her feet; there were no beach shops or cafés for miles in any direction. A hundred yards out to sea, her son floated on his back, drifting, clutching something over his belly, which must be some kind of flotation device; it was brightly coloured, and must be intended for children. There was some wind in the afternoon; the water in the bay ruffled, and the son was rotating slowly. Thyme waved, and settled himself a hundred paces or so from the Swiss grouping. The sea must be cold; the salt must sting the man Florian's red-raw skin. Thyme himself was brown by now; he took off his T-shirt and shorts and, after a moment's consideration, put his swimsuit on. There was a sort of delicacy in him that made him decide that he would not swim until Florian got out: he would not divide the whole bay with Florian if there were only two of them. A curious sort of intimacy, of bold advance or flirtation, arose in their sharing the billions of litres of salt water, and Thyme thought of something he had once been told in school, that the atoms of H_2O that filled his glass of water had once passed through Napoleon, through Lord Byron, through Metaxas and Venizelos and King Otto the First. The litres that held Florian's body would also hold Thyme's, and he waited until the Swiss might get out before getting in. And yet the Swiss manager of the coffee concession did not acknowledge him and had not noticed him. He swam, he floated, in the sea as if this element offered him a break from his real life, as if the life that he had for the other weeks of the year, the rest of his existence, mattered. His recreation was grave and formal in its celebrations.

The Swiss woman noticed him and waved at him. Thyme went over. She offered him a drink of water from the three unopened bottles underneath her chair – Thyme wondered how she and Florian had managed to get all this stuff to the beach.

'Florian should not be in the sun,' she said fondly. 'I have told him and told him. But he says he is fine.'

'It can be dangerous,' Thyme said. 'When did you get here?'

'Only three days ago,' the woman said. 'We are here for two weeks – I think he has really done too much in his first two days. He was always like that. Because he has the sort of skin that goes brown in the end, after a period of going bright red, he does not remember, and goes into the sun immediately, for hours and hours. My husband was much more sensible, and I know how to handle the sun.'

'It's nice to come back to the same place,' Thyme said.

'This was always our favourite beach,' the woman said. 'It is always so quiet here. No one disturbs you, you can read or you can sleep, you can just sit and look at the sea for hours. Look, Florian, he's so peaceful lying there in the sea, he's hardly moved for an hour.'

'Is he asleep?'

'Asleep?' the woman said, alarmed. 'No, that is unsafe, to fall asleep in the sea. You could easily drown or be swept out to sea.'

'I'm sorry?' Thyme said. He didn't think anyone would be swept out to sea today: there was only a very mild wind, and Florian was only a hundred metres out. Thyme came here often too, and for the same reason: there were few people who made it as far as this, and the four bays that preceded this one were perfect as far as most islanders and visitors were concerned.

'Do you think he could be asleep?' the woman said. 'Please, we should wake him, ask him to come back. Could you swim out to wake him?'

'I'm sure he's absolutely fine,' Thyme said, but in any case he waded out, breaking into his lazy stroke, splashing water about like the village boys. From here, the beach was a thin line of white with a dark shape at the centre of it called Mother; behind her, the far pale hills fell from the skies like a curtain. Out here, there was only Thyme in the sea, and in a moment, the Swiss boy, floating, unconscious, every limb as relaxed as could be, floating like a jellyfish. Thyme stopped where he was, out of his depth, treading water five metres from the floating man. His splashing had not disturbed him, and now he trod water quietly, and looked at him. It was no more than ten seconds before he was almost overwhelmed by a sense of what Florian was, and what his body was. In the sea, there was a density and a lightness of spirit in his body, a conviction in the loose-ness of limbs that it would do as well to float out to sea, to stay just where it was. Thyme had often been whelmed by a sense of the erotic in a man's body in the sea, on the beach. It was an ordinary joy of incompleteness to him. You could satisfy it by walking out here and knowing there would be a man to look at and, sometimes, to engage with. This was that and not that. The sensation of incomplete excitement was there in him, but before it had always been an emotion of gazing, of an encounter with an indifferent object that could somehow move and breathe, like an untethered hill. Now the sudden and unheralded sensation he had, treading water at the edges of the vast ocean, was of being embraced in the warmth of another body and another consciousness, as if it were scanning him and taking him in. I must have him, Thyme thought, and corrected himself: he must have me. For the first time he felt himself aware of the desire and possession of another person as of a limitless field or space containing a fluid and the strength and density of that desire; the strength and density of the loose-limbed body floating confidently in the still cold sea made him feel how little he knew. Florian was there; he was asleep or unconscious; he knew nothing about Thyme's presence within his sphere and still his sphere enveloped, crushed, seized Thyme. He did not know how he could speak if Florian woke up. Like an irrelevant and insignificant detail, Thyme noted that Florian was quite naked. It hardly seemed to matter, and it was out of a habit of assessment and enthusiasm that applied to other men that Thyme now tried to assess the weight and heft, the heavy substance of Florian's cock and balls. The centre of his power was there and it was somewhere else. Thyme trod water.

There was calling coming from the beach. It was the Swiss man's mother. Thyme had had no idea she was still there. He splashed at Florian, with no result, then swam towards him, almost feeling the waves of pressure and loose personal confidence around Florian's floating personality, and with a sense of daring reached out one arm and shook Florian's shoulder. It was not a very safe thing to do. Florian woke, his arms flailed and he swallowed water. Thyme had gripped Florian's shoulder, but he almost immediately righted himself and, like Thyme, sank and trod water. He took a handful of water, snorted it up his nose and out again, splashed it all over his face in a strong

and decisive way. He grinned at Thyme as if he had expected nothing else. To be taken into Florian's arms would
not be to be overpowered, but to have a sense of your place
in his world, and Thyme shut his eyes to remind himself
that he knew nothing about this man, saying to himself
that he was just another good-looking tourist. But he was
not good-looking in any way that Thyme could understand or would be able to explain. It was that density and
the radiant lightheartedness. In a moment Florian lightly
punched Thyme on the shoulder, as if they had known
each other for years, as if that annual holiday of the Swiss
man on a Greek beach, from early childhood, could be said
to amount to knowing each other for years. 'I shouldn't be
here,' Florian said. 'I should be in the shade. I thought you
would come out this afternoon.'

'Your mother,' Thyme said, 'thought – you were asleep
– thought it was – dangerous – so I came out to wake – you
up. Aren't you cold?'

'The lake at home is colder in August,' Florian said.
'Come on and we will swim back to the beach. Come and
sit with us.'

But they swam together, treading water, and grinning at
each other, and by the time they had drifted slowly towards
the beach and Florian had got out, kneeling on the sand,
puffing, pushing himself up, the mother underneath the
umbrella had herself gone to sleep. 'Don't disturb her,'
Florian said, shaking himself, naked, like a large Swiss dog.
'She'll wake up in her own time.'

'It must be strange,' Thyme said, seizing Florian's towel
and rubbing himself, 'being here without your father for
the first time.'

'We have a task to carry out,' Florian said. He did not seem to be answering Thyme, but in a minute he said, 'My mother, she talked to my father before he died, and he said that he wanted his ashes to be here. We didn't come last year because it was too soon, but this year, she said to me, Florian, we need to go to Antidauros, to empty your father – empty your father? That does not seem correct.'

'Scatter your father's ashes,' Thyme said. 'I think that's what you say.'

'Scatter – scatter? – your father's ashes. I see. Yes. But she wants to do this, and she said first, Oh, not today, we can't do it on the first day, then not again after that, and she has not said anything about it today. I think she is scared to do it. Or something like that.'

'You probably need to take charge,' Thyme said. 'Where are you going to do it?'

Well, Florian said, that was the problem. There was no particular place they had decided on, and it seemed wrong to deposit the ashes in the town on the streets, outside the taverna, or on the beach, or in the sea, or … Well, they had not decided. It was difficult. For Thyme it was not difficult, and he knew where they should go. The hills that rose behind the village looked steep, but could be quite easily walked in a morning, and at the top of the hill, Dauros could be seen across the strait, and beyond that Naxos in the looming, swimming Aegean air, like a whale surfacing. Up there it was peaceful, and up there were wind and flowers. Thyme liked to go up there. And before he knew it he had agreed to walk with Florian and his mother the next morning, to wait while they perhaps read a poem, and

Florian should open the lid of the box, and let his father scatter – scatter? – on the wind.

'It would be good if you came,' Florian said. 'My mother – she appreciates very much the portrait of your father, the picture of my father. She often shows it to visitors and tells them it was how my father was. You can help us to a good place on the mountain.'

It was five o' clock. Thyme had to go. The mother's mind had been penetrated by her son's voice. The afternoon wind had subsided towards a still warmth: the beginnings of the evening. She woke, her mouth opening and smacking with thick saliva, like a much older woman, and in a moment composed herself, smiled at the English boy without saying anything. He dressed slowly, looking all the time at Florian. They seemed to be staying a while longer. He wondered if he should offer to help them carry their beach possessions back – the towels, blue umbrella, chair.

Oak was there at the café, and had opened it up. He was sitting behind the desk, tapping away. There were no customers, and he carried on, paying no attention to Thyme as he came in until Thyme dropped his wet towel on the desk.

'Where've you been?' Oak said flatly.

'It was so quiet,' Thyme said. 'There was no one in all morning, so I went down the beach. I was with Florian.'

'Who's that?' Oak said.

'That Swiss boy,' Thyme said. 'You remember.'

'Oh, yeah,' Oak said, but absently. 'There's those friends of Charlie arriving in a bit. I've been getting the house ready. It's a nightmare.'

'It'll be fine,' Thyme said.

'Charlie says one of them's a real interior-design queen,' Oak said. 'He's been wandering round for days getting the curtains to hang just so. And an arrangement of pebbles on a white marble plate and – oh, you don't want to know. He's done no painting for about a month.'

'Yeah, that's what you do when you stay with a friend,' Thyme said. 'Say straight off, Charlie, I'm sorry, but I can't sleep somewhere where the curtains are hanging so badly. And those pebbles, the way they're arranged – it's an *insult to your guests*. You're mental.'

'Well, Charlie's friends might say exactly that,' Oak said. 'I'm nervous, to be honest. They haven't met me, apart from one of them called Henry who was in Paris when we went. They're coming to inspect me and inspect the house about equally. I thought Charlie was going to start going through what I was going to wear for the next ten days when he'd finished rearranging the willow branches in the vase. He had a sort of look, but I think I'm OK.'

Thyme giggled and Oak, in a way, joined in; since Oak, these days, only ever wore cream linen shirts and white linen trousers, with a cotton jumper in blue or cream for cold days, it was hard to see what Charlie could object to.

'Close the café tomorrow and come over for lunch,' Oak said. 'I could do with a hand. That's another thing – trying to make something that looks Greek and typical and seasonal and all that crap that Charlie doesn't mind eating. It's a challenge, I don't mind telling you.'

'I'll do my best,' Thyme said. 'I promised Florian I'd spend the morning with him. He's got something he needs to do tomorrow morning.' But then it occurred to Thyme that he had made no arrangements with Florian, and Florian had not seemed to think it at all necessary. They could only be staying at one of three hotels in the village; perhaps he was just expected to come and find them.

'Florian,' Oak said, in a superior, Charlie-like way. 'Remind me.'

'He's that Swiss boy,' Thyme said. 'I spent the afternoon with him. And his mum.'

'Oh, his mum,' Oak said.

'He's really nice,' Thyme said. 'Pa painted his father's portrait a couple of years ago. He was dying.'

'Oh, yeah, the Germans,' Oak said. 'I remember. Pa kept going on about how awful they were. I don't remember a son – just a husband and a wife, and the painting they went off with. It would have given me nightmares.'

'Well, there's a son,' Thyme said. 'He's here now. He works as a manager of Starbucks in Switzerland. Swiss, not German. He's really nice.' Something made him insist on this. There was no reason to insist on Florian's job, but he knew the thing that would specify Florian for his brother, as for all his family, and that was the possibility of open contempt. He offered the possibility to Oak.

'Oh, the deputy manager of Starbucks,' Oak said. 'I remember now, and Ma going on and on about it. She does go on,' he finished languidly, and the contempt in his voice covered his mother, and Starbucks, and the Swiss manager of the concession that he had no recollection of ever having met.

'He's the manager, these days,' Thyme said blandly. 'He's been promoted in the meantime. He's like me, managing Drys, except that he's got some staff, and a pension plan, and he's not employed by his brother in a shop named *after* his brother, or anything.'

A bold single howl filled the air of the evening; a huge trumpet, echoing and resounding, playing its single note over water, and Oak stood up.

'That's the ferry coming in now,' Oak said. 'So fuck off. I'll see you tomorrow, about lunchtime.'

They were at the first hotel he went to in the morning, and finishing their breakfast. It was the cleanest of the three hotels in town. In a rough period between patches of profit, Ma had worked as the receptionist, trying out her O-level German and A-level French on the customers, struggling through Greek with the handymen. She'd quite enjoyed it, she said. But afterwards she always said, when they were a bit hard up, 'We haven't got to the point where I'm going to have to work at the Aphrodite, I'm pleased to say.' It was an efficient and well-run hotel, the Aphrodite, at the hands of Mr Matsoukas or, these days, his shipshape daughter Anna; the hotel was painted white top to bottom every other year, and the beds renewed. There was talk of her installing a cocktail bar, even a swimming-pool; Anna Matsoukas said it would appeal to the better sort of holidaymaker. Florian and his mother were sitting outside on the terrace underneath a bougainvillaea, eating yoghurt and honey: the mother was drinking Greek coffee but, Thyme noticed, Florian was stubbornly drinking something that looked like instant. They greeted him as if they had had an appointment and he was slightly but forgivably late. After offering him a coffee, the three left. The mother patted her canvas bag, in which there was something hard and metallic that clinked. It was the container of the man's ashes. The single road out of the village that went up the hill was quickly steep, and Florian and Thyme soon found themselves a hundred metres in front of Florian's mother. They waited; Florian wordlessly put his hand out and took the bag from his mother, and they started to walk again. By the time they were out of the village, and past the last of the unfinished villas, rusting steel rods running across the roof, they were ahead of his mother again. They looked back, and she waved in an encouraging style. She would catch up, Florian said, and Thyme pointed out that there was only one road and it went to only one place, the top of the hill.

It was quite a hot day already, and Florian pulled off his shirt. His skin was not so brilliantly red as yesterday, but still burnt and painful-looking. After the beginning of the hill, he was sweating. There was a gust of animal odour when he pulled his shirt off. Thyme was seized by desire, and by a desire that was not just lust, but a feeling of magnetism, as if he were being pulled towards the weight and substance of this body. The world had disappeared for him. He had to turn away.

'What are you going to do?' Florian said. His expression could not be read, behind the sunglasses.

'I'm supposed to go to my brother's for lunch,' Thyme said. 'But it doesn't really matter. He just wants me to help out with some guests and probably with the cooking, too.'

There was a puzzled pause. 'I really meant – what are you going to do generally?' Florian said. 'Are you working here as a summer job? What comes after that?'

'It's my brother's shop,' Thyme said. 'He can't be here every day so I look after it for him. What did your mother do with the painting of your father? Is it on the wall at home?'

Florian laughed. 'Of course it is on the wall – where did you think she would put it? She likes it. It's the first thing she shows anyone. She talks about my father a lot and about Antidauros. They liked this island a lot, you know. Me …' He shook his head.

'You don't like it so much,' Thyme said.

'It is a painting by your father,' Florian said.

'I don't care,' Thyme said. 'I hate some of his paintings and I don't have any opinion about almost all the others. I can't even remember seeing that. I remember him working on it. He kept talking about it, about whether he should start up a portrait business. He's like that – he does one thing and then he thinks he can make his fortune. He was like that the year he managed to grow beans in the patch behind the studio.'

'But he didn't start a business painting portraits.'

'He's back where he started now,' Thyme said. 'Views of the harbour and teaching people and his own stuff in the winter or in the evenings in the summer, sometimes.'

'I don't know,' Florian said. 'The painting – it looks like my father, but towards the end, he looks very old and very ill. I sometimes think your father was making, not a joke, but a comment on someone he decided he did not like. What is this hill called, this hill we're going up?'

'I don't know,' Thyme said. They had climbed out of the town. The sea was expansive and a rich blue beneath them. A donkey in the field by the road swished its tail, taking no notice of them. Thyme felt that he should know the name of the hill, and also the field, and perhaps even the donkey. Everything had a name, but not on this island; it was all how things could be accounted for – the hill, the town, the beach, the road. 'I don't know what it's called.'

'You don't paint,' Florian said.

'No,' Thyme said. 'No one taught us. My elder brother, my father started to teach him when he was five, but he lost patience and Oak didn't have any interest. So then he didn't teach any of us.'

'That is so strange,' Florian said. 'Your father not wanting his children to do what he does.'

'It wasn't really that he didn't want it,' Thyme said. 'It was more that we weren't really interested and it just didn't happen. We had some kind of art lessons at the school, but it was really the music teacher showing us slides of Velázquez and talking about them. My pa was always too busy, and he wouldn't want little kids messing about with his easel and palette, or whatever.'

'But it didn't happen,' Florian said. It was as if he had made his mind up about something. 'Your father – does he want to be famous? I think maybe he wants to have children so they can be his fans, his admirers, and then he can win in life. You know, I never see any of you reading a book, never. So what are you going to do in your life?'

'I don't know,' Thyme said. He could have said that they read books, but against this man there was no resistance.

'The café, the internet café,' Florian said. 'Why is it called Drys? Does it mean something?'

'It's my brother's name,' Thyme said. 'My brother's name in Greek, I mean. *Drys* is an oak tree. It was his idea. My brother, Oak, I mean. It's a nice name for a café. I don't think anyone's ever asked why it was called that before. You're the first.'

'And why is he called Oak? Is that a name in English?'

'I don't really know,' Thyme said. 'We all have strange names. My parents just thought of them as we came.'

'*Drys*. I see. You have to do something,' Florian said. 'You grow up here, you want to be artistic. Your father is artistic, your mother is artistic, and so everyone thinks you will be artistic. But what is it that you can do on this island? It is very nice for two weeks each year. But to live here, to grow up here, to grow old here, to stay here. And you do not belong. You are English, they all know that. You speak Greek but you are always the son of the painter, the English painter.'

'What do you do?' Thyme said. He meant in general, what ought a person do in response to this fact of parentage? But Florian took it for the ordinary, the polite question.

'I am managing a coffee shop in Solothurn, which is a town in Switzerland. And it is very nice, a very good job. I like it. I arrive before seven, and the shop opens at seven thirty. We make coffees of very many sorts. People like them. And there are cakes and sandwiches, snacks, and similar things. If you make and sell things that people like, and you understand what it is that they like, then your job is satisfying. I am satisfied with my job. I have learnt a lot working for a multinational company, and one day I am going to go to work for a different multinational company, for more money, in a larger town. There is nothing so wrong with that. My father managed to be proud of me before he died.'

There was nothing to say to that, except what Thyme's mother would have said. She had supplied him with responses when a person explained what they did for a living, and the responses were polite, and noncommittal, and spiritually prophylactic; they allowed no contamination of the upper world by commerce, or the words *deputy manager*, and they did it with politeness and an empty sneer. The way they would respond when the person was out of the room was not so polite. They would talk about them and dwell on the words *deputy manager*, like ore that might contain gold, turning them over and over with laughter and scrupulous consideration. The upper world would remain uncontaminated. But as Thyme walked, silently, by the side of this man, the density of his physical presence a proof of his decency, and of the life that was opening up before him, that upper world had never been so empty. What was there in his mother's words, his mother's manners, the way of life his father had chosen and – Florian was right – had jealously guarded from his children? The island was beautiful. He could see that. He had never looked at it and never let it fall into his mind other than as the place where he lived. But today he was looking at it and finding it beautiful, with the eyes of a visitor who would soon leave it, and the beauty of the place was a guarantee of its emptiness. There was nothing to say in response to Florian, explaining his work. His mother and father had supplied him with no means of responding and finally he said merely, 'That sounds really nice,' inadequately and bathetically. Florian looked at him with amusement. They fell into silence.

At the top of the hill, you could see so far. They scrambled off the road, and up onto what should have been the final tussock but there was another one, and they scrambled up that, to find themselves on what, really, was the peak of the hill. It was a small, flat stretch of sand and stone. In one direction, there was the village; in the other, there was the small settlement where his brother and Charlie had settled. Beyond that, the sea, not framed by land and land's requirements, but all around them, like an element. It was so blue; more blue than, even, the sky. Down in the village, the air had been nearly still, but up here, the wind was marked and warm. There was the sound, far off, of a motorbike. The smells of the island, of the undergrowth and of wild herbs growing, were all around them. Florian put his arm round Thyme's shoulders. It was as if he had been doing it for ever. Thyme felt heroic, like a poster of sporting deeds, up there on the top of the hill, but also on the verge of a loss of control. Next to Florian, he was dissolved, cloudlike, insubstantial, and from the top of the hill he could roll or melt or float away. Florian's arm was a tether on his lightness. He felt that. They stood there for a long time. He could not understand it when a woman came into view. Nobody came up here, and certainly no tourist. Then he remembered it was the mother of Florian, and what they were here to do.

Florian lowered his arm from Thyme, and, taking the shirt from his waistband, put it on. Perhaps he understood that it was a solemn moment. Thyme knew he should walk away and leave the man with his mother to say goodbye, but he simply could not, and he stood there while the mother spoke in German, musically, almost flirtatiously, to her son. He took a folded piece of paper from the pocket of his cargo shorts, and opened it.

'This is a poem that my father liked,' he said to Thyme. 'He wanted it to be read before we emptied – before we scatter – his ashes. It is very nice. But I am going to read it in German.'

Florian started to read, soberly, without much expression. *Ich denke dein/wenn mir der Sonne schimmer/Vom Meere strahlt.* His tone was that of a man not used to poetry, with not much display of poetry in him, but who knew that poetry had its place in the world, and would treat it with respect. Thyme understood nothing of what he heard, but he could hear it was a poem, with rhymes, and he could see that Florian's voice went through it with the music of his accent, a song that belonged to its place of birth and not of this particular invention. He was not embarrassed in the slightest. His mother touched his arm, her two fingers touching his sore forearm, like a shy child, trying to attract attention. Her eyes shone. The poem came to an end, and, like a coda, Florian said, 'Mama?' and, leaning down, passed her the casket from her bag. It was an anonymous object, cylindrical in polished steel.

'*Zusammen*,' the mother said. Thyme understood nothing, but together Florian and his mother unscrewed the lid of the casket, and together they shook it into the air. Thyme feared that the winds would blow the ashes back into their faces, but Florian had thought of that. They were standing at exactly the right point, facing the right direction, and the ashes blew away from them, into the air and towards the sea. Thyme was part of this farewell, and it was his farewell too. He felt that.

They had almost reached the hotel when Florian said, 'I'm very burnt. I feel so sore. Mama dressed me with yoghurt last night, but I need some more.'

'She probably wants to rest now,' Thyme said, and they said goodbye to Florian's mother until dinner time. It was three o'clock. There was no point in going to Oak's for lunch. He would face that fury later, or perhaps not face it at all. He went with Florian through the lobby of the hotel. Anna Matsoukas was behind the desk. She looked up at him, a disapproving presence with a tight-drawn, almost military bun, tapping the lid of her biro on the volume of bookings. He said nothing to her, but just went on with Florian, up the stairs, along the corridor, into his room. Florian went to the little fridge, and took out a tub of yoghurt, unopened. With two or three gestures, unembarrassed and even mechanical, he pulled his shirt over his head, unbuckled his belt and dropped his shorts, kicking his sandals off. Thyme took the tub of yoghurt, and, opening it, scooped out handfuls of the stuff. Florian's skin was sore and red, but to Thyme smooth and beautiful. He painted Florian's back, and his hands, as they went over him, lost any sense of separateness. He felt as if he was dissolving into Florian, the sunburnt rough skin and the relaxed play of muscles. There was in Thyme an impersonal lust as he moved over Florian, a hot blaze in the eyes, but also something unique that he felt was like love. The thick neck with its folds and the little ears, sticking out and, on top, encrusted with burn scars; his hands went, laden with yoghurt, over Florian's face. He could feel the eyes shut, the mouth pursed; gently, he swivelled Florian, and painted his chest. The collarbone, the shoulder seemed loose and relaxed; it was hard to think that Florian was in pain from his burns. Thyme's hands went over chest and arms, stomach, Florian's burnt cock and balls, his thighs, calves and even his feet, though his feet were brown and not sore. Florian sat and let him do it. At some point he said, musingly, *Ich denke dein*. After that, there were no words spoken between them. He was smooth and painted and cured of his pain by Thyme. He could do this for Florian as Florian could do something for him. In the evening they went up together to see the painter and his wife in their house on the hill.

Rose had had a difficult day. The twins had come home from school crying. Rose knew perfectly well what it was but, in their ten-year-old way, the twins liked to get their story straight before one of them was allowed to tell their mother. Rose had carried on around the kitchen, putting things straight, chopping onions for the dinner tonight – she was making *stifado* in a big pot, whatever bloody Charlie might have to say about it. In the end, Thistle had come to her, her sister Borage standing behind silently, reproachful, and had said that they never wanted to go back to that school. People there were horrible, they stole your things and they tore up your books and they were going to throw you in the sea and watch you drown. Rose had heard it all before. It was part of growing up on the island, and probably anywhere else at all. It had happened to Oak and it had happened to Thyme, and they were more obvious targets; it had happened to Rosalys and to Juniper. They had all come through it OK. It was probably character-forming. Rose said, 'Oh dear,' from time to time, hardly listening to Borage's explanation, apparently worked out in detail, of how they could be educated at home from books and never have to go to that horrible school ever again. If she listened she knew she would grow exasperated with just one more thing.

Because this was a time and a day when she could hardly bear to engage with any of it. The bookings for the school were thin to the point of non-existence this year. The Germans who normally came with such largesse were gone. They had heard what the ordinary Greeks thought of their chancellor, and they did not want to be made to feel unwelcome in a country. It wasn't helpful for Thorpe to say that he didn't know what the country was that would make them feel welcome, before saying, brilliantly, 'Germany, probably.' The fact remained that they weren't coming. It was last year when someone else had said to Rose that Greece used to be lovely and cheap, but now … It was true, she supposed. It wasn't just the Germans that weren't coming; there were few bookings of any sort. The people who complained about Greece being too expensive hadn't thought that people who lived here would find it expensive too, and more expensive if their main source of money decided on a whim to take it away. If she only had five minutes with those people complaining about the expense, she'd bring it home to them.

But Thorpe didn't seem to be taking anything at all seriously. That day, she was supposed to be cooking and preparing an immense *stifado*. Oak and Charlie had some posh friends from England staying with them in the Winter Palace, as she'd christened their house in Hora. For some reason, Oak had said that they'd bring them over for dinner. She resigned herself to being seen as the picturesque bohemian living up the hill on a Greek island in a muddle of green and purple skirts. She knew that one of them would be certain to ask if they had any dope. Thorpe had said he would help, but had disappeared after breakfast to the studio. He hadn't been seen since. Around three in the afternoon, just after Oak had phoned to ask in a rage where the bloody hell Thyme was, she'd gone over to see if he wanted anything to eat. She had found him at work in front of an immense canvas, smearing and slashing. The canvas was wild, she had to admit that, but it was one of his winter canvases. It was the sort of thing he worked at when there was no pressure on him. In the store room, there were thirty or forty winter canvases, all exhibited, all unsold. She had asked him, as politely as she knew how, whether the saleable views had all been done by now. The visitors would be here soon, and would want to start buying.

But Thorpe had said, quite crossly, that he understood where he was going wrong now, that his real painting couldn't be produced in the gaps between commercial work. The commercial work had got into the bones of his work, the painting he'd only been playing at. He needed to walk away from views, from realistic portraits, from chocolate box, from the *quality of light*. If he did nothing else but this, he said, gesturing at the huge Twombly exercise, then in a month or two, his work was going to lose that taint. It would get somewhere. He could feel—

She left the studio, slamming the door, in case he said that he could feel greatness in him. How they were supposed to live through this summer and next winter without any saleable art to sell – with hardly any students for the art school. They were going to have to move, the lot of them, into the flat over the top of Oak's internet café, or back to England to live with her old mum. She just could not see it. 'Oh, for God's sake,' she said now to the twins, still going on about the terrible things that were going to happen to them. 'Just shut up.' She devoted all the energy in her body to the vegetables beneath the blade of her knife.

It was then that the door opened, and Thyme came in. Behind him was a man she didn't recognize, and she gave what must have been a tired smile.

'You're in trouble,' she said. 'You were supposed to go over and help Oak out with lunch for eight.'

'This is Florian,' Thyme said, making a gesture to bring the man into the kitchen. He was dark, and startlingly red in colour. His face and arms were streaked with some kind of lotion; his eyes an intense blue. She looked at him: there was something familiar about him.

'Are you hoping to get invited to dinner?' Rose said. 'There's fourteen of us, but I expect we can squeeze two more in, if you don't mind sitting on garden chairs. It'll be a squash.'

'No,' Thyme said. 'We're not staying. We're going to have dinner with Florian's mother.'

'That's nice,' Rose said. 'Are you here on holiday?'

'In a way,' Florian said. 'But now it doesn't seem so much like it.'

She let this go. She had had enough of enquiring into other people's lives. He had a German accent, and she felt at least pleased that not every German had decided they couldn't risk the collapsed state for a holiday, that they would be targets for hatred because of Frau Merkel. They would still come, after all.

'I want to take Thyme away,' Florian said.

'Well, he's a grown man,' Rose said. 'Take him off. Show him a good time. It's nothing to do with me. I'll see him when you bring him back and hear about the whole thing. What is it – Mykonos?'

'No, Ma,' Thyme said. 'You don't understand. I'm going away. I'm going with Florian to Switzerland, to Solothurn. I want to be with him. I can't stay here knowing that Florian is in another country.'

Rose stopped what she was doing. The twins were sitting underneath the table. She wished they would go away. They had a knack of understanding whenever something important was going to happen, and staying very still and listening. The man was looking levelly at her, with a gaze not hostile or even unfriendly, but one that was made of some tensile, resistant, flexible material. She felt the power of his gaze; she looked away, at her son. But there she did feel some hostility.

'I know who you are now,' she said, but not looking at him. 'You're the deputy manager of a branch of Starbucks.'

'That's nearly correct,' the man said. 'But a little out of date.'

'That sounds wonderful,' Rose said, now jeering openly. 'It won't last. Thyme, you don't know what you're doing. There's no way that you could settle down with someone like this. After the way of life you're used to, watching someone put on a little badge, watching them go over the accounts, watching them—'

'It's fine, Ma,' Thyme said. 'It's going to be absolutely fine.'

'We've brought you up to think and be yourself,' she said. The door to the kitchen opened. Thorpe came in, standing there with something like shyness. She remembered the awful things she had said to him, an hour or two before. 'Have you heard this?' she said to Thorpe. 'Thyme's going to run off with a deputy manager of Starbucks. You want to listen to this.'

'We don't know how to do anything,' Thyme said, ignoring his father. 'We don't know anything about art, even, except that de Kooning is God and Stanley Spencer is the devil. And the only time I ever saw a painting by either of them was that one time we went to England and we had a day in London. And that was only so that Pa could talk loudly in a gallery and impress lots of people. I'm sorry, Pa. We don't know anything. I can't remember the last time I read a book. I couldn't write a letter in Greek without worrying that I was saying something you'd only say to kids on the street. I don't know anything. And what am I going to do? You know what Charlie is going to make Oak do? He's going to adopt a baby, get one made by paying a surrogate. A baby – two babies, three expensive little babies in that house, puking over the white sofas. It's all going to be so expensive. How are they going to manage? I'm going to go over there and do it all, be a nanny, a brother and a nanny, with my stuff in the spare room upstairs. That's what those friends are here for – they're

307

not friends, they're people who are taking Charlie and Oak through the whole process. What is my life going to be?'

'You're a free spirit, Thyme,' Rose said. She was as solemn as she knew how to be. It was a sentence she produced on high occasions, when her children complained of bullying, of people who were richer or cleverer or more beautiful than them. She had used it three times this week, to Borage, to Juniper, when she was saying that she wished she lived in a house as nice as Charlie's only without Charlie in it. She said it now to Thyme, with a solemn intonation: 'You can't go to Switzerland, get a job in a Starbucks and expect it to suit you. It just isn't going to work. How on earth are you going to live?'

'The minimum wage in Switzerland—' the sunburnt man began, but Rose interrupted.

'Oh, for heaven's sake,' she said. 'We're not talking about money. Money is just—'

'I think we're going to go,' Thyme said. 'I don't have so much to take with me. I'm just going to go when Florian goes. You see, Ma, the thing is, I love him. I love him. I don't know why.'

'I've never heard of you before,' Rose said. 'Never, never, never. And my sons tell me everything. When was this? When is this supposed to have happened?'

The man looked at Rose, and it seemed to her that he looked at her with calm interest, as if he wanted to know what her response to an event would be.

'It is the case, what Thyme says,' he said. 'I love him. It happened and it is still happening. He has to be with me and now my home is with Thyme. We are here to explain and to say goodbye.'

'I don't know what I'm supposed to say,' Rose said, but then she went too far. 'What are people going to say here, when they hear that the son of the painter, the one who brought real art, real values to this place, he's gone off and he's living with someone who works in a branch of Starbucks? How are we going to tell anyone that? You can't be happy, Thyme. Tell him, Thorpe.'

'That's what you've always said,' Thyme said. 'You can't be happy. All of you. We're going to go now, Ma. I'll come and say goodbye before we go.'

Thorpe gave a small, feeble smile, a whipped child hoping to placate his tormentor. They went, watched by the bullied twins, huddled underneath the table that seated fourteen and would stretch to sixteen. Their brother and the Swiss man left, and found themselves negotiating the door with the other brother, Oak, and Charlie, trying to come in. They were with some people they didn't know. Where the hell were you? Oak was saying, but Thyme said something short, dismissive, and was gone. They saw Charlie, a little man, rich and tiny, a pathetic, ill-fed scrap, looking about him as if he had never seen anything so awful as their kitchen, and turning to his rich friends, who were coming for dinner, with a shrug and a face. Their mother said they were early. Oak said they thought they'd come early and see the paintings, too. And then it all kicked off.

'I didn't know how it was going to be,' Thyme said.

'It was fine,' Florian said. They were walking down the hill.

'Are you sore? Your skin?'

'It's better. Your mother—'

'Forget about it. She'll tell Pa. They'll be a long way away soon.'

'Are you sure?'

Thyme laughed, incredulously, drolly. 'When can we go?'

'We've got a flight from Naxos. Come on the same flight.'

'They fill up, those flights,' Thyme said. 'If I can't fly with you, what then?'

'We'll get a ferry to Athens,' Florian said. 'There are flights all day long from Athens to Zürich. There's a train from Zürich to Solothurn. It's easy. Do you want to come to Solothurn with me?'

'It must be beautiful,' Thyme said.

'I don't know,' Florian said. 'I've stopped seeing it. It's just where I live now. I suppose it's nice.'

'All right,' Thyme said. 'Let's go tomorrow to Solothurn.'

A Lemon Tree

The terrace here has plants on it. Lavender, jasmine. It smells nice. They are the plants from the terrace at home. At home my mother waters them every night and every morning. She comes out and says something about the heat of the day. Then she waters the plants. The kind people who work here have brought the lavender and the jasmine from the terrace at home in Naples to make me feel at home.

Nothing is too much trouble for the kind people. It is nice to be at a spa. This spa is not like the spa my father took us to last year and the year before. We always go to Montecatini Terme in Tuscany. This is not Montecatini Terme. There you drink the waters and talk in the streets to the same people you see every year. The waters are good for your digestion. Sometimes in Montecatini Terme you or your parents are talking to a friend in the street and then suddenly the friend is not there any more. He has gone to the lavatory to answer a call of nature. In Montecatini Terme it is not necessary to say 'goodbye' or apologize for leaving. Everyone knows you just turn away and absent

311

yourself. And one day you realize that your three weeks' stay is over and tomorrow you, too, must leave, it is over, and you must go back home to Naples.

In Naples we have lavender and jasmine on the terrace and my mother waters them every day, twice a day. The kind people who work here have brought the lavender and jasmine from our terrace and put it outside where I can see it. It makes me feel at home. Some time I will have to leave the spa and go back home. It has been a nice holiday. There have not been any waters to drink. But the kind people have made me comfortable. There is risotto to eat sometimes, and sometimes soup, a cold, bright green vegetable soup, very nice. The vegetable soup is my favourite to eat and I look forward to it. Last year I went with my parents, and the year before that we went to Montecatini Terme in Tuscany. This year I came here, and my parents did not come. They went to Montecatini Terme. There is plenty of time left before I have to go back home. My brother is here, I see him sometimes at the other end of the room, where the television set hangs on the yellow wall, but once I went over to say hello, and found myself about to speak to an old man by mistake. I don't know where my brother went.

The kind people who work here make us comfortable and talk to us. Sometimes it is the kind ladies, the ones from Africa, who bring us our lunch and our supper. There is a kind lady from Russia who does not talk, who hits us when we are slow to get into bed and she is in a hurry. There are some strict gentlemen and strict ladies too, who come and ask me questions. I have told them these things before, but I don't mind telling them again. I am between forty and fifty years in age. It is 1974. (Sometimes I make a small joke, and I tell them that the year is 1975. The strict ladies write this down just the same.) The name of the pope in the Vatican is John Paul, and he is Polish. They ask us the names of other people. They are different questions. But they always ask us the name of the prime minister of the country. Silvio Berlusconi, I always say. I look down when I say this. Berlusconi is a very good friend of my husband, Pierluigi, who is away at Montecatini Terme with my parents. In the past, he has come round to our house, and sat and told us about what he wants to do, and sometimes he has sung a song. I do not tell the strict ladies and gentlemen about this; there is no need. In the mornings they ask us what Silvio Berlusconi does for this country and in the afternoon Silvio Berlusconi comes to the spa and he visits us.

There are mostly old people at this spa. I am the youngest here, thirty or forty years younger than the rest of them. The old man who sits in the chair next to me, he dribbles in his risotto at table and we pretend not to notice. They ask all of us one by one who the pope is and who the prime minister is. The old man in the chair next to me, the risotto-dribbler, he gets the answer right about the pope but then he says that the prime minister is Craxi. The strict lady writes the answer down. She does not correct him. She goes on to the next old person, who knows, like everyone else, that the prime minister's name is Silvio Berlusconi. I want to ask the old man how he can say something so stupid. But I don't. In the afternoon the prime minister sometimes comes to visit us. Bettino Craxi has never been to visit us and he never will.

On the terrace, the lavender and jasmine come from the terrace in Naples. The kind people who work here brought it, to make me feel at home. I like to smell it when the windows are open and it makes me feel homesick and it stops me feeling homesick. The kind people brought the lavender and the jasmine here.

Silvio Berlusconi does not look as he looks. But now I know that is what he looks like. His hair is black and smoothed down and his skin is tanned the colour of the risotto. He smiles at us but I did not think he recognized me at first. Now he has remembered me and he talks to me sometimes when he comes. Once he sang the line of a song to me, and he held my hand and I knew the tune. *Volare … Cantare …* Other famous people come to the spa to visit us. Eros Ramazzotti comes. He is the grandson of one of the old ladies. Sophia Loren has come with her pet dogs, one under each arm, and Gina Lollobrigida, very beautiful, as beautiful as ever. I recognized her immediately, but I said nothing. Nino Brunacci comes very often. He was my favourite star when I was young and it is so nice that he comes very often to visit us. He comes so often because he is one of the kind people. He is a big star but he does not mind cleaning up when one of the old people has an accident. He has not grown any older. But the most regular one who comes is the prime minister.

It is nice that the prime minister comes. He comes because he wants to hear what ordinary people think and what ordinary people like us are saying. He does not clean up after accidents but he sometimes brings us our risotto or our vegetable soup, putting them down in front of us. Vegetable soup is my favourite. Silvio Berlusconi sets it down and he asks me if I'm good to go. Sometimes I am not sure what Silvio Berlusconi means, but I agree, and pick up the spoon to eat it. Sometimes Silvio Berlusconi says that I am his favourite old dear, and if he ever runs out of talent, I'll be at the top of his list. Silvio Berlusconi is an old friend of my husband, and so he talks to me like this, and neither of us minds it. My husband would not mind it if he was here. My husband is in Montecatini Terme with my parents. He did not want to come here. We will meet again in Naples. I will tell him all about the things that Silvio Berlusconi has said to me and how nice it was that I and Silvio Berlusconi were at the same spa and Silvio Berlusconi was a kind person giving me some soup to eat.

Sometimes a kind man comes to visit me. He calls me Nonna. He sits with me and sometimes he talks and sometimes we sit and we watch the television together. Today Miss Lollobrigida came on the television and I explained that she had come to visit us all only that morning. He shook his head, the kind man who calls me Nonna. But I explained again about all the people who come to visit – about Sophia Loren, and Gina Lollobrigida, and Marcello Mastroianni, and Nino, but he had not heard of Nino Brunacci. And not just stars but the prime minister too, I explained. Silvio Berlusconi comes to visit. I often talk to him, I said. He gives me risotto to eat if it is a risotto day and vegetable soup if it is a vegetable soup day. Oh, Nonna, the kind man says. Soon it is time for him to leave.

But quite soon after he leaves, Silvio Berlusconi comes into the room. He has been at the spa all day. Just now he was working in the kitchen. He takes off his washing-up gloves and comes over to me to say goodbye for the day. I want to say something to him, because behind him I can see the kind lady from Russia just taking off her coat and I do not want to be left alone with the kind lady from Russia. I ask him if he knows the plants outside; they come from my father's terrace in Naples. The lavender and the jasmine. They smell here just as they smell in Naples. I was thinking of leaving them here – it would be kind to all the old people. But Silvio Berlusconi says something. You didn't bring the lemon tree, then, he says. I am very surprised that he should remember that we had a lemon tree on the terrace at home, but he is right. They have brought the lavender and the jasmine from home but they have not brought the lemon tree. My father will be very disappointed at that. I agree with Silvio Berlusconi. Then Silvio Berlusconi puts on his own coat, and the big blue car that sits outside the spa sometimes takes him away.

I close my eyes. I pretend to sleep. The Russian kind lady is in the room. I don't want her to know that I see her. I don't want her to catch my eye. Some time soon it will be time to return home; some time soon the holiday will be over. I have had a good time. It has been a long time. Soon it will be over and time to go home.